Gold Fever

Gold Fever

LOUISA FRANCIS

BLACK
lace

Black Lace novels are sexual fantasies.
In real life, make sure you practise safe sex.

First published in 1995 by
Black Lace
332 Ladbroke Grove
London
W10 5AH

Copyright © Louisa Francis 1995

Typeset by CentraCet Limited, Cambridge
Printed and bound by Mackays of Chatham PLC

ISBN 0 352 33043 0

Chapter One

*T*he ship rolled gently on the almost calm sea. A benign breeze lifted and filled her sails, carrying her steadily eastwards across the Indian Ocean. It was a warm breeze – a soft breeze – kissing and caressing the face and hair of the young woman who stood alone on deck, gazing in rapturous wonder at the star-spangled sky above.

If she had not seen them with her own eyes she would never have believed there could be so many stars in the heavens. Nor would she have imagined they could shine so brightly. Their sparkling, twinkling brightness made her think of blue-white diamonds scattered across black velvet.

Smiling to herself at her fancifulness, she continued to stroll along the deserted deck. It was late and all the other passengers were asleep below, but the tropical night had filled her with restlessness, with a yearning for something to which she could put no name. Now as she strolled the deck and felt the warm caress of the breeze against her skin, she realised there was something magical in that tropical night which was making her very aware of her body.

A gasping, groaning sound made her halt. She listened

carefully, hearing only the scughing of the wind in the sails and the normal creaks and rattles of the moving ship. No, there it was again; a gasping 'Ah – ah – aah', like the cry of a woman in distress. It appeared to be coming from behind a pile of ropes and, thinking to offer her help, Ginny hurried forward.

When she reached the place a few moments later, shock brought her to an abrupt standstill. Then fascination made her press herself back into the shadows to watch the actions of the pair who had previously been hidden from view.

The woman's buttocks were supported on a strong, twelve inch high, coil of rope. Her body was arched backwards and downwards, her skirt hitched high and her knees opened wide to expose her most private parts to the man who knelt before her.

'Oh do it again, ple-ease,' moaned the woman, and Ginny's eyes opened wide as she watched the man bend his head forward and saw his tongue snake out to lick slowly up and down between the crevices and folds of the woman's sex place. Every few strokes the exploring tongue would pause on one particular spot to wiggle quickly, at which times the woman moaned and writhed with gasping approval of his actions. 'Oh yes, yes. Oh God yes. I'm going to come. Ah, give it to me, give it to me, I can't wait.'

The man raised his head and fumbled with his trousers to allow his hard, engorged penis to spring free. He grabbed the woman's knees to lift her buttocks higher and bring the moist and puffy lips of her vagina closer to the gleaming tip of his penis. Then he drove into her with a sudden, violent thrust. The woman exhaled sharply. He pulled almost out, thrust in again, out, in, out, in, out, in; his movements slow, hard, systematic until with a loud gasp he began pumping into her with frantic rapidity, using his grip on her knees to jerk her against him so that each thrust was deeper and more penetrating. With loud cries of release they both climaxed. Even then he continued to jerk and pump into her.

Ginny crept quietly away. Her heart was beating rapidly and her mouth felt dry, but the secret place between her legs was moist, warm and tingling. It was not the first time she had watched a man and woman together, but she had never in all her twenty years, experienced the act herself.

Her aged parents had been straight-laced to the extreme and after she learnt, thanks to a garrulous maid, how children came into being, she marvelled that her parents could ever have engaged in such an activity. For as long as she could remember they had occupied separate bedrooms and displayed no affection, nor made any physical contact, either with each other or the daughter they kept secluded from contact with any man.

It was about a year after she learnt how a man and woman came together to make babies that Ginny discovered some also did it for pleasure.

One afternoon she had gone to the kitchen on an errand for her mother. The pantry door had been open and on passing it she could see the couple who stood close together, kissing. About to continue on she realised that was not all they were engaged in doing. The maid's hand was fondling a large bulge at the crotch of the groom's trousers, and his hand was somewhere underneath the skirt she held hitched up with her free hand.

'Lor, Maisie, you sure know how to stir a man.' The hand that was not under her skirt had been busy freeing her large white breasts from the confines of her bodice, and his mouth now went eagerly to suckle them.

The maid giggled. 'As if you be needing stirring. You be as randy as a stud bull all the time.'

'A randy bull what can hardly wait to stick his rod between your legs and screw you good and hard. But I've got to get back to work. Nine o'clock in the stables Maisie. Don't you be late.'

Ginny hurriedly continued on her way to the kitchen,

delivered her message then, like the dutiful daughter she was, spent the remainder of the afternoon helping her mother stitch an intricate patchwork quilt. Her thoughts, however, were wholly occupied with the little scene in the pantry and she puzzled over the meaning of the interchange. It seemed highly unlikely Maisie and the groom were planning to make a baby for they were not married, and Ginny could not understand why else they would want to do the 'thing'. And then there was that breathless sort of anticipation in their voices which intrigued her no end.

Just after the ninth chime of the huge grandfather clock in the hall reverberated into silence, Ginny pulled a robe over her nightgown and crept quietly downstairs and across the yard to the stables. The small door was slightly ajar and she quickly slipped inside. At the far end, in an empty stall, a trimmed lamp cast a soft glow, and by listening carefully she could hear, above the snorting and stamping of the horses, the sound of feminine giggles.

Ginny knew there was a large crack in the exterior wall of the empty stall. She slipped back outside and hurried around to the rear of the building where she quickly located the crack by the glimmer of light from within. Breathing rapidly and with her heart beating, nervously she pressed her eye to the small aperture.

She barely suppressed her gasp at what she beheld. The groom had already shed his clothing and was standing – stark naked – in the middle of the stall with that odd looking male part of his anatomy jutting stiffly out in front of his body.

Maisie was not completely disrobed. She was still wearing her corsets and pantaloons, though her camisole had been pulled down to expose her large round breasts to the groom's exploring hands. He squeezed and worked the twin mounds as though he was kneading dough, then took each dark nipple between a thumb and

4

forefinger to roll and tweak them until they became hard little peaks.

While he did that Maisie stood watching him with an impish smile on her face, extending the tip of her tongue to pass it lightly over her lips. Her hand moved down to stroke his penis, curving down under to cup his balls before moving back up. She knelt down, still caressing with her hands, her tongue darting out to tease the crack at the tip. Her lips slid over the shaft taking about an inch of it into her mouth. Very slowly she drew her lips back up to the tip before she slid them down a second time to take more of it into her mouth, repeating the action until the entire shaft was encompassed.

The groom gave a shudder. 'Cor, Maisie, you're too much. Lay off woman or I'll be all done before I gets inside you.'

His hands pulled her head away and in a fluid movement she turned onto her hands and knees. He dropped to his knees behind her, found the opening in the centre seam of her pantaloons, pulled it wide to expose her vagina and inserted two fingers. He pushed in and out, stroked up and down, while Maisie wiggled and squeeled with delight. Taking one hand off the floor she twisted around to grab his penis, circled her fingers around it and began to jerk them up and down while his – three of them now – twisted and screwed inside her.

He extracted his fingers and taking his penis in his own hand guided it between her sex lips to begin pumping and thrusting, banging against her buttocks so hard that her large breasts swung backwards and forwards with each movement. Faster and faster he pumped until he let out a cry and gave one, two, three slow, hard thrusts.

Maisie's knees gave way and she collapsed onto the floor with her partner, still joined to her, on top of her. They lay like that for half a minute then he pulled away, rolled her on her back, and, spreading her legs wide, entered her again.

Watching all with a mixture of shock and fascination Ginny suddenly became aware there was considerable moistness between her legs and that she had a peculiar tingling feeling in her private parts. Back in her room, in bed, she hitched up her nightgown and felt down there with her hand. Her fingers encountered the softness of the curly patch of hair then lower still the folds and creases of her woman's place. Quivering a little from curiosity and the fear of doing something forbidden, she cautiously inserted a finger. The place inside was wet and warm and her finger slid experimentally in and out in pleasurable sensation.

Quite soon after that, a particularly severe epidemic of influenza devastated their village and left Ginny an orphan. She could feel no real grief, rather relief that she was free of her parents' restrictive domination. But the greater shock came when her father's will was read. Everything had been left to a second cousin, the only possible male heir. Ginny was penniless unless she married the cousin. And that was something she vowed she would never do. He was several years her senior and she had always thought him both repulsive in looks and sanctimonious in nature. She held no doubt any woman unfortunate enough to be bound to him in matrimony would find herself treated as a lowly drudge.

Ginny had long since decided that if she married it would be for love, and if that was not possible, then she would make certain her husband was a kind-hearted man who could provide her with both wealth and position. That being highly unlikely with the social strictures of Victorian England, she gathered what little money she had, fled to London, and gained an assisted passage to Australia, determined to put her past firmly behind her.

Now as she walked back along the deck after watching the fornicating couple she was feeling more disturbed by the wetness and tingling between her thighs than at any time ever before. She longed to slip her hand down there, knew it would be difficult to do so unobserved in the narrow, 'tween-decks, sleeping space she shared with another girl.

A quick glance revealed no other person in sight, and she rested against a bollard, spread her legs and fumbled beneath her petticoat to insert her finger into her sopping wet hole. But although she was pleasured by the action of sliding her finger in and out of her secret place she had a notion something was missing. Enjoyable though it was it did not induce in her any desire to cry and gasp and moan, like the women did who had a man's thing sliding in and out of them.

'Cor blimey! Now ain't this something. Looks like you be wanting a good hard cock there to help you.'

Ginny's eyes flew open – she had not realised she had shut them – when she heard the rough voice followed by a lascivious chuckle. At the sight of the common sailor with his bloodshot eyes, stubbled chin and gap-toothed grin, she hastily extracted her hand and stumbled to her feet only to find herself imprisoned in a brawny pair of arms with the man's fetid breath hot on her face. When his hand began fumbling beneath her skirt she struggled violently and opened her mouth to scream only to have his, revolting and lustful, clamp over hers.

He pushed her backwards down onto the deck moving one hand to cover her mouth while he held her pinned by the weight of his body and the hard pressure of his rigid cock against her thigh. His other hand had found its target between her legs and rough fingers were twisting and screwing inside her.

'Cor, you wet and hot for it all right, and I got it right here for you.' His hand left her mouth to fumble with the opening of his trousers and Ginny screamed. She might be curious, even eager, to know what it was like to have a man thrust that hard, fascinating part of his

7

anatomy deep inside her but she was not about to allow a smelly, unwashed sailor to be the first.

'On your feet, man!'

The angry command startled them both. Flat on her back Ginny stared upwards in wide-eyed relief at the looming figure of the first officer. For a moment it appeared her assailant was intending to ignore the command. Full of booze and crazed with his sexual urges, he remained as he was until the officer levelled a rather deadly looking pistol in his direction. Then he released his captive and lumbered to his feet.

'She were asking for it,' he declared in sullen defence of his actions.

'That was not the impression I received. Get back to your station immediately and I will see that you are appropriately dealt with tomorrow.'

With a scowl and barely audible curse, the sailor staggered away, and Ginny's saviour bent to assist her from the sitting position she now occupied to her feet.

'Are you all right, Miss Long? Were you hurt at all by that animal?'

'Not really. Oh, but I am glad you came for I believe he would have, have . . .' She was trembling so much from fear and reaction she could say no more. The officer took her arm with gentle solicitude.

'You have received a terrible shock, Miss Long. If you will allow me to take you to my cabin I will give you something to calm your nerves.'

'You are kind, sir, and I thank you, for I do feel in need of something.'

First Officer Jonathon Salter was barely able to suppress a smile of triumph. His heart was beating a little faster as he escorted the trembling girl along the deck to his cabin. He could hardly believe his luck. A connoisseur of women, he had noticed her soon after they sailed from Southampton and he had been itching to get his hand, and more, beneath her petticoats ever since. Her beauty was unusual; gold-brown hair, brown eyes and a figure which curved and swelled in all the right places in perfect proportion to her medium height. During the first weeks of the voyage he had spoken with her several times but until now had never been able to devise a plan for getting her inside his cabin. This night it appeared fate had played into his hands.

Once they were enclosed in his cabin he settled her in a chair and poured generous measures of brandy into two glasses, one of which he presented to her.

'This will make you feel better,' he said. 'Have you ever drunk brandy before?'

'Yes I have,' she admitted. Not that her parents ever knew. On more than one occasion she sneaked a drink because she enjoyed the warm and languorous state the fiery spirit induced. It was no different now. As she sipped slowly she could feel the warmth spreading through her veins to re-stimulate that part of her that had never been opened to a man.

The arousal of desire made her aware she was alone with a man for the first time in her life. Ginny was ripe and eager, and the young first officer, with his wavy blond hair and eyes the blue of the morning sky, was handsome indeed. His physique was splendid; tall and slim but firmly muscled with a most interesting bulge at the crotch of his trousers.

Suddenly afraid she was staring rather too obviously at that part of his anatomy, she raised her head to find him smiling at her.

'Are you feeling better now?'

'Yes thank you, Mr Salter.'

'Johnny, please. And may I call you by your Christian name, Miss Long?'

'It is Virginia, but I prefer to be called Ginny.'

'Virgin-ia. Are you a virgin, Ginny?'

Ginny hesitated before nodding her head. For some reason she felt reluctant to admit it was so. Her lack of

9

experience made her feel like a naive child instead of the sensual woman she believed she could be.

'You are very beautiful, Ginny. I have admired you from the moment I first saw you.' He deposited his glass on the table and moved nearer her chair. 'May I kiss you?'

Before she could gather her wits he cupped her face with his hands and pressed his lips against hers; softly, without pressure. When he drew away he was gazing at her with a faintly puzzled and greatly intrigued expression. 'Have you never been kissed either?'

'I fear I am very ignorant. I have much to learn about the ways of a man and a woman.'

'Would you like me to teach you, Ginny?'

His lips were moving softly over hers once more, his arms curving around her to draw her to her feet whereupon he kissed her more deeply, drugging her senses. Then, just when she was beginning to feel she was drowning in his kiss, his lips released hers to trail a sensuous passage across her cheek, up to her eyelids, then down the other cheek and around to nibble the tiny pink lobe of her ear. Delicious shivers ran down Ginny's spine.

'You enjoyed that didn't you, and they were only kisses. Do you want to learn how good it is to really be with a man?'

Ginny wanted to – desperately – but twenty years of strict moral upbringing were difficult to toss lightly aside. 'I – I don't think it would be proper.'

Johnny continued to trail kisses over her face and neck, his voice husky and persuasive. 'You are too beautiful. There is no way you will reach the end of the voyage with your virginity intact. You were fortunate I came along when I did tonight.'

'Yet from what did you rescue me if you plan to do the same to me yourself,' she protested.

'Hardly the same. I will tutor you in all the delights of making love, of giving and receiving pleasure.' First

Officer Salter prided himself on his powers of seduction and was becoming impatient with her resistance; a reluctance he suspected was totally feigned. 'Allow me to make love to you Ginny, or next time I will let the sailors have their way. Imagine what it would be like with them sticking their filthy cocks into you, one after the other. There would be no tenderness, they would simply use you.'

Ginny was finding it difficult to concentrate for those sensuously tantalising lips were finding every erogenous nerve ending to stimulate and tantalise. And for some reason, instead of repelling her, his words caused an increase of the dampness between her legs. His hands began moving over her back to release the lacing of her gown. 'Take it off, Ginny,' he ordered, and kissed her full on the lips again, working his mouth expertly over hers until she began to tremble from the quickening in the pit of her stomach and the heightened sensations in her woman's place.

Feeling as though she was in a dream she discarded her dress and petticoat so that she stood before him clad only in her camisole and pantaloons, for she had given up wearing stays in the heat of the tropics. He reached out to cup her breasts through the thin material of her camisole, then he adroitly released the drawstring bow and pushed the garment from her shoulders so that her breasts, full, firm and exquisitely shaped, were exposed to his lustful gaze.

She was even more beautiful than he imagined and his breath sucked in sharply. He stroked the smoothness of her skin, cupping her breasts and curving around their shape, with his thumbs circling over the rosy nipples to coax them into rigid peaks.

Suddenly he stepped back, his hand moving down to his trousers, and his engorged manhood sprang forth, hard and erect. He ran his hand lightly along its length. His gaze never left her face while hers was fastened on that fascinating shaft of muscle. She noted the veins that ran up its length and the smooth shiny head with its tiny crack at the tip.

'Touch it, Ginny.'

Mesmerised, Ginny reached out a tentative hand, her fingertips barely touching the hot skin. Grasping her wrist he drew her closer, closing her fingers around his rod. It felt warm and hard, so-o hard. Becoming more daring she slid her hand up and down its length as she had seen the maid do with the groom, marvelling at the way the skin rolled in her hand, amazed to discover the shiny head would almost disappear if she rolled the skin up far enough.

Johnny reached between her thighs to explore the wetness and when he slipped a finger inside it was totally unlike anything she felt when she did it for herself. His experienced finger not only slid in and out it stroked and wiggled finding a spot she never knew existed to send a shivering spasm through her body.

He scooped her into his arms and deposited her on his bunk. Then he released the tape at the waist of her pantaloons and drew them down her legs and over her feet, so that she was naked except for the camisole which remained draped around her midriff. Leaning forward, he kissed the flat plain of her stomach while his hands parted her thighs. Then his head moved lower until he was kissing her special place to send shivers of exquisite sensation coursing through Ginny's body. When his tongue darted out to explore her woman's secrets she gasped with shock, continuing to gasp as he licked and stroked, tickled and teased.

His tongue found the place his finger had touched, stimulating it with rapid movements which sent her into an erotic frenzy. Suddenly the world exploded and she was soaring high into the heavens then drowning on the waves of her orgasm, as he sucked hungrily of her juices until her shuddering abated.

Rising from the bed, he rapidly shed his own clothing while she lay there still bewildered by what had happened to her. It did not seem possible that there was anything else he could do which would pleasure her so much. She discovered there was. He straddled her body and with a hand on his rigid member guided it through the sopping wet curls of her mound and into her hole. He pushed in a little and pulled out again, each time pressing a little deeper until he felt the resistance. Then he continued to push with gentle pressure until he broke through the membrane.

The unexpected pain caused Ginny to cry out, as much in distress that her pleasure should be destroyed as from the pain itself. Once he began stroking rhythmically in and out, Ginny forgot everything except the pleasure of feeling the hard rod of his manhood moving inside her. Instinctively she tensed her internal muscles, gripping him so tightly that he was the one to gasp. He began to thump vigorously, slamming deeply into her, driving her into an ecstatic frenzy. With a supreme thrust and great cry of release he climaxed and Ginny again experienced the explosion of indescribable sensation and the warm flow of her juices.

First Officer Salter collapsed panting on top of her before he raised himself slightly to stroke languorously inside her a few more times.

'Did you enjoy that?'

'Oh yes, yes.'

'Did you imagine it would be anything like that?'

'Never!'

'Would you like to do it again?'

'Oh yes. Please.'

He was still moving gently within her, but when she reached her hands to his buttocks to urge him to faster movement he held her off. 'Not yet, we have all night. Let's have another drink first.'

She felt bereft when he pulled out of her, and when he returned to the bed she was both disturbed and disappointed to note his formerly rampant shaft was hanging limply downwards. A gleam entered his eyes when he observed the direction of her gaze and the pout of disappointment she was unable to hide.

'Don't worry, love,' he assured her. 'He'll come good again.'

And he did.

In between sips of brandy, Johnny fondled her breasts, tipping a drop of the spirits onto each nipple and licking it off. Ginny had nowhere near finished her drink before he tipped her onto her back and entered her again. This time he was more impatient, banging into her with a frenzy which rapidly took them both to another climax. Only then did he allow her to finish her brandy and to dress.

Before she left his cabin he took her in his arms and kissed her deeply. 'You were magnificent, Ginny love. Will you come to me again tomorrow night?'

Ginny went the next night and every night after. She found she was impatient with the days, longed for the nights. Now that she had been initiated into the joys of sex she could not get enough, yet she never considered giving herself to another man. In complete naivety she believed her Johnny was the love of her life and that he was equally enamoured of her. Not even the advice of the far more worldly young woman who shared her sleeping space disturbed her belief in the romantic nature of their liaison.

Well aware the first time Ginny had returned in the wee hours of the morning, she presumed her companion had found a lover among the male passengers. When she realised the truth she felt bound to issue a warning.

'I hope you know what you are doing, Ginny. There is no future in this affair for you.'

'What do you mean? I love Johnny and he loves me.'

'You imagine you love him because he is the first man to have bedded you, and I admit he is a handsome devil. But you have to realise that he does not love you. You are merely his companion of pleasure for this voyage.

Once we reach Melbourne and you leave the ship, he will put you out of his mind. And you may be certain there will be some other woman to accommodate his shaft on the return voyage.'

'That's not true,' cried Ginny, red faced with rage. 'You are jealous because he has not looked at you.'

'Oh he has looked at me all right, very closely, the second night out. And I am not the only one. Our handsome first officer is a randy devil but you certainly have the honour of being the one to have held his interest.'

'Doesn't that prove he cares about me?' Ginny was on the defensive, discovering she did not like to be reminded there were other women who had experienced the pleasure Johnny was capable of giving. Her friend merely scoffed.

'It certainly proves how he feels about you, but love has nothing to do with it. Look, Ginny,' she added when she noted the angry expression in the other's eyes, 'I am only trying to prepare you so that you don't get hurt. You are still such an innocent. And that's another thing. Has it ever occurred to you that you could end up expecting a child?'

'I – well – no.' Ginny suddenly felt terribly unsure. At no time had she given any thought to that possible consequence. When she was with Johnny revelling in the feel of his hard rod slipping, sliding, slamming in and out of her special place and being carried away on mindless explosions of ecstasy, the begetting of babies was the last thing on her mind. Now she frowned and bit her lip in anxiety. 'Is it possible?'

Her friend sighed. 'It is not only possible, it is highly probable unless you take precautions to prevent it happening.'

'What sort of precautions?'

Another sigh. 'It's as well you have me to look out for you or goodness knows what sort of mess you would be in by the time we get to Melbourne. It is quite simple really. All you need is a soft piece of wool soaked in vinegar.' She raised a hand to forestall Ginny's words. 'I know, you have no idea where to obtain such things. I will get them for you and show you how to insert the pad. And Ginny – don't place too much importance on any man's declaration of love. All any of them ever want is to get us on our backs with our legs in the air so they can screw us with those insatiable cocks of theirs. And the damnable part is they know how much we enjoy it.'

While Ginny was grateful for the advice on how to avoid an unwanted pregnancy, she refused to believe she meant no more to her Johnny than an object of lust. So whenever they were together and not actually engaged in driving each other into a sexual frenzy, she began to make seemingly innocent but questioning statements about their future. Not wanting to ask her lover straight out if he planned to marry her, she sought to discover his intentions by more indirect means.

His answers, more cunningly indirect than her questions, allayed her doubts, though it never occurred to her to wonder how they were going to conduct their married life unless he resigned from his position.

Johnny Salter was, however, becoming tired of her possessiveness and assumption of any permanency in their liaison. She was a beautiful woman, sexy, sensual, magnificent to bed and quick to learn all the tricks he taught her. He was still thrilled to have been the first man to have had her, but he had no intention of ever tying himself down to any woman. He decided there was one more lesson for Ginny to learn.

It was their last night of sailing. On the morrow they would reach Melbourne where most of the immigrants would disembark. Convinced the time had come for Johnny to ask her to marry him, Ginny was impatient to go to his cabin. She undressed in the tiny sleeping space, stripping off every garment except her chemise, which she covered with a robe. Eagerly she made her way to the main deck and along to Johnny's cabin.

Not bothering to knock she opened the door and entered only to halt in uncertainty when she discovered her lover was not alone. The second officer and steward were seated at the small table on which were scattered several cards. Feeling a trifle embarrassed she mumbled an apology and would have retreated except Johnny rose hastily to draw her into the cabin and close the door behind her.

'Come in, my dear, we are just finishing our game.' He pressed a glass of brandy into her hands and returned to the table to pick up his cards. Ginny had no idea what game the three were playing, but Johnny dropped his cards with a sigh. 'Well that does it, you've cleaned me out. I'll have to give you an IOU.'

The second officer frowned. 'No IOUs. We want payment now.'

'We-ell.' Johnny appeared to be thinking, then he stood up, walked behind Ginny and before she realised his intention pulled her robe open. 'What do you think gentlemen?'

Ginny's face felt hot. So too did the place between her thighs because there was something about the way the two men were looking at her. Uncertain just what was going on she did not know whether or not she should protest at being thus displayed. She had the notion she was being viewed as some sort of trophy.

Rather nervously she gulped the remainder of her brandy and heard Johnny chuckle. The second officer was sizing her up very carefully, his hot eyes inspecting her inch by inch.

'She's not bad, not bad at all, but we can't see enough to judge whether she will cover the debt.'

Ginny began to realise what was intended. 'What is he talking about, Johnny?'

Johnny shrugged his shoulders. 'I am woefully

unlucky at cards my dear. I have nothing left to offer except –'

'Me?' squeeked Ginny. Full realisation dawned and anger surged through her. 'You're offering me, like a common whore, as payment for your debts? You bastard!' She hurled the brandy glass at him. He saw it coming and ducked so that it shattered against the door. The other men laughed. 'Fire and spirit, eh?'

Still in a rage she turned, picked up the nearest object, which happened to be a heavy paperweight, prepared to hurl it at the one who spoke but strong arms pinned hers to her sides and Johnny's amused voice was near her ear. 'You want to see what she's got, Harry. Come and take a look while I hold her. She will stop protesting soon I promise you.'

Ginny opened her mouth intending to scream only to give a gasp of pain when her arms were jerked roughly behind her. The second officer, Harry, had lumbered to his feet to stand before her, his great hairy paw fumbling at her breasts through the thin material of her chemise. A swarthy man, he was of average height, his eyes being on a level with hers, and she suspected the rest of his body was probably covered with the same dark hairs as the back of his hands. He was strongly muscled and without being aware of it her gaze travelled down to his trousers where she could see the bulge of that other muscle.

He gave a lascivious chuckle, 'Interested, eh?' And before her startled eyes he dropped his trousers so that his engorged member sprang rampant and unrestrained in front of him. Ginny found herself unable to tear her gaze away. It was so different from Johnny's – for some reason she had imagined all men would look the same. Harry's tool was nowhere near as long as her lover's but it was thicker, darker, springing out from a dense mat of tightly curled black hair.

'Like it do you?' he asked. 'Want to feel it?'

He lunged forward to slide his hands under her

18

chemise and around her thighs, lifting her forward and up. She felt Johnny's arms move under her armpits, and his hands cup her breasts as she was lifted off the floor and impaled, without any preparation, onto Harry's throbbing shaft of manhood. His hands shifted her legs so they curled around his waist then returned to grasp her buttocks, working her up and down on his shaft while Johnny supported her under the armpits and squeezed and tweaked her breasts.

It was an experience unlike anything Ginny could ever have imagined. While her mind was trying to tell her she was being used and degraded, her body was responding with pleasure and she could feel the moistness inside her increasing with every thrust. Suddenly he withdrew even though she knew he had not come for his shaft still remained hard and erect.

'She'll do Johnny, but no point in hurrying things. I'm going to have another drink. Your turn, Frederick.'

As Johnny had also released his hold of her, Ginny started for the door, shaking it in frustration when she found it locked. The steward had risen to his feet and followed her. When she turned to glare wildly back at the men he reached out to grab her. She dodged sideways but he lunged after her, caught hold of the back of her chemise and as easily as an angler drawing in a fish, reeled her back to him. With a swift movement he ripped the garment from her body and spun her into his arms, his mouth closing hungrily over hers.

One hand shot down between her legs where his finger began rubbing frantically up and down her slit then pushed inside, frigging and screwing, bringing her close to a climax. Ginny sagged helplessly against him. She no longer cared which of the three men took her, as long as one of them did – in a hurry. Then she felt someone behind her and the pressure of a hard cock against her buttocks. The fingers were withdrawn and the rod of muscle took their place.

Frederick ceased kissing her to push her shoulders

19

down so that she was bent forward at the hips and in that position he held her while Harry slammed his rod deeply into her, grabbing her around the hips to pull her back and magnify the impact of each forward thrust. Faster and faster he worked. Ginny could feel the heat and fire building within her and she came to a shuddering climax only moments before he reached his.

Without realising how she got there she was on her back on the floor, her legs being held high and wide by Harry and Johnny, one on each side, while Frederick had his turn with her. His technique was different, more of a tease. He slid into her then almost out in an action that was smooth and tantalising. The slow, controlled movement which took him right into her then drew almost completely out tingled her already vibrantly attuned nerve ends into heightened awareness.

Just when she thought she could stand no more he withdrew completely, rested back on his knees, and with his shaft in his hand proceeded to rub the tip up and down her slit, finding her special spot, teasing it until she began to moan and writhe, wriggling her hips to get more of it. He pulled away, then slapped it against her, the unexpectedness of the action making her gasp. There was another slap and another. This was something Johnny had never done to her, and she found the sensation of his cock being slapped against her sex lips wildly stimulating. She could feel herself building towards another orgasm and gaspingly begged him to put it inside her.

He obliged, sliding deep inside her as far as he could go then twisting and grinding as though he would work his shaft in further. He withdrew only a fraction, twisting and grinding within her a second time, a third time, a fourth time, and Ginny came. Arching and rearing against him she slipped her hands under her buttocks to lift herself up to him while he continued with the same movement of withdrawing slightly then pushing in with a twisting motion.

Ginny's orgasm did not pass. It went on and on, waves and waves of exquisite pleasure unlike any she had ever experienced before. She did not even know when he climaxed for the steady rhythm of his body moving inside hers never altered. She was only aware that eventually he withdrew, her legs were released and she lay naked on the floor in near exhaustion.

Then she was rolled onto her stomach. Hands she knew well clasped her hips, lifted them from the floor and Johnny entered her, doggy fashion, as he had done many times before. It was a position she usually enjoyed. Now she was too spent to feel anything except a shadow of the pleasure she had just experienced, and a certain relief when he thrust into her three times with extra force and she knew he too had climaxed.

That was all three of them; she hoped they were now satisfied. They were not. They gave her wine to drink then each had his way with her again and again, using every imaginable position, and Ginny lost count of the number of times she climaxed.

Whatever her thoughts when she first realised the men's intentions, Ginny knew, when she eventually dragged her exhausted body back to her own sleeping quarters, she had never enjoyed a night of sex so much. Having three men at once was not something she would like to do every night – too exhausting – but it was certainly exciting.

There was something else she had discovered. She was not in love with Johnny as she supposed. She was in love with what he did to her – with having sex. After her many varied experiences of that night Ginny decided she wanted to make love with as many different men as possible. While she had no intention of becoming a paid prostitute she decided she could use her sex to gain both the wealth and social position she desired.

Chapter Two

Wattle Creek was much like any other colonial gold mining town. It had sprung up virtually overnight and where there had once been only virgin bush, there now stood a town of over a thousand inhabitants, with an estimated additional thousand living on the surrounding gold fields. At this particular time, in the late 1860s, it was at the height of its prosperity. No fewer than sixteen hotels stretched along its dusty main street with another half dozen or so scattered along the side streets. Various shops, general stores, grocers, blacksmiths, wheelwrights and banks filled the spaces between.

On a sweltering February afternoon Dan Berrigan and his mates lounged in the shade against the wall of the Post and Telegraph office. They were occupied in doing nothing other than watching the passers-by, for already the Saturday crowds were beginning to come into town. By evening there would barely be enough room to walk along the main street. A skittish horse, ridden by a newly arrived city gent, stirred up a small cloud of dust in front of them, eliciting a few choice oaths from the three men.

'Hell!' declared Charlie, whose six feet of muscled

frame and flaming red beard made him noticeable in any crowd, 'A man could bloody choke just standing in the street. I vote we go wet our whistles down at the Grand.'

'Yeah,' agreed Josh. 'You coming, Dan?'

'Not yet. You two go ahead. I'll maybe join you later.'

His companions gaped at him. Josh, who was a good six inches shorter than the other two, stretched himself to his full height and waggled a finger in his ear. 'Reckon I must be going deaf.'

'What do you mean, you're not coming? You sickening for something?' demanded Charlie, for Dan had never been known to turn down a drink.

A quick infectious grin split Dan's face, strong white teeth a startling contrast against the tan of his skin. He lifted his hat, ran his fingers through his unruly black hair, and said, 'Just got something better to do.'

'Now what could be better than – oh, I see,' Charlie gave a wicked chuckle. 'That cock of yours will get you into trouble one of these days, old boy. Don't think she's going to lift her petticoats for you, not without a wedding ring on her finger.'

Dan merely grinned again. 'We'll see. Go on you pair, I'll catch up with you later. If not I'll see you back at camp.'

When his mates departed, with a crude parting jibe over which they chuckled all the way down the street, Dan returned his attention to the girl who was approaching along the other side of the street.

Miss Jenny Townsend was a picture to behold. Dressed in a summery gown of pale lemon she appeared unaffected by the heat and dust of the afternoon. Petite of build, her sweet, heart-shaped face was topped by tresses the colour of corn silk and her eyes were the deep blue of a precious sapphire. Her voice, Dan knew, was as sweet as her face. She was young, innocent, absolutely adorable, and he had known from the moment he first laid eyes upon her that he had to have her.

That had been five weeks previously when her father

had arrived to take over as manager of the Bank of New South Wales. Ever since then Dan had been endeavouring to find some way of being alone with her. All he had ever managed were brief conversations in the very public main street, and his desire to bed her had become almost an obsession. He drifted off to sleep at night visualising what it would be like to have her. He was a tall man, solidly built, and his manly asset, when aroused, conformed with his other dimensions. And she was so tiny!

He watched her now from beneath drooped lids, making careful note of the trim thrusting breasts, the diminutive waist and slender hips. He visualised the whiteness of her skin, the golden hairs that would cover her mound, and imagined how tight her hole would be, how it would grip his shaft and make his passage into her even more stimulating.

Christ! He shook his head to clear the image and straightened up away from the wall. If he wasn't careful he'd explode inside his trousers just thinking about it. Taking a few deep breaths to steady himself, and willing his rampant member to a quiescent state, he sauntered across the road to intercept her.

'Afternoon, Miss Townsend.'

'Good afternoon, Mr Berrigan.'

'Are you shopping?' he asked, indicating the basket on her arm.

'I am on my way to the Chinese garden. Mother needs some fresh vegetables for dinner.'

'It would give me the greatest pleasure if you would allow me to walk with you, Miss Townsend. Perhaps', he suggested with a quirked eyebrow, 'we could go by the river path for it will be cooler than walking through town.'

'I would like that,' she agreed with a shy blush. 'It really is far too hot today.'

Dan suppressed a triumphant smile, fell into step beside the petite Miss Townsend, and escorted her along

24

the street and down to the river bank. The market garden lay a good distance beyond the main part of the town and by the time they had gone half the distance Dan had brought them to first name terms. Once they were out of sight of the other people who were taking advantage of the cool shade on the river bank, he took her arm and drew her to a halt.

'Why don't we rest here awhile and enjoy the breeze?'

Her mouth formed into a little O of uncertainty and her beautiful blue eyes held coy hesitation. Dan swiftly assured her he meant her no harm.

'Oh, I did not think you did,' she replied hastily, 'but my mother will be wanting the vegetables and if I dally she may become concerned.'

'A few minutes, that is all I ask.' He had taken her hand and was slowly circling the pad of his thumb around its palm, knowing well how sensual a caress that could be. His words held a seductive huskiness. 'I have been wanting to get to know you better, ever since we met.'

'I would like to know you better too,' she admitted shyly, 'but my father does not want me to associate with the miners.'

'We are not all ruffians, some of us are quite respectable.'

He had coaxed her to sit down on the ground beside him and was kissing her knuckles, turning her hand over to press his lips first against her palm then the inside of her wrist. He felt her tremble, and placing both hands on her shoulders kissed her on the mouth. It was only a soft touch, a tentative tasting. When she did not object he kissed her again, more deeply, moving his mouth over hers, exploring and enticing with his tongue, tasting her, drugging her with sensation until she was quivering in his arms.

One hand moved down to cup her breast, his thumb stroking its peak through the material of her dress. His mouth continued to hold hers captive giving her no

25

chance to protest. Only when he succeeded in releasing some of the buttons to slip his hand inside to lay it against the smoothness of her flesh did she twist her lips free, her beautiful eyes wide with shocked innocence. 'Oh no, you must not.'

'It's all right,' he gentled her, knowing no man had ever touched her in such a manner before. 'I am not hurting you am I? Do you like this?'

His thumb was stroking her nipple, circling and teasing it to hardness. Feeling its response and receiving a moaned appreciation of his actions, he hurriedly released the remaining buttons of her bodice to expose her breasts to his view. They were as he had imagined, small, firm, milky white mounds just waiting to be suckled.

She moaned her pleasure as he sucked gently on them and teased the nipples with the tip of his tongue. One of his hands began feeling its way beneath her gown and petticoats to caress slowly up a stockinged calf until it encountered the frilled edge of her pantaloons. Why, he wondered, did women have to wear so many damned clothes. He fumbled for the crotch of her pantaloons and slipped his hand inside, silencing her small protest with another drugging kiss.

His fingers found the soft, downy hair of her mound then stroked down across her slit. He continued stroking her externally until he felt her wetness. Only then did he insert his finger. He probed gently, working in and out, caressing her, agitating at her clitoris, then sliding in again, thrusting and circling until he felt her shudder and the warm juices flowed over his hand.

Without removing his finger he lifted his mouth from hers and stared down at her, 'Did you enjoy that, Jenny?'

'Oh yes,' she breathed, her face aglow with wonder. 'What did you do to me?'

'I showed you the pleasure a woman can only feel with a man. But it can be better than that. A thousand times better. Let me take you somewhere.'

26

'Do you mean some place where we would be quite alone?'

'Yes. Perhaps we could go to one of the hotels.'

'Oh no! I could never do that.'

'Then where?' he demanded, impatient, now he had got this far, to strip her of her clothing, spread her legs wide and slide his rigid, throbbing shaft into her tight, wet hole.

'You could come to my house tomorrow night.'

'Your house? What about your parents?'

'They always go visiting. I could plead a headache and remain at home.'

Dan's heartbeat quickened and he felt his shaft jerk inside his trousers. After five weeks what was another day. Anticipation would only heighten the thrill of his eventual possession. He withdrew his hand from beneath her skirt, rebuttoned her bodice and kissed her again. 'Until tomorrow then.'

He was smiling broadly when he walked back into town. It had been easier than he thought. Having expected to engage in a drawn out wooing process, he could hardly believe the readiness with which she had capitulated. Eager for the next thirty odd hours to pass, he decided he might as well get rid of the load he was carrying. He did not want to spoil it by coming too soon when he finally got to screw the dainty Miss Townsend.

Down at the Grand, Charlie and Josh were making good work of a bottle of rum and had reached the stage where they were not completely inebriated but their senses, particularly their sexual ones, were pleasantly heightened. Charlie's gaze was attracted by the considerable expanse of plump white bosom which became visible when one of the barmaids leaned forward over a neighbouring table.

'You know, Josh, we've both screwed Liz and Betsy more times than we can count and I reckon it's getting a wee bit boring, don't you agree?'

'What have you got in mind?' Josh knew no remark of Charlie's was made without reason.

'Why don't we get the both of them together. You know, the two of them and the two of us.'

'Why not?' agreed Josh. 'It could be fun.'

The girls apparently thought so too, and half an hour later the four were in one of the Grand's upstairs bedrooms sharing the last of the bottle of rum.

'Well, who's first?' asked Charlie, unsure now they were together what to do next.

The girls giggled and exchanged mischievous glances. 'Why don't you boys just relax and finish your drinks. You said you want something different so we'll give you something different.'

Betsy was a buxom redhead with bulbous breasts and a thatch of gold-red hair between her thighs. Though not so well endowed in the mammary department, Liz was well proportioned. Being olive skinned her thatch was a veritable jungle of black curls. The girls had quickly shed their garments, their contrasting colourings stimulating arousal in the two men. Before their astounded eyes, Liz lay back on the bed with her legs opened wide and Betsy, parting the thick thatch with her fingers, promptly darted in with her tongue to begin licking and sucking for all she was worth.

Both Charlie and Josh felt their cocks jerk to instant rigidity. The sight of Betsy's plump white backside wriggling in front of him while she licked and slurped at Liz's fanny was too much for Charlie. He lurched to his feet, dropped his trousers and took the couple of steps required to enable him to slip his fingers between Betsy's legs. Inside she was wet and warm and his cock quickly replaced his fingers. Grabbing her by the hips he pushed into her, excited by how slippery she was. Muttering forceful oaths to express the unbelievable arousal he was feeling, he slammed his rod in and out and gyrated it around while she continued to slurp and suck at Liz.

Josh, already stripped naked, was looking frantically around for a place to stick his throbbing shaft when Liz beckoned him to the bed. He knelt up beside her and, propping herself on one elbow, she used the other hand to guide his hot and randy organ into her mouth. She slid her lips up and down it, sucking him in then easing him out. The tip of her tongue teased the sensitive head until he thought he would go mad from the effort of trying not to come in her mouth.

Just when he thought he could hold on no longer she turned onto all fours and he rammed into her from behind, slamming into her so hard his balls were slapping against her. Grunting and groaning like a rutting bull he jerked frantically back and forth, spilling himself into her with a great groan of release.

Meanwhile Charlie had somehow managed to pull Betsy back with him so that he lay on his back on the floor and she was kneeling astride him with her back to him. In that position she worked herself up and down on him. She would lift up, almost off him so that only his tip was still inside her. Then she pushed down again, right to the hilt, completing the movement with a small circular motion before lifting up again. Then down hard, circle, lift up, down, circle, lift up, down, circle – Charlie shot his load with a shouted, blasphemous oath at the wrenching intensity of his explosion.

The four of them rested awhile and cracked open another bottle of rum. Betsy began stroking Josh's poor limp rod back into life, her skilful hand rapidly achieving the required result. He pushed her back onto the bed and rammed it into her warm, receptive hole. Hooking her hands beneath her knees, she held her legs high and wide to give him unrestricted access, enabling him to drive into the very hilt. Once there he began to circle his hips, screwing and twisting his shaft inside her just as she had been circling and twisting over Charlie minutes before. His hands grasped her large breasts, rotating them in conjunction with his hips. Three times clockwise, three times anti-clockwise, then clockwise again, his shaft growing bigger and harder the more he worked. He knew he would be a long while coming a second time, however, his gyrations gave Betsy not one, but two, shattering orgasms.

It did not take long for Charlie, who was relaxed in a chair watching them, to come alive again. Seeing his rod grow erect, Liz straddled him and eased herself down over it. 'Geez,' thought Charlie, it was the first time he'd ever done it sitting in a chair. Grabbing Liz's hips he jerked her up and down, enjoying the novelty but becoming frustrated because he could not manage to push himself fully into her. Down on the floor it was better, with him on his back and Liz sliding herself up and down. He pulled her forward so he could suck and nibble her tits at the same time.

Limp and exhausted, Betsy was begging Josh to let her be. Even though he still had not reached a second climax, he gave into her pleas and withdrew his rock hard rod. He got off the bed, moved to where Charlie and Liz were in high time on the floor and shoved a finger into Liz's rear. Her gasp of approval was all the encouragement he needed. He worked her a little more with his finger, positioned himself behind her and the next time she slid backwards on Charlie's shaft, pushed his rod into her arse. Its tightness was all he needed. Josh spurted into her rear hole, Charlie spurted into her sex hole and Liz, sandwiched between them, thought she was dissolving with the most shattering orgasm of her life.

Dan lay on the bed stretched out on his back with his hands pillowed under his head, and allowed Michelle to do her job. She was an expert, there was no doubt about that. Whether it had anything to do with her being French or not he did not know, but she possessed the most erotic tongue he had ever come across. She always kissed first, moist sensual kisses, before working her way slowly downwards. Her tongue moved down his neck, his shoulders, his chest, etched erotic circles around his nipples. It trailed feather-light across his hard muscled stomach, investigated his navel, then moved further down, circling the base of his shaft and licking up to the head. When it began to tickle the sensitive tip Dan groaned his pleasure. She took just the head between her lips, sucking gently before sliding her tongue down to the base again and around to his balls.

'It is good, mon ami?' she lifted her head to ask.

'It is good,' he agreed.

'Then it is my turn, non?'

'No,' he answered. He had sucked and tasted her juices before but this afternoon he was not in the mood. While his body was enjoying the expert ministrations of her lips and tongue, his thoughts were wholly with Miss Jenny Townsend. All he wanted of Michelle was for her to empty his load.

Shifting their positions, he turned her onto her back and entered her carefully. He knew it was not easy for most women to accommodate his size and he had learnt not to be over eager. Always careful, he would ease into his partner bit by bit so he would not cause hurt. He took it gradually, pushing in a little, pulling back and pushing in a little further, repeating the process until he was able to penetrate deeply, by which time the recipient of his tool was usually reduced to a state of mindless pleasure simply from having all that male hardness filling her.

It was the same now. Michelle's sensual moans of delight heightened his own pleasure. He took her large white breasts in his hands, squeezing and massaging them while he worked his shaft back and forth in her warm and slippery hole. When he felt himself close to his climax, he withdrew and thrust his massive rod hard against her breast bone squeezing the twin mounds of her breasts together. Thus encompassed he thrust up and down between them until his juice spurted out to cream onto her throat.

Sundays were rest days. No one did any mining. The religious walked into town to attend whatever services were available and the others, like Dan and his mates, tidied their camps, washed clothes and repaired equipment. While Josh and Charlie delighted in recounting the activities of the previous afternoon – and found themselves becoming re-aroused in the process – Dan remained reticent on the subject of Miss Jenny Townsend. He steadfastly ignored the good-natured jibes of his mates, especially when he fetched a bucket of water from the creek, stripped, and proceeded to wash himself. That done, he shaved, put on a clean shirt and combed his unruly black hair into temporary order.

It was all too much for Josh who was becoming goggle-eyed, with disbelief. 'Geez mate, I've never seen you go to that much trouble before just for a bit of skirt. You sure you're not meeting the parents, like is right and proper?'

Dan laughed, his eyes twinkling with merriment. 'Her old man would not let me so much as get a foot in the door, so there'll be no right and proper about it. It's in the back door for me as soon as her folks have gone out – and she being a lady of class she'll appreciate a man taking the trouble to make himself clean.'

'Well if you're planning to sneak in the back door you had better make sure her old man doesn't catch you or there'll be hell to pay.'

Again the irrepressible grin. 'It isn't the first back door I've been in and out, nor window for that matter. I've managed to evade more fathers and husbands than I can count and I don't intend to get caught this time either. But don't wait up for me,' he added with an even broader grin.

His mates both laughed. 'We won't, cause you'll probably wear yourself out with the pure Miss Townsend and we'll have to do all the bloody work tomorrow.'

Dan walked briskly from the diggings into town. He decided against riding his horse, figuring the animal's presence would be a dead giveaway. The night was warm, a faint breeze preventing it from being uncomfortably hot. There was a pleasurable feeling of anticipation in his gut that was rapidly spreading to his loins. He could not recall when he had last taken a maiden's virginity, and as a rule he was not particularly interested in doing so. Women with more experience and fewer inhibitions were more to his taste. But he just had to have Miss Jenny Townsend and the knowledge he would be the first added extra titillation. He was looking forward to initiating her into the joys of sex.

When he reached the town he avoided the main street, veering instead towards the lane which ran along the rear of the shops. The manager's residence was on the top floor of the two-storied bank building, its rear access an external flight of stairs. Dan paused in the shadows of the yard to make certain there was no witness to his presence before he began, as stealthily as a burglar, to mount the stairs. Very cautiously he turned the knob of the door, relaxing when it swung noiselessly inwards.

The room into which he stepped was a kind of parlour, but he took little note of how it was furnished. Miss Jenny Townsend stood in its centre waiting for him, clad only in a blue silk robe with her golden hair cascading over her shoulders. Dan realised she was naked under the robe, the knowledge sufficient to make his loins throb and his shaft swell to its maximum size. He experienced an animalistic urge to seize her and take her immediately, without any foreplay.

With an effort he controlled himself and allowed his gaze to rove slowly over her body, pausing slightly at every feminine curve as though he could see through her garment to the hidden treasures beneath. The rise of pink colour in her cheeks brought a smile to his lips. He knew she would already be feeling wet between the legs for he had yet to meet the woman who was immune to the warm, seductive intensity of his dark eyes.

Forced to again remind himself she was a virgin he stepped forward, took her in his arms and pressed his firm mouth against the petalled softness of her lips. When she kept them together, passive beneath his, he curbed his impatience with her innocence. An expert in the art of kissing he coaxed her lips apart, moving his mouth on hers until she parted her lips in breathless response. He slid a hand down her back to mould her against his body, pressing his rigid shaft against the flat of her stomach. Positive she was wearing nothing underneath, he worked the material of her robe up to enable him to slip both hands under, clasp the tight cheeks of her buttocks, and press her even closer.

'Your bedroom,' he whispered urgently.

Without a word she eased out of his hold and led the way down the passage. Dan followed her into her room and carefully shut the door behind them. Only then did she speak; a shy plea for him to be gentle, not to hurt her. He reassured her, his hands already at the front of her robe, releasing the fastenings. It slid easily from her shoulders to subside, crumpled, to the floor.

Dan felt a stab in his groin just looking at her. Standing naked with her hair cascading over her body and waves of blue silk at her feet, she was the personification of some exquisite water nymph. God but she was tiny. And so perfect; from the rosy tips of her taut little breasts to the cluster of pale golden curls where her thighs joined. He scooped her into his arms and carried her to the bed.

'Will you do what you did to me yesterday?' she asked.

'If that's what you want.' Already his finger was feeling its way, stroking and parting her folds to find its way inside. 'I will do other things too, that you will enjoy even more.' He bent his head to take her tiny breast into his mouth, nibbling on her nipples with gentle pressure of his teeth. She moaned her pleasure and he worked his finger more rapidly in her juicy hole. To his surprise she came almost immediately with panting little oohs of ecstasy. When she opened her eyes their normal clear blue had become stormy with desire. In a husky voice she pleaded for more.

It took Dan only a few moments to shed his clothes. Kneeling on the floor he grasped her legs and swung her sideways across the bed, pulling her towards him until her buttocks aligned with the edge of the mattress. Using gentle pressure he spread her knees wide, parted her soft pink sex lips and plunged his tongue deep into her crevice, revelling in her salty taste. She jerked once in shock, then began to gyrate her hips to magnify the impact of his caressing tongue.

This time it took longer for her to come. When she did, it was with a frenzied, animal-like cry. Dan licked and sucked going almost crazy with the taste of her. He raised his head, inserted two fingers and frigged her rapidly. His other hand he clasped around his hot, throbbing shaft. Then he sucked her again, drawing out her passion's liquid until her twitching body became quiet and her moans faded.

He lifted her straight on the bed, clambered between her legs and guided the head of his impatient rod into her. Christ! She was every bit as tight as he had imagined. The tautness around his shaft almost made him come immediately. By exerting considerable willpower he held himself in check. If he was not to hurt her he would need to take it extra carefully, for he doubted she would be able to accommodate all of him.

Working gently, he pulled back and pushed in half a dozen times, giving her only the head, teasing himself with the feel of her. Then he began to push in more deeply, though still with controlled care, waiting for the resistance he knew he would feel. After a dozen or so strokes he suddenly realised he had almost penetrated her fully, and the expected resistance had not been there.

35

Up till then he had been watching the movement of his shaft penetrating her sex. Now he looked at her, noting the way she lay with her eyes half closed, her lips parted, a self-satisfied expression on her face. The truth hit him with shock force.

'Why you deceitful little slut. You're no more a virgin than any of the whores in town.' And he slammed the entire swollen length into her, ignoring her cries of protest.

Dan was an easygoing bloke most of the time. But if someone did the wrong thing by him or deceived him in any way he had the very devil of a temper. Miss Jenny Townsend was feeling the full force of that temper through the giant rod of hot angry muscle he rammed savagely in and out between her legs. Once he gained his release he moved from the bed, pulled on his clothes and stormed out of the house without a word. Jenny was left bruised, aching and vengeful.

When her parents returned two hours later they were perturbed by the sound of muffled sobs, and on opening her door were aghast to find the room in disarray, with an upturned chair and shattered vase indicating a vicious struggle had taken place. Worse was the sight of their beautiful daughter curled in a shivering, sobbing heap on the bed. Jenny shuddered and whimpered when her mother reached a comforting hand to her, pulling her robe protectively tight around her body. Only after considerable gentle coaxing did she raise an anguished tear-stained face to cry in a wretched voice, 'Oh Mummy, Daddy, I've been raped!'

Dan was in the filthiest of moods, unable to believe he had been taken in by her false innocence. His anger both with the deceitful Miss Townsend and with himself for being so easily duped affected his attitude towards Charlie and Josh. The three were the greatest of friends with never a cross word passing between them, but by mid-morning both Charlie and Josh had endured about as much of Dan's ill humour as they could take. Figuring he was going to be no company until he worked whatever was bothering him out of his system, they decided they might as well go into town to collect the stores they originally set out to buy on the Saturday before they had become distracted by their sexual high jinks.

Deciding a cold beer would not go astray they headed for the Grand. There were about a dozen men in the bar, all of whom ceased talking to stare at them the moment they walked through the door. The publican glared at them. 'You can take your custom elsewhere. I don't want any trouble with the law.'

'What the hell are you talking about?' demanded Josh. 'Why should we cause you any problems?'

Charlie was noting the sombre, unfriendly expressions of the other customers. A frown puckered his brow. 'What the hell's going on anyway?'

'It's what went on last night that's the trouble,' one man informed them. 'Your mate Dan broke into the bank and raped the Townsend girl.'

For a moment both Charlie and Josh simply stared at the speaker with their mouths agape. Then they both spoke at once.

'What the devil do you mean?'

'Why, you bloody liar!'

Seeing that the two were prepared to launch into a physical, and probably violent, defence of their absent mate, the publican hastily intervened. 'It's true all right, the news is all over town. The sergeant rode out a few minutes ago with a warrant for his arrest.'

Charlie and Josh did not hang around to ask any more questions. There was a short cut through the bush which they took at a breakneck speed, hoping to reach camp before the law. Dan, his curiosity initially aroused by the sound of thundering hooves, was startled to realise it was his two mates who were galloping towards him as though there were demons at their backs.

Charlie was yelling at him even before he hauled his

37

mount to a stop and jumped from the saddle. 'You bloody fool! I told you that cock of yours would get you into trouble one day.'

Dan's voice remained steady despite the prickling warning of danger that crawled up his spine. 'What's the matter?'

'The Townsend chit screamed rape,' Josh informed him in a hard voice. 'The cops are on their way here with a warrant for your arrest.'

'The bitch!' Anger rapidly replaced Dan's initial shock. No deceitful, whoring little slut was going to get the better of him. Noting the light of battle enter Dan's eyes Charlie swore.

'For Chrissakes, man, you've got to make a run for it. Nobody is going to believe your word against hers.'

'He's right, Dan,' agreed Josh. 'You won't stand a chance in court.'

Reluctantly Dan recognised the validity of their argument. With their help he rapidly gathered a few things together, mounted his horse, and was barely out of sight over the ridge before the sergeant and his trooper rode up to the camp. Charlie and Josh quite skilfully sent the police on a wild goose chase in the opposite direction then stared gloomily at their mine shaft and wondered what was going to happen next.

As he rode deeper into the bush, Dan was brooding over the same thing. The three of them had enjoyed a pretty good life with their mine giving them more than enough to live on, even if it was not making them rich. He was just 27 years old and now, thanks to that lying little bitch, his life appeared to have been ruined. He vowed then that somehow, someday, somewhere, he was going to get even with Miss Jenny Townsend.

Chapter Three

Ginny picked up the crystal goblet, sipped the golden wine, and pretended an interest in the pontifications of the elderly gentleman seated on her left. She glanced along the table taking little note of the expensive silverware, glittering crystal, fine china and delicate hothouse flowers which sat upon the perfectly starched, snowy damask cloth. From the other end her wealthy, estimable husband gave her a faint nod of smiling approval. With a barely suppressed sigh Ginny took another sip of the imported German wine and told herself she should be content.

Everleigh was one of the grandest mansions in Melbourne and its owner, William Leigh, had taken Ginny for his wife some four months earlier. His position in colonial society was of the highest standing, and Ginny's life was a pleasant succession of dinner parties, balls, theatre outings and all the other activities deemed entertaining and suitable for the elite and wealthy. She wore gowns of the latest fashion and jewels of considerable value, yet she was becoming increasingly restless and discontented.

William Leigh was an impressive figure of a man. Tall, well built, with only the slightest of paunches, his thick grey hair enhanced his distinguished features. His appearance gave the impression of a man barely fifty rather than one rapidly approaching his sixty-sixth birthday. Just six months after her arrival in the colony, Ginny had exchanged her vows with her husband, for it had taken very little time to bring him to that stage once she decided he would be able to give her everything, and she meant everything, she wanted.

Unfortunately his manly shaft did not match the rest of his splendid physique and the fact his heart, in spite of his virile appearance, was less than strong, rendered him disinclined to engage in any strenuous bedroom capers. On the few occasions he came to his wife's bed it was for a quick coupling in the dark, which left Ginny aroused and totally unsatisfied.

At least he was a kind and generous husband and if it were possible for her to take a lover, or preferably lovers, then she would find no complaints with her life. Ginny knew there were many among their acquaintances who would be only too eager to satisfy her sexual needs except, without it being in any way obvious, her husband managed to keep her under close and jealous surveillance.

The conversation at the table had drifted to politics. Totally bored by a subject about which she knew little and cared less, Ginny allowed her gaze to rove over their guests. Playing an amusing little mind game she tried to imagine how each would act in the bedroom. All of the women, she decided, were so corseted and correct they were probably, without exception, relieved if all they were forced to endure were quick copulations beneath the blankets in the dark.

Of the ten male guests, four could be deemed too old to have either interest or ability in the act and the priest could definitely be discounted. Ginny was positive no licentious thought ever crossed that pious man's mind. The doctor was too fat and she rather imagined the thin, effeminate-looking man talking to him held little interest in women. That left three.

The number conjured erotic memories of her wonderful last night aboard ship. As clearly as if it had been yesterday, she recalled how Johnny and the second officer held her legs high and wide, opening her up for the steward. She remembered how he had rubbed the head of his organ against her slit then slapped it against her sex lips until she was at the throbbing threshold of a climax. So vivid were the memories she realised she was becoming rather wet between the thighs.

'They say it will be a hot summer again, Mrs Leigh. What do you think?'

'It – I – oh yes.' Ginny brought her disturbing thoughts back to the table to smile at the man who addressed her. 'Oh yes, Mr James, a very hot summer indeed,' she agreed, with a direct stare of open-eyed innocence which brought a quirky smile to the corners of his mouth.

After dinner the guests adjourned to the drawing room where most soon became engaged in various card games. Seeing that her husband was thus occupied, Ginny turned to Mr James who, with the doctor, had declined to play. 'I believe you have an interest in rare books, Mr James. Perhaps you would be interested in seeing my husband's collection. You too, doctor,' she added with perfect propriety.

'No, no,' declined the doctor, 'too replete to get up.' He accepted another glass of port from a servant. 'You two go along, I don't mind.'

Walking sedately Ginny led the way out of the drawing room and down the hall to the library, her companion following silently behind. Inside she lit a single lamp and turned to smile at him. 'It is unfortunate, Mr James, but we must be quick.'

'I understand, Mrs Leigh. If you would be so good as to bend over the desk.'

Ginny obliged.

Mr James deftly lifted her skirts, spread the seam of

41

her pantaloons and inserted his finger, not surprised to find she was already dripping wet and becoming wetter with every stroke he made.

'Oh do hurry,' Ginny begged, impatient to have a decent shaft inside her, fearful they might be discovered.

Mr James withdrew his finger, and a few moments later a gasp of pure pleasure left her lips when she felt his warm shaft slide into her pulsing sex. Oh God! It was heaven! He was big and hard, thrusting into her to stroke places which had been deprived of stimulation during all the months of her marriage. It was too much. She came quickly, violently, biting her knuckles to prevent herself from crying out loud her excitement at both her wonderful orgasm and the magnificent feel of his randy shaft sliding in and out of her long deprived channel.

In less than ten minutes they were on their way back to the drawing room. Outside the door he paused and raised her hand to his lips. 'You have done me a great honour, Mrs Leigh. It is a pity I leave Melbourne tomorrow for I would have liked to have had the opportunity to become better acquainted.'

The greater pity, Ginny mused several weeks later, was that such brief encounters only exacerbated her dissatisfaction with her sex-starved life and heightened her longing for something more exciting. As she had done when an unawakened virgin, she resumed the habit of using her own fingers, except now she knew how to rub and stimulate herself to achieve a climax. It afforded her some relief even if it was not the same as having a man.

Thus it was she lay one afternoon resting on the chaise longue in her private sitting room, thinking of the dinner party they were giving that evening. Which of the guests she wondered, giving them a mental review, might be interested in being shown the library. The afternoon was hot and she was clad only in a robe, her near nakedness and erotic imaginings stimulating an awareness within her sex place. She opened her robe, fondled her breasts with one hand and positioned the other between her legs.

Resting her head back she closed her eyes, relaxed in the enjoyment she was giving herself. In no hurry to climax she stroked languidly, soothingly, almost lulling herself into a half sleep. In that state she did not hear the light knock on her door and was unaware her maid, Tessa, had entered the room until the girl spoke.

'Would you like me to help you, ma'am?'

Ginny's eyes sprang open and with a gasp she hurriedly removed her hand and attempted to close her robe. The maid, however, had already sunk to her knees and rapidly inserted her fingers in the place of Ginny's. Her actions were so perfect the protest Ginny had been on the point of making was immediately forgotten. She closed her eyes again and gave herself up to the maid's expert ministrations.

Tessa removed her fingers, lifted one of Ginny's legs over the back of the chaise longue, spread her thighs wide, and applied her tongue in the same manner as she had applied her finger. Shivers of satisfaction ran through Ginny's body. She would never have believed she would enjoy having another woman do such things to her, but enjoy it she did. Oh, how adroitly the girl stroked, licked and tickled her clitoris.

Ginny felt the quickening deep down, the flow of warmth inside. She writhed and twisted, jerking herself against the erotic tongue until her juices seared forth in a flood which the maid licked and sucked until Ginny's twitching ceased and she relaxed. The girl rose to her feet, wiped her mouth on her apron and looked down at Ginny with an insolent smirk.

'I can solve your problem, ma'am. You have need of a lover and I know my brother is eager to have you.'

Ginny had pulled herself to a sitting position and gathered her robe over her nakedness. Something in the way the maid was watching her filled her with unease. Instantly she regretted what had just taken place for she realised the girl intended to use it to whatever advantage she could.

'You are being presumptuous', she stated, in her haughtiest voice, 'to even make such a suggestion. You will forget – completely – everything which happened in the last few minutes or you will be dismissed.'

The girl gave a slight shrug, the insolence remaining in her expression. 'Dismiss me, ma'am, and Melbourne society will have much to talk about. And you would not want the master to learn just how you show your guests the library.'

Ginny's gasp was a mixture of outrage and shock. For how long, she wondered, had the girl been spying on her? There was no doubt her threats were very real. Ginny shuddered; not only at the thought of becoming a social outcast, the laughing stock of Melbourne, but with the knowledge of how such disclosures would humiliate and hurt her good, kind husband.

'Very well – ' she sighed, 'what is it you want?'

'I want my brother to have what he desires. I will tell him to be waiting for you tonight, after the guests have left.'

It was blackmail! Straight out blackmail. Any intention of resting for the remainder of the afternoon now totally abandoned, Ginny paced her room, her emotions fluctuating between regret at what had occured, anger at her maid for taking advantage, and an uneasy fatalism. She was aware Logan wanted her; but she had never meant him to have her.

When she first laid eyes on her husband's stablehand, Ginny had known a stirring of interest. There was a certain indefinable something about his dark features, and a strange intensity in the depths of the black eyes; piercing black eyes which seemed to challenge her. A familiar quivering had shivered from Ginny's stomach to down between her legs. Quite casually she allowed the back of her hand to brush across the front of his trousers when he was assisting her to mount.

Looking down at him from the height of her horse's back, she pursed her lips in amusement at how easily he had been aroused. Then she looked into his eyes and what she saw there faded her smile. A small jolt of fear hit her stomach and she urged her horse forward, aware he stood watching her. From then it seemed he was always watching her, with a brooding sentience which stimulated her sexual awareness of him yet filled her with unease. Even though her body told her he would be able to carry her to the heights of passion she treated him with disdain. Some deep instinct told her he was a dangerous man, a man to whom she must never give in.

Now, because of a moment of weakness, it appeared Ginny had no choice but to go to him, and in spite of her chagrin the prospect induced a warm tingling reaction in the place where their bodies would be joined. But she determined she would make it very plain to Logan she was condescending to do him a favour. He would be left in no doubt she viewed him simply as the instrument of her pleasure.

It was midnight before the guests had departed and Ginny and her husband retired to their respective bedrooms. By that time she was in a state of highly aroused anticipation. With only a robe to cover her nakedness she crept cautiously downstairs. True to her word, Tessa was waiting to open the back door for her, though Ginny did not like the way she said, 'I will be here to let you back in when Logan has finished with you.'

Then Ginny was outside in the cool night air. The blue light of a full moon enabled her to easily see her way to cross the yard to the stables. A steep, external flight of stairs led to Logan's quarters above, and Ginny's legs were trembling almost too much to carry her to the top. The door was opened just as she reached the landing, and Logan stood staring at her with a dark brooding expression.

45

'So you came,' he said and drew her into the room, shutting the door behind her.

Ginny glanced curiously around. There was not much furniture in the room. A chest of drawers, a small table and chair, a washstand and narrow iron bed. That was all she had time to notice.

Logan twisted one hand cruelly in her hair and pulled her to him. His mouth closed savagely over hers, possessing rather than kissing. The other hand gripped her buttocks to press her hard against his body, against the rigid evidence of how much he wanted her. The brutality of his actions angered Ginny and she began to struggle; a futile effort which only caused her greater discomfort when the hand in her hair twisted the strands more savagely.

'You have played with me long enough,' he said. 'Now it is my turn. I am going to watch you squirm and make you beg.' He released her and stepped back. 'Take off your robe, I want to see you naked.'

A little frightened by the cold deliberation of his words and hint of malice in his voice, Ginny did as she was told. With his eyes narrowed to black slits, Logan exhaled his breath through his teeth in a slight whistle. 'By God, you are something. You have a body designed to drive men wild, but you know that, don't you?' He was walking slowly around her, inspecting her from every angle. Ginny could almost feel his gaze caressing the most intimate parts of her body. Certainly she felt the dampness between her legs.

When he again stood in front of her he reached his hands to her breasts and began to fondle them. Ginny sucked in her breath. It felt good, so good. His hands were instruments of exquisite pleasure as they kneaded, squeezed and rolled her breasts. The pads of his thumbs stroked delicate circles over her hardened nipples. With a soft moan Ginny closed her eyes and gave herself up to the marvellous sensuality. Gradually the pressure increased and pleasure metamorphosed into pain. She

46

opened her eyes with a cry of protest when her nipples were viciously pinched, saw he was watching her with his lips thinned in a sadistic smile.

'You bastard,' she spat, and turned to pick up her robe. There was no way she was going to tolerate being hurt.

His movement was quicker; he grabbed her and threw her backwards on the bed, kneeling astride her to prevent her escaping. When he drew some rope from his pocket, Ginny realised his intention and cried out in protest, swearing at him, as she twisted and turned in an endeavour to free her body.

Her futile efforts appeared only to amuse him and with slow, deliberate movements he tied both her wrists to the bedhead. His mouth remained thinned in the same hard line and there was a gleam of cruelty in the jet black of his eyes. Ignoring the oaths she screamed at him, he stood up to shed his shirt and trousers.

Ginny ceased her struggles to look at him. Her mouth went so dry she found it necessary to wet her lips with her tongue. He was impressive to look at – God no – he was beautiful. The darkness of his skin enhanced the sinewy muscularity of his body. His hips were slim, his legs long, and where they met, his rampant manhood drew her admiring gaze. Her insides lurched and she experienced a sharp stab of longing between her thighs. To hell with the fact he had her tied to the bed, she wanted him to take her, wanted his magnificent shaft thrust deep inside her.

Then he straddled her chest so that the proud organ was close to her face. She raised her eyes in question only to be captured by the mesmeric intensity in his. Placing both hands behind her head he pulled her forward. 'Suck me,' he ordered, thrusting his shaft into her mouth before she could object.

He worked her backwards and forwards, encouraging her to slide her mouth up and down his shaft. Realising

47

he was doing this to prove his domination, Ginny rebelled and brought her teeth sharply down.

Her triumph at his cry of pain was short lived. A vicious slap across the face knocked her sideways and she recoiled beneath the black malignancy of his expression. He wrenched her legs apart and jabbed two fingers inside her. Ginny cried her protest at the manner in which they pushed, twisted, tweaked and pinched her, then gasped because they were inflicting just sufficient pain to stimulate her nerve ends and stoke the flames of desire. Relentlessly they worked to bring her burningly close to an orgasm. His fingers were removed.

There was nothing!

Her nerve ends were screaming; she was hanging on the edge of a chasm – and he simply sat there watching her. On the verge of begging him to give her release she recalled his words and clamped her mouth shut. The glint of battle entered her eyes. There was no way she was going to give him that satisfaction.

A grim smile twisted his lips in acknowledgement of her silent challenge. Her eyes were telling him that no matter what he did he would never hear her beg. He leaned forward to mould and squeeze her breasts again. His head came down and he suckled first one breast then the other, sucking up and dragging the nipple through his teeth with just enough pressure to hurt, then gentling the aching tip with his lips.

The eroticism was too much. Ginny moaned and lifted her hips upwards, twisting and gyrating them to indicate her readiness to have him inside her.

Again he sat back – and waited. Ginny almost screamed in frustration. She knew exactly what he was doing. Quite sadistically and deliberately he was drawing her to the very edge of an orgasm then removing the stimulation to watch her writhe.

'Bastard!' she swore at him.

He shrugged his shoulders as if it was no concern how many names she called him. Going across to the table he picked up a bottle and poured some type of strong spirit into a mug. Returning to the bed he lifted her head, held the mug against her lips, and commanded her to drink. Ginny was forced to swallow, gasping and choking on the fiery liquid. Whatever it was it sent a sensual warmth flooding through her veins. A warmth heightened by the light caress of his fingers as they trailed over her body, teasing her nipples before carving a sensuous path over the flat of her stomach, down between her legs then back up again. It was a butterfly touch, so light, yet so, so – dear God! She was nearly ready again.

Logan walked back across the room, drank the remaining spirit in the mug and watched her with that darkly mesmeric, taunting gaze which was sapping her will. Angrily she closed her eyes to break the spell and turned her head away, twisting on her side and pressing her legs together to ease the terrible ache in the core of her being.

Her thighs were pulled open, spread wide apart. His fingers parted her sex lips to give his tongue easy access. It was an exquisite tease. It licked and darted, tickled her special spot, worked quickly then slowly, then quickly again, driving her into a crying, gasping frenzy. Surely this time.

But it was not so. For the third time he deprived her. Her plea was uttered with a sob. 'Do it, damn you, do it.'

He eyed her with mocking satisfaction. 'Are you begging me?'

'Yes, you bastard,' Ginny cried, the tears spilling down her cheeks, 'I'm begging.'

He straddled her; rammed hard into her, each controlled, forceful thrust banging into the very depths of her. She came immediately, the release more violent for having been so long denied. Her tears flowed rapidly, precipitated by the exquisite, searing agony of her orgasm. She felt as though she was in some strange netherworld. There was no reality except for the magnificence of Logan moving within her and the warm surge of love juices which spilled in crashing waves from her body.

When he pulled away she was bereft, crying a protest. He lay down beside her, lifted her leg over his hip, re-entered her, so she again felt complete. From that position, somewhere between the side and the back, he worked her expertly, reaching over her body to finger her clitoris at the same time. Ginny burned from the fires flaring within, cried his name, 'Logan! Logan!' and he increased the rapidity of movement both with his shaft and his finger to bring her to a second climax.

Again he withdrew. Realising he still had not come she marvelled at his supreme control. This time he untied her wrists, rolled her onto her stomach and, lifting her hips, drew them back towards the edge of the bed so that her knees were bent under her and her face was down on the mattress.

Standing next to the bed he thrust into her from behind, viciously pinching her buttocks at the same time. He thrust and pinched again and again, the pain which made Ginny flinch increasing her awareness of the hard organ that was pleasuring her. Then he held her by the hips and, remaining perfectly motionless, moved them in circular fashion, rotating her love tunnel around his shaft.

Even though Ginny understood the manner of his handling was intended to underline his assertion she was simply a tool for his pleasure, her own enjoyment was indescribable. Every nerve in her body was vibrantly alive. Dear God! It was superlative. She was coming again! At that moment he pulled her buttocks back hard against his body and began slamming vigorously in and out, his movements increasing in speed and force. With his name a sob on her lips she felt the rush of his fluid and knew, that time, he too had climaxed.

But even then he was not finished. He turned her onto her back, pushing and twisting his shaft inside her until it finally began to relax. Dormant within her he kissed her savagely on the mouth. When he lifted his head, his dark eyes gleamed down at her. 'This is how it will always be, Ginny. You are mine now and will always be mine to have as I will. Every time I want you, any time I want you, you will come to me. And you will come', he assured her, 'because your body will know it can not be otherwise.'

Ginny was too distraught – and too sore – to get out of bed the next day. Upset and confused by the way her mind and body conflicted with each other, she dreaded the coming night. If he intended to use her in such a manner every night her body would soon be worn out. Yet just thinking of him set her afire with remembrance of the heavenly heights – or was it hellish depths – to which he had taken her.

He did not send for her that night, nor for the next week. Although initially relieved, Ginny soon began to wonder why. With a little flare of triumph she hoped he had discarded his threat to use her as he would; then she despaired that it might be so. The need within her was like a creeping malaise, increasing with each night she was left to ache and toss alone.

If Logan had changed his mind so had she. Ginny wanted him, more than she had ever wanted any man before. Inventing whatever excuses she could for going to the stables, she suffered the chagrin and humiliation of having him ignore her presence, while the cynical twist to his mouth told her he was well aware of her reason for being there.

When his summons did come, anger consumed her. With heightened colour and flaming eyes she informed Tessa she could tell her brother to go to the devil – if the devil was willing to take him. But the hours of darkness slowly wove their spell. At midnight, convinced Logan was the very devil himself, she took her throbbing, eager body to his room.

51

Logan was a master in the art of sadistic pleasure. The skilfully inflicted pain heightened her sexual arousal, drove her into a frenzy of desire. He used her, abused her, and his powerful shaft carried her away to hitherto unknown realms of erotism. She was enslaved. Her body belonged to him in a way it could never belong to any other man. The enormity of her need frightened her more than the power he wielded. It was as if he held her in a thrall from which she was unable to break.

Tessa held her with blackmail. Ginny was forced to part with both money and jewellery to ensure Melbourne society did not learn the truth about Mrs William Leigh.

Three months passed in that manner. Three months during which she felt as if she was two different people. One was the charming social beauty, wife of William Leigh. The other belonged to Logan, became whole only when her body was joined with his. How easy it was to believe his declaration she had belonged to him in a previous life, that she would belong to him again in the next. She did not love him, she was closer to hating him, but he was a part of her and she of him. In an endeavour to regain some control of her life, Ginny determined she would, for once, decide when and where she would give herself to Logan.

Everleigh was set in several acres of parkland which blended into the virgin bush that clothed the foothills of the ranges. One of Ginny's greatest enjoyments was the rides she took into that bush; rides on which she was always accompanied by the elderly groom for her husband felt even that activity to be too strenuous for his heart. On her chosen day she contrived for it to be Logan who was her escort.

They rode beyond the parkland and up into the foothills with Ginny leading the way. When they reached a grassy clearing beside a tiny moss-lined stream she called a halt. She announced her intention of remaining there awhile, dismounted, and ordered Logan to secure the horses. By the time he had done so she had discarded her hat and gloves and was in the process of removing her riding habit.

His dark eyes observed her actions yet he said nothing. With a haughty tilt of her chin she demanded that he undress. 'For once you will do what I want and I want you now.' When he did nothing except stand staring at her with a cynical twist to his lips she lost her temper and struck him across the cheek with the leather strap of her riding crop. Although he flinched and his eyes smouldered with rage he did not even lift a hand to the reddening welt. Using deliberate movements he began to unbutton his shirt. A triumphant smile curving her own lips, Ginny continued to undress. Naked, they stood facing each other.

'Touch me,' she ordered, taking his hand to guide it between her legs, exhaling a deep breath when he slipped a finger inside her and began to leisurely stroke and caress. Dear Lord, but he was incomparable; knew just when to cease pushing in and out; when to begin stroking her externally; how much stimulation her special spot could take. Her nerves tingled. She felt wet, warm and so wonderfully aroused she was becoming weak-kneed from pleasure. It became necessary for her to clasp his shoulders to keep herself upright. Her voice came as a husky plea. 'I want you to suck me, to lick me and suck me until I come.'

He removed his finger, pulled away from her, and stared at her with cold black eyes. 'And if I refuse?'

She hit him hard across the chest with the riding crop. His breath sucked in with the pain and something menacing flared in his eyes again. 'I see,' was all he said.

'I'm glad you do.' Ginny lay down on her discarded clothing, bent her knees, and spread them wide in readiness. Her complacency vanished when Logan bent forward, grasped her knees and pulled sharply upwards. In that position he held her, upside down, with only her head and shoulders on the ground.

53

His mouth lunged at her moist sex lips, nibbling and sucking hard. When his tongue began to lick back and forth between her folds Ginny stretched herself up towards him, thrilled by the shameful display of her inverted position. With her hips so raised and her sex place opened wide to him she was doubly sensitive. She wriggled her hips, pushing her slit against his tongue, crying out her delight when the fiery quickening told her she was about to come.

Her legs were dropped. At first she was startled then, believing he intended to mount her so she could climax with his shaft inside her, she spread her legs and smiled eagerly up at him. She did not care how he gave her the ultimate satisfaction, as long as he did. To her utter astonishment he turned away and picked up his shirt. Ginny shot to a sitting position. 'What are you doing?'

'Getting dressed. You thought you could force me to your will, but you cannot. I give you your pleasure only when, and if, I am prepared to give it to you.'

'You bastard,' Ginny cried, scrambling to her feet and going for him with the riding crop raised in her hand.

This time he caught her wrist and twisted the crop out of her grasp. Keeping both her wrists captured in the vice-like grip of one hand he hit her sharply across the buttocks with the leather strap; a stinging slap which brought tears to her eyes. Then he turned the crop in his hand and pushed it down between her legs to rub the rounded heel of the metal head against her sex. At the cold touch of metal Ginny gasped, then moaned, the carnal contact making her sag at the knees.

'Are you ready to beg?' Logan asked.

Ginny raised her eyes; stared defiantly into those cruel black ones. He twisted the crop and she felt the hammer head push inside her. 'Beg,' he ordered, circling the head of the crop inside her with the shaft tilted so that it pressed against her clitoris and seared her with sexual fire. 'Beg me, Ginny.'

'God damn you! I hate you, Logan,' panted Ginny,

going almost wild from the immensely erotic experience of being invaded and stroked by cold metal instead of warm flesh.

He pushed her away, down on to all fours, dropped to his knees behind her and pulled her back onto his shaft. At her cry of fulfilment he gave a cruel laugh. 'Is this what you wanted me to do, Ginny?' he asked, easing back and slamming savagely into her. 'And this?' reaching around her body to roll and squeeze her nipples with a measured brutality, which inflamed her already vibrant response to his deeply embedded shaft.

When he clasped her hips to rotate her around that shaft, she almost swooned from the sheer intensity of sensation. Taking control she moved her hips herself, grinding over him, wanting more and more. The stinging slap on her buttocks made her jerk. With one hand grasping her hips, he forced her to continue her movements; slapped her repeatedly with the other hand; pushed and worked his shaft to the depths of her gyrating hole.

Sobbing his name and panting her need, she jerked at every stinging slap, grinding frantically against him. He bent over her, kneading her breasts. When a finger moved down to stroke her clitoris Ginny cried out in wild delight, working herself feverishly over his shaft to induce waves and waves of rapture.

Then he lifted her away, rolled her on to her back. Still kneeling he raised her hips, impaled her on his shaft. 'You see, Ginny,' he said, 'you must always do what I want you to do.' And he slammed vigorously in and out of her until he achieved his climax.

That he should order her to come to him that night surprised her, for he derived sadistic pleasure from leaving her alone until she was going almost mad from need of him. Sore and bruised from the things he had done to her that afternoon, she obeyed his command. And, although she swore at him and told him how much she hated him she was aroused by his delicate torture.

Frenzied with desire, she begged him to fill her with all his hard muscle and make her complete.

Just one week later William Leigh sat down at his dining table, clutched frantically at his chest, and died.

Chapter Four

The late afternoon shadows were slanting, dark pools across the road when the Cobbs coach thundered along the flat. There were another twenty miles to go before it reached Wattle Creek, with almost a third of those to the final staging post. A crack of the whip, flicking near the rump of the leader, urged the horses to a faster pace.

They were well behind schedule, delayed by a broken shaft, and the prospect of driving in the dark filled the driver with unease. Up ahead the road began to ascend, curving its way between two hills. Soon he would need to pull the team in, for on that narrow, twisting section of track, with the dense bush encroaching to its very edge, any pace faster than a walk was downright dangerous. With the hills blocking the last rays of the setting sun, the gloomy passage between the trees held a threat of menace, and the hairs on the nape of his neck were standing on end when he began to pull the team in to a walk.

Inside the coach the eight passengers were relieved when the sickening swaying eased, and they were no longer being jolted so roughly against one another. They were a mixed group; a fresh-faced youth, a sailor, a portly middle-aged couple with a young daughter, a priest, a rather plain young woman and an unwashed, rough looking individual whom the others eyed with both distaste and distrust. For ten dusty, sweaty hours they had endured each other's company within the stuffy confines of their conveyance and each one longed for the terrible journey to be at an end.

Their reactions, when the sound of a pistol shot was followed by the command to 'Stand and deliver', ranged from shock and surprise then indignation from the priest, a scream from the matron, and cynical acceptance from the ruffian. It was he who spoke. 'I reckon we're about to make the acquaintance of Dan Berrigan and his mates.'

The young woman, who had paled with fear, turned to him with a glint of excitement in her expression. 'I have heard he is quite handsome and such a gentleman.'

The man grinned, showing broken yellowed teeth. He quite deliberately stared at the shape of the girl's jutting breasts, with a lascivious gleam in his eyes. 'Well, he ain't hurt no one yet, he just takes what he wants if you get my meaning.'

It being impossible not to 'get his meaning', the woman flushed bright red and the portly man gave a derisive 'hmphh' of disgust. 'The man is a criminal and a rapist.'

'And I reckon there's more to that story than's ever been told.'

Just then the door was pulled open and a tall man with a flaming red beard ordered them all out.

Seated astride his horse with a revolver in each hand, Dan assessed them as they hastily emerged. He found no satisfaction in the almost petrified fear the matron exhibited and regretted the necessity of causing such distress. Unfortunately, of all the passengers, the middle-aged couple appeared to be the only ones who might have anything of value. In his own peculiar code of ethics, men of the cloth and young ladies were exempt, and the other three passengers were undoubtedly all on their way to the gold fields to seek their fortunes.

Suddenly disgusted with the whole sordid business, he ordered Charlie and Josh to relieve the driver of the cash box, while the passengers prayed he was not about to discharge either of his deadly looking revolvers. To the immense relief of all, he wheeled his horse around, and the three bushrangers galloped away with their booty, leaving their victims shaken but unharmed.

Dan was silent on the ride back to their hideout high in the hills. He had taken to bushranging while governed by anger and suffering from a seething sense of injustice. But now it had become merely a way of life. That Josh and Charlie possessed temperaments more suited to such activities he was well aware. He also knew, that while they would never question any decision he made, they were wondering why he had not robbed the passengers.

'The trouble with you', offered Charlie, when they were back at the slab hut, which had been their home for the past nine months, 'is that your cock is starved of action. Why don't you pay Molly a visit?'

Dan grinned, forked another piece of meat into his mouth, and shook his head. 'Not my type.'

'Hell! What's type got to do with it? All a bloke needs is a nice wet hole and Molly's got one that's ve-ery accommodating.'

Dan laughed outright at that. 'Exactly. Maybe it has been a while since I've had a woman, but I'm not so desperate as to become as depraved as you pair of sex maniacs.'

Josh winked at Charlie and protested with mock indignation. 'He's calling us sex maniacs – us! Whose cock got us into this anyway?'

Immediately Dan became sober. 'You didn't have to, you know. The law was not after either of you.'

'No, but they revoked our mining licence and confiscated our bloody mine, didn't they?' snarled Josh. And we couldn't leave you on the run on your own.'

'I know,' said Dan quietly, 'and I'm grateful to you both for sticking by me.'

'Well, that's what mates are for,' declared Charlie. 'You're the best Dan, and me and Josh will always stick up for you no matter what.'

The three men regarded each other somberly for a moment, then, deciding the conversation had become somewhat maudlin, Charlie gave a chuckle. 'Well Josh, what do you say to us paying Molly a visit even if Dan's not interested?'

'Why not? I wonder if she'll draw straws tonight to see which one gets to lay her? Maybe we should make them all the same length.' They guffawed loudly, grabbed their hats and sauntered out of the hut.

Left alone, Dan sunk onto his bunk and pillowed his head on his hands. Staring up at the rough bark roof of the hut he bleakly reflected on his current way of life and wondered where the hell it was all going to end.

Miss Jenny Townsend ran her hands over her body, smoothed the material of her skirt and pouted at her reflection in the mirror. There was no sweet innocence in the blue eyes which stared back at her, only frustration and ill temper. Since the night she had invited Dan Berrigan to her room, little had gone right. Not only had her intended revenge amounted to nothing when he evaded the law, but now her parents maintained such a close protective watch over her it had become impossible to engage in any other sexual adventures. If she did not manage something, soon she would surely go mad with frustration.

Her malicious resentment towards Dan Berrigan had been for the manner in which he had taken her. Jenny enjoyed playing the innocent young girl who was being seduced, the pretence heightening her enjoyment when her partner was finally allowed to thrust his eager shaft into her tiny hungry hole. Usually her lovers, once they realised her act, were happy to play along with the pretence. Except the tall miner. He had become angry with her and been almost brutal. But oh, how he had stretched and filled her, thrusting that massive rod into the very depths of her being until she was near to swooning from the sheer power of that magnificent shaft.

Just to think about it – which she did frequently – made her vulva ache with remembrance and set the warm juices flowing between her thighs. It was no different now and she pressed her legs tightly together. She needed a man – desperately – and in the state she was in, just about any man would do.

With a petulant scowl on her face, she joined her parents for dinner. Resentful of the fact they kept her so cloistered that she could do nothing to ease the ache between her thighs, she spoke little throughout the meal. Her mother asked if she was feeling unwell and wondered if she might rather stay at home than accompany them to the School of Arts.

Although she considered a scientific lecture would be the epitome of all that was boring, Jenny hoped she might be able to make some interesting acquaintances before the evening was over. About, therefore, to answer in the negative to her mother's concerned queries, she hesitated when her father arose with the announcement he was going downstairs to speak with the accountant.

Carefully shielding the speculative expression in her eyes, she looked back at her mother. The bank's accountant was young, rather handsome, and the material of his trousers always appeared to be so interestingly stretched around the region of his thighs. Jenny envied his wife and frequently wished she could take her place in his bed. 'Is Mr Alexander working late tonight, Mama?'

'I believe so.'

'Then – perhaps I will stay at home. I do feel a little unwell but with Mr Alexander working downstairs I will feel perfectly safe from any – ' she gave a delicate shudder, 'any intruders.'

The last statement was a miscalculation. Reminded of the terrible ordeal to which she had been subjected, her parents began to fuss. It took some time and considerable guile for Jenny to persuade them to allow her to remain at home. However, they eventually departed for the lecture and with a feline smile of satisfaction, Jenny returned to her room to prepare herself.

Admiring the perfection of her dainty body in the mirror, she unpinned her hair and combed it into a silken swathe around her shoulders. With a narcissistic smile she gently combed the golden hairs on her mound, lifting the fine hairs away from the skin so they also shone with a silken glow in the lamplight. It was an erotic vanity which induced a gentle pulsing in her sex lips. Next she took a small jar of rouge and very carefully enhanced the colour of her nipples, knowing well how the sight of such rosy tips excited men to greater desire.

A musky, sensual perfume, applied at her throat, on her breasts and on the insides of her thighs completed her bodily preparations. The nightgown she slipped over her head, a gossamer fine garment with low neck and capped sleeves, revealed far more of her charms than it concealed. She moved experimentally, satisfied with the way the floating material spread and draped. Through a sheer single layer her breasts and golden mound became clearly visible only to be teasingly hidden beneath multiple folds. Nerves fluttering with libidinous anticipation, she made her way silently downstairs.

Mr Alexander was seated at his desk, frowning over his ledgers when Jenny pushed open the door. Initially startled, he arose in confusion and consternation when she moved into the light and he saw that her blue eyes were wide with fear and her sweet mouth trembled. He tried not to notice how little she was wearing. 'Why, Miss Jenny, is something the matter?'

'I am being silly, I know, but I felt afraid upstairs on

my own.' She forced a tear to her eye. 'I thought I would be all right. You see it is the first time I have been alone at night since – '

The accountant reddened and swallowed uncomfortably. He knew to what she was alluding and he was experiencing great difficulty in keeping his gaze away from the hard peaked outline of her taut little breasts beneath the thin material. 'Do you want me to fetch your parents?'

'Oh no, I do not want them to worry. If you were just to put your arms around me, Mr Alexander, I am certain I would feel greatly comforted.'

Somewhat awkwardly Mr Alexander did as he was bid, his attempt to avoid any unnecessary bodily contact destroyed when Jenny pressed against him in a manner designed to make him even more aware of how little she was wearing. With the apparent simplicity of a trusting child, she rested her head on his shoulder.

'Your arms are so strong. I feel safe now.' Jenny snuggled closer.

'Miss Jenny – I – you – I think it – '

'I think I would like you to kiss me,' invited Jenny. She raised soft pink lips and moved her body innocently against his, although it was difficult to maintain her ingenuous act when she felt the stirrings of his arousal.

'Miss Jenny, please.' Mr Alexander released her and took a hasty step back hoping she would not notice the embarrassing bulge in his trousers. 'You don't know what you are doing. It is fortunate I am a man of honour for surely you would not want to be brutally taken advantage of again.'

'Oh but, Mr Alexander,' pouted Jenny in wide-eyed innocence, 'I think I might like being taken advantage of. If the man had not been so rough, I believe I would have enjoyed the experience immensely. Every time I think about it I become all wet and warm in my private place and I am at a loss to know why. Perhaps you could explain it to me.' She took his hand and placed it between her legs. 'Do you feel how wet it is?'

Mr Alexander did. When he pushed against the material to better ascertain the degree of wetness, Jenny sucked in her breath and wriggled herself into position. He pushed harder, working the material encased digit deeply into her dripping hole. At her squeal of delight he rapidly discarded his inhibitions and his clothing, managing to do the latter while relieving Jenny of her nightdress and continuing to work his finger in and out of her wonderfully slippery crevice.

It was even better than Jenny had hoped. Wildly excited, she grabbed his hot shaft and began working her hand up and down at the same enthusiastic rhythm as she was being frigged. When she looked down at it and saw the gleaming droplet on the reddened tip she pushed his hand aside, dropped to her knees and licked the globule off.

At the touch of her delicate tongue, his shaft jerked a violent response. Jenny was rapidly pulled away and lifted up to be sat upon the desk in front of him. He opened her legs wide, parted her sex lips with his fingers and bent his head to lick at her moisture. Jenny rested back on her hands and opened her legs even wider. With her head lolled back and eyes closed, she gave herself up to the enjoyment of his teasing tongue as it licked and searched between her folds and invaded her eager hole. It felt good, so-o good; something like being given a drink when one was dying of thirst.

She pushed herself up so she could watch his tongue waggle frantically at her sensitive nodule. The sight of her glistening golden curls and wide-spread thighs with a man's face buried between always aroused her to incredible excitement. Jenny licked her lips; held herself in panting readiness. Oh yes, yes! She was coming! At the moment when her juices spurted forth she clutched his head, holding his mouth against her swelling tissues. Her body jerked wildly from the joy of her orgasm. She wanted him to draw her juices out until she was empty, would not allow him to lift away. 'Suck me, suck me,' she cried.

At last she was ready for him, panting for him to give her his shaft. He pushed her back on the desk, lifted her left leg high over his shoulder, stretched her right one wide and thrust deeply into her canal. 'Oh yes!' shouted Jenny. 'Push it right in. Harder, harder, oh yes, yes.'

With libidinous avidity, Mr Alexander slammed his rod in and out and twisted it around, growing harder and more excited as she writhed and gasped her approval. 'Oooh, it's so good so big – so hard.' She lifted her head to watch his shaft working in and out noticing how shiny and slippery it was from her juices. 'Yes, yes! I want you deep in me. Oh, oh harder, harder.'

A horrified cry penetrated her lust inflamed senses. Her head dropped back and she turned glazed eyes towards the door. An expression of incredulous shock on his face, her father stood there supporting the fainting form of her mother.

'Oh Daddy,' she gasped in a faint voice, then, 'Oh, ooh, oooh,' in ascending volume as Mr Alexander thumped frantically into her and they exploded into simultaneous climaxes.

A week later she was being escorted, under the strictest chaperonage, to an aunt in Sydney, to be married as quickly as possible to the first respectable man willing to take her.

Molly Jones and her husband operated an unlicensed bush inn far enough away from any settlement for them not to be bothered by the law. They provided a rough hospitality. Sleeping accommodation consisted of a couple of bunks in a lean-to extension, meals were tasteless stews of mutton or kangaroo meat and the liquid refreshments were the product of a still kept out at the back.

Not that the few travellers who called at the inn were

likely to complain. Almost without exception they followed callings which found little favour with the law. But whatever their profession, or indeed their age, they could be certain of finding favour with Molly.

A plump, bawdy woman of moderate attractiveness, she possessed an insatiable sexual appetite undiminished by thirty six years of rough living. During the early years of their marriage, Mr Jones had been more than capable of keeping her satisfied and their energetic lovemaking had been confined neither to the bed nor the night time. Then came the day an unfortunate accident with a gun rendered him impotent, his once randy tool a limp, pathetic fraction of its former glorious size.

Unable to tolerate such an abrupt cessation of her sexual pleasures, Molly soon sought fulfilment elsewhere. And it so happened that one day, when Mr Jones caught his wife and her partner in the final throes of a frantic humping, he discovered he could, even if his diminished tool could no longer rise to the occasion, still achieve an orgasm.

Husband and wife came to an agreement. Molly could engage in whatever sexual activities took her fancy just as long as Mr Jones was able to watch, in secret if necessary, and thereby gain a vicarious satisfaction.

A small peephole allowed Mr Jones to see quite clearly everything which took place in the back room of the inn. New customers always attracted Molly's interest and it was not uncommon for her to take two or three lovers in the course of a night. Never one to simply lie on her back and open her legs, Molly constantly surprised her husband with her ever more daring activities. He thought he had seen everything until the night the two bushrangers arrived at the inn. Unable to decide which of them she wanted first, the big man with the flaming beard or his shorter, cheekier mate, she had them both at once.

Molly also remembered the night with perfect clarity for it made romping with a single partner tame by comparison. They undressed each other with much jocularity and touching then the men picked her up and plopped her on the bed. Sprawled on her back in naked abandon she bent her knees and opened her legs wide to display her plump and hairy fanny.

Immediately he saw it Josh parted the dark jungle of hair and darted his tongue into her slit to lick and tease. Charlie offered his swollen shaft to her mouth and Molly slurped her lips and tongue up and down its length, unbelievably excited by having two men who were randy and willing. When she realised she was reaching a climax, she relinquished Charlie's shaft and screamed wildly for Josh to jam his into her throbbing canal. He obliged, humping her vigorously several times before rolling over so she was on top. Then to her surprise and very vocal excitement, a finger was twisted into her rear passage and Charlie climbed on the bed to guide his cock into the prepared opening.

Molly felt herself being stretched and the muscles of her other passage contracted tightly around Josh's rod in automatic reaction. Charlie eased in slowly until she was opened sufficiently to take him. He held her hips and began to work in and out while Josh screwed his rod in a circular motion. Molly, flat on top of Josh, and almost swooning from the incredible sensation of two hard cocks working inside her at once, came in a screaming, raging flood.

Molly was thinking about the two and wondering when they would next pay her a visit when they sauntered through the door. She poured them each a drink of the latest brew then took one for herself.

At first she thought it lacked the potency of the usual brews, but by the time she was halfway through her second drink she realised she was feeling uncommonly randy. Nor did it take long for her to realise the brew was having a similar effect on all three of her customers.

They sat together at the single rustic table, Josh, Charlie and the man whom, because of his bushy black beard and the patch he wore over one eye, they called Black Jack. Molly was well acquainted with the sexual abilities of all three and knew their tastes bordered on the bizarre. And she was becoming so hot for a cock, for all their cocks, she was game for anything.

Easing the already plunging neckline of her blouse even lower so that her large brown nipples were barely covered, she walked across to the table to pour each of them another drink. The scent of her lust wafted over the men, arousing them even more.

'What did you put in this stuff?' demanded Josh. 'My bloody cock is pushing at my trousers like a bull trying to get in the cow pen.'

'Mine too,' agreed Charlie. 'It's your blimming brew that's caused this Molly, so I reckon you've got to do something about it.'

'Yeah,' added Black Jack. 'I don't reckon it would be fair if only one of us gets to lay you tonight seeing as we're all in the same stiff state.'

The three were eyeing her with such lecherous expectation, Molly was growing hotter and wetter by the second. She had had two men at once, why not three? Hitching her bodice down to fully expose her fat white breasts she gazed at them with fever-bright eyes. 'Well, which of you wants to be first?'

They lunged at her. Charlie grabbed at her breasts squeezing and pawing them while Josh and Black Jack quickly stripped her naked. They took every opportunity to touch and feel her all over as they did so, and she was soon panting with excitement. Forced to relinquish his grasp on her breasts, Charlie rapidly shed his trousers. The sight of his rigid tool drove Molly into such a frenzy she almost threw herself at him and pushed him down to the floor.

There she straddled his body, heaved her plump vulva over his shaft and slid herself all the way down to his groin. She immediately began pounding herself on it with such vigour her huge breasts bounced madly up and down.

'Christ, Molly,' panted Charlie, astounded by the vehemence of her actions, 'you'll break me bloody cock off. Will you blokes come and give me some help.'

Josh and Black Jack hurried to his aid. 'Do you want another one in you as well, Molly?'

'Ooh yes,' she cried, continuing to pound up and down on Charlie in a drink befuddled state of frenzied carnality. 'I want three big fat cocks in me.'

'Then I'll have the back end,' Josh grinned at Black Jack, 'and you can have the front.'

Molly bent forward to give Josh access to her rear hole and hungrily took Black Jack's shaft into her mouth. It took a few moments to coordinate all their movements. Molly worked up and down over Charlie's rod, while Black Jack slid his in and out of her mouth and Josh thrust into her rear hole.

The first one to come was Mr James. Slack mouthed and goggle-eyed, he watched from the other side of the room. With the limp remnant of his poor manhood gripped tightly in his hand he spurted all over the floor. Charlie was next, his shaft relaxing inside Molly's canal in spite of her efforts to work it rigid again. Josh pulled out of her and rubbed his shaft between the cheeks of her bottom to spill his juice all over her white flesh. Her hungry sex hole wanting still more she slid off Charlie, rolled on her back and opened her legs wide to receive Black Jack. She panted and heaved against him unable to get enough. For some reason, maybe the effect of the brew, she could not reach an orgasm, hung agonisingly on the edge.

When Black Jack shot his load and withdrew his softened rod she reached both hands down to her swollen, throbbing fanny. Thrusting three fingers as deeply as they would go she twisted and frigged, at the same time frantically rubbing her rigid nodule with a finger of the other hand. Oblivious of the three men who watched in amazement she jerked and rubbed, panted and moaned, until an orgasm, so violent it was painful, wracked her body. Its force was so exhausting that when it was over she gave a great sigh and passed out on the floor.

The next morning Charlie's and Josh's recollections of the night's debauchery were somewhat unclear. About the only thing of which they were certain was that their heads felt as though they were being pounded with the blunt edge of an axe. Their hangovers lasted for three days, and when they sobered up enough to realise they had brought a bottle of Molly's powerful brew home with them, they pushed it out of sight into the corner of the hut, declaring they would be a long time touching the stuff again.

Chapter Five

*T*he funeral was over and William Leigh's last will and testament had been read. Although disappointed to receive only a very small settlement, Ginny was in no way unduly perturbed by her altered circumstances. The bulk of her late husband's estate, including Everleigh, had been left to William's only nephew. Francis Leigh was in his early thirties, pleasant of appearance in a fair, fresh-faced manner, amiable in nature, and single.

Not that Ginny's reaction to her husband's death was in any way callous or mercenary. Her natural grief at the passing of a man of whom she had been quite moderately fond was exacerbated by a guilt not present when he was alive. Ginny castigated herself for not curbing her lusty nature and remaining faithful to a man who had always treated her with the utmost respect and kindness.

To her immense relief, Logan allowed her to grieve in peace, and given that respite from the obsessive passion of their relationship she determined to break free from his masterdom. William could no longer be hurt; any scandal would be just a nine day society wonder. And it would not even be that if she was cunning enough to lay foundations for discrediting anything Tessa – or Logan – might disclose.

The one bright aspect of the fretful weeks following William's death was the unexpected companionship she found with Francis. From the day prior to the funeral when he arrived at Everleigh with his friend Harold, Ginny felt at ease with him.

A man as good natured as his uncle he displayed a compassionate sensitivity to Ginny's emotional needs. Almost daily they took long walks together through the parkland; long, healing walks after which Ginny always felt more at peace with herself. Francis possessed the rare ability to know when to talk, when to listen, and when to just simply be there offering silent support.

There came the day they were returning from a particularly pleasant walk when he stopped her and took her hands lightly in his. 'You know that I am happy for you to remain here Ginny. Everleigh is your home for as long as you wish.'

She smiled a tremulous gratitude and soon after began to seriously consider Francis's unmarried state.

Then came the call from Logan. Ginny did not even send a reply. She simply would not go to him. But it was a decision more easily taken than carried out. By dinner time she was almost physically ill from the conflict between spirit and flesh. She retired early to seek the comfort of her bed. Her head was aching and her body was crying out for Logan's.

Sleep, however, proved elusive and when the clock chimed midnight the stab of desire which seared her body made her cry out in pain. Tossing back the covers, she left the bed, walked over to the window and drew the curtains wide. With her arms wrapped around her shivering body, she stared out at the moon-shadowed grounds, fighting the invisible pull of Logan's will.

Midnight – the witching hour. Was it purely coincidence it was always midnight Logan commanded her to go to him, or was he indeed some kind of warlock?

Certainly he was an enigma. Why did a proud and powerful man who spoke in the manner of the educated work as a lowly stable hand? She had called him a devil more than once and consigned him to hell. His only response had been that cruel, thin smile and a flame pricking the depths of his black eyes.

When she heard the movement at her door and saw the knob being slowly turned her nerves tensed. Almost fatalistically she watched the door open and the dark figure of Logan step into her room. As soon as he saw her silhouetted near the window he paused, and Ginny sucked in her breath. His expression was shadowed, yet she felt the sinister threads of his displeasure.

'You did not come to me, Ginny,' he stated in a voice which was all the more menacing for being seductively soft. 'Why didn't you come?'

He was standing in front of her, close enough for her to reach and touch him, or for him to touch her. She was trembling, her body vibrantly alive to his proximity, her throat so dry her voice was barely a croak. 'You must know why. Everything has changed.'

He reached for her then, touching her hair, lifting it and allowing the silken strands to run through his fingers. A sob caught in Ginny's throat. 'Please go, Logan. Leave me alone.'

'You know I cannot do that.' Very casually he draped a strand of her hair across her throat. The action was almost a caress, yet undeniably sinister.

With a rapidity of movement which took her by surprise, he grasped the neckline of her nightgown with both hands and ripped the garment from her body. The sound of the tearing material caused her to flinch.

Twisting a cruel hand in her hair he pulled her against his body. His mouth took savage possession of hers, his other hand slipping around her buttocks and between her legs. When he thrust a finger deep inside, Ginny's nerves jumped in recognition. She began to struggle fiercely, fighting both Logan and herself. But the more

73

she struggled, the more vibrantly she was aroused for her frantic movements complemented the action of his finger.

Her arms were trapped between their bodies. Realising her struggles were futile she spread her hands, located his nipples, and through the material of his shirt pinched them as hard as she could. His sucking intake of breath at the pain not only pleased her, it aroused her. Seeking release of her inner tension she worked herself against his violating finger.

Logan moved and she was thrown onto the bed. As on the first night he straddled her and tied her wrists to the head of the bed. Then to her utmost shock he spread her legs wide and tied an ankle to each extremity of the bed end, her struggles to prevent him so doing giving him sadistic satisfaction.

With a tantalising touch he began to caress her body. His hands trailed lightly over her breasts, her stomach, down between her legs, expertly bringing alive every sensitive nerve end. Unable to move, to evade the erotic passage of his fingers, Ginny began to tremble. With her legs so tied she felt vulnerable, exposed, needing him to cover her nakedness with his own and fill the burning chasm of her desire with the throbbing perfection of his manhood.

When he did she revelled in his possession, clenching the muscles of her womanhood around his magnificent shaft. She wanted to hold him against her; bound as she was, she could not. Ginny used her hips, lifting them, bucking against him, wanting more and more of him with every violent thrust of their bodies.

Quite suddenly he left her – bereaving her. He untied her wrists and ankles and walked away from the bed.

'Logan?' Ginny, her body aching to be fulfilled, was perplexed, his name a question on her lips.

'I bound you to the bed only to punish you for daring to defy me. I have no need of ropes to bind your body to

74

mine. If you can tell me now to go away and leave you alone then do so.'

He stood silhouetted in the moonlight, dark and beautiful with his wonderful shaft projecting proudly from his body; like some pagan god carved of lustrous wood.

Ginny could not speak. She could only look at him, admire him, want him, her body aching with her need of him. He gave a soft triumphant laugh. 'You see, you cannot send me away. You want me Ginny, but you must come to me.'

As though being drawn by some invisible thread, Ginny left the bed and walked slowly to where he stood. The epicentre of her womanhood was throbbing with desire and she pressed herself against him, lifting her arms around his neck.

Logan's hands moved to her buttocks. She felt herself lifted; sucked in her breath when the head of his shaft touched her sex lips; exhaled with rapture when her moist channel slid down over the length of it. With her arms around his neck and legs around his waist, she clung to him. He was in complete control, holding her buttocks to slide her love-wet sheath up and down his shaft.

Ginny dug her fingers into his back; knew her burning readiness; cried his name when the fire consumed her; a fire which raged uncontrolled as the soft flesh of her buttocks was bruised by his grip. He worked her rapidly. He did not stop even when she was burnt out and clung limply to him with her head lolling against his shoulder.

Just when the embers of her fires were being fanned to new life, he lifted her free and carried her back to the bed. He set her on her side and lay down behind her. Lifting her leg high in the air to open her wide, he entered her again. Ginny lay quietly, giving herself up to the wonderful sensation of fulfilment created by his easy rhythmic stroking. But when he pulled out and began to caress her hard peak of desire with the tip of

75

his shaft, she reacted convulsively, rubbing against it to bring herself to the edge of another climax. 'Oh God, now,' she cried, and he thrust hard, driving into the very depths of her body. He used his finger to maintain the stimulation at her clitoris and the world exploded around her. She was drowning, floating, burning up, and when he gave a last violent thrust she was welded to him, his shaft deeply embedded in her womanhood.

They lay as one for some time and when he pulled away it was as though part of herself was being removed. She cried her protest and he rolled her onto her back to stare at her with a mocking, dark intensity.

'Nothing has changed Ginny, yet everything has changed. The time is approaching when I will keep you with me forever, but until then I will have you when I want you. Day or night.'

The pale light of dawn was in the sky before Logan left her room. Emotionally and physically exhausted from the hours of torrid, passionate coupling, Ginny fell into an exhausted sleep from which she did not awaken until early afternoon. Stiff and sore, she rang for Tessa and ordered a bath, not liking the smirking insolence of the girl's demeanour.

The warm scented water helped ease her aches, and when she dried herself on the fluffy towel, she did so gently. There were dark bruises on her body; bruises knowingly inflicted by Logan. As though to reaffirm his mastery and her subservience, he had been sadistically brutal in the manner of his handling. And, as always, the carefully calculated, stimulating pain had driven her into a frenzy of desire. She fought wildly with him when he hurt her, swore at him, called him the devil, but ground her body against his, bucking and thrusting in savage conjunction with his movements, unable to get enough of him.

Ginny studied her naked body in the full-length mirror. Her breasts were full and firm, her stomach flat, her hips gently rounded, and where her long, slender legs joined, soft, gold-brown curls guarded the secrets of her womanhood. 'A body to drive men wild,' Logan had said. And he had taken her, possessed her, bound her to him by invisible threads of lust. She was caught in the web of sexual passion he wove around her. 'The time has almost come for me to keep you with me.' Ginny had not questioned his meaning, she only knew that if she did not break free – now – there would be no escape, either from Logan or her own soul-destroying passion.

She dressed carefully, took several deep breaths to steady her nerves, and went in search of Francis. He was in the library, sorting through William's papers. His smile of genuine pleasure on greeting her giving her confidence for what she planned to say.

'Francis, will you marry me? After a decent period of mourning of course.'

He gazed at her with a quizzical smile, not at all put out by her blunt proposal. 'Do you pretend to have fallen in love with me, Ginny?'

A faint smile of relief curved her own lips when she shook her head. 'You know I have not, though I am very fond of you. I do want to continue living at Everleigh. I know', she hastened to add when Francis started to speak, 'you have said I may do so, but it would appear to be, in all ways, far more practical for us to marry.'

'I admit I have thought on those lines myself. You are a beautiful woman and would be a credit to any man.'

'Thank you, Francis.' Ginny was genuinely pleased by his compliment. 'Do you agree then?'

'I agree, if you have no objection to Harold also living here at Everleigh.'

'It is your house, Francis.'

'I would like you to think of it as yours too. Harold and I have been close for several years. I know he is very attracted to you.' He smiled again. 'You are a very sensual woman, Ginny, and I do not mind sharing.'

At first Ginny thought she must have misunderstood Francis. Then she realised she had not and her heart tripped over a beat. It appeared Francis was not only happy to marry her, but he had no objection to her taking his best friend as a lover either. Life might become fun once more. A husband and a lover; neither of them brutal.

The mental allusion to Logan clouded her expression. There was another favour she needed to ask of Francis. 'There is another matter on which I feel troubled and would seek your advice.'

'Anything, my dear.'

'For some time now I have suspected my maid has been stealing money from my room and lately I have missed certain items of jewellery.'

'Good heavens! Have you confronted her with your suspicions?'

'No, for the girl is insolent and would only lie. I beg you to have her room searched. If the jewellery is there, it will prove her guilt.'

Francis frowned. 'An unpleasant task. I believe the servants find me an easy master, but I will not tolerate dishonesty. Do you wish to come with me, Ginny?'

'No, have Mrs Mason accompany you.'

Ginny paced restlessly around the library waiting for Francis and the housekeeper to return. Now that she had set her plan in motion, she was terrified it might fail. She needed to clench her hands together to stop them from shaking when she heard the two pairs of footsteps coming back down the hall.

'You were right, Ginny,' said Francis, holding out the two brooches and necklet Tessa had demanded in blackmail. 'Do you wish to confront the girl yourself?'

Ginny shook her head. 'I would prefer you to handle it for me, Francis.'

'Do you want her charged with theft?'

'No, I simply want her dismissed.'

Francis frowned in disapproval. 'Are you certain that is all the action you want to take? These are valuable items of jewellery.'

'I know, but I do not believe time in gaol would make her mend her ways. I would have her dismissed without a reference. And I feel you would be wise, Francis, to dismiss her brother as well.'

'Her brother?'

'The stablehand – Logan.' It was impossible not to hesitate before voicing his name, nor close her eyes against the sudden turmoil of emotions. She hoped Francis noticed neither.

'He is a good man with the horses,' Francis demurred.

'His sister is a thief and it would not be wise to trust him once she is dismissed.'

Francis sighed an agreement. 'You are undoubtedly right, Ginny, and I must confess that for all his ability with the horses, there is something about the man I have never quite trusted.'

'That is how I feel. Dismiss them both without references. If they show any inclination to cause trouble, I think the threat of the police will be sufficient to make them leave quietly.' And so it proved. By nightfall both Tessa and Logan were gone from Everleigh.

There began for Ginny a second period of grieving. Though she could never regret her action in driving Logan out of her life, she felt almost as if she had destroyed a part of herself. But deep inside she believed Logan would not let her go so easily. Daily she lived in fear of his return; a fear precipitated not so much by what Logan might do to her, but by how she would react to his presence.

Two weeks went by before she began to pull herself together. The very reason she wanted Logan out of her life was because he threatened to take control of it, yet she was allowing thoughts of him to do just that. In an endeavour to exorcise him from her mind and her body, she began to speculate on the sexual potential of both Francis and Harold.

Francis's remark about sharing intrigued Ginny

immensely; especially as he continued to treat her in the same friendly manner as before. Of course he might think, it being only a matter of weeks since William's death, she was not yet ready to have another replace him in her bed. Dear Lord! It was not her husband she needed to replace, it was her cruel lover.

Quite deliberately, she began to encourage Harold's interest. Frequently she caught him watching her with a decided gleam in his eye. Almost as fair as Francis, Harold could not by any standards be considered good looking. Nevertheless, he possessed a certain charm and Ginny endeavoured to make it plain she was willing for them to become better acquainted.

Ginny dreaded the nights. The hours of darkness were filled with memories, and a yearning for her aching womanhood to be soothed by the hard thrust of Logan's body. During the daytime she could find ways of occupying her mind. Lying in her lonely bed at night her longings became almost unbearable. Not even masturbating could alleviate the need.

Feeling more than usually disturbed one evening, and thinking she would read until she became sleepy, she slipped a light robe over her nightgown and made her way downstairs to the library. It was very late and she presumed both Francis and Harold would also have retired. However, on opening the door, she discovered Harold was seated in one of the wing-backed chairs reading a novel. He glanced up when he heard her and set his book aside.

'This is a surprise, Ginny. I thought you had retired for the night.'

'So I had, but I found myself unable to sleep and thought to take a book to read for a while.'

'You need to relax, Ginny. You appear to have been a little agitated of late. Perhaps a glass of port might help.'

He lifted the decanter with a questioning expression, waiting for her 'Thank you' before pouring each of them a glass. As the glass passed from hand to hand, he allowed their fingers to touch and his eyes posed an unmistakable question.

The wine warmed Ginny, eased her tension. Seating herself on the sofa she sipped it slowly, gazing up from under her lashes at Harold. A faint provocative smile played around the corners of her mouth. With his heart beating faster, Harold drained the port from his glass in one swallow. Going quickly to the sofa he sat beside Ginny, took her in his arms and kissed her.

Ginny was not certain how to categorise that kiss. Too demanding to be brotherly, yet it fell far short of being either passionate or lustful. And it certainly was not sexually inducive. At least it was not one of savage possession like Logan's kisses. Oh, to hell with Logan! Ginny opened her mouth and returned Harold's kiss with more expertise than he displayed, and far more arousing effectiveness.

Harold's hand moved from her shoulder to her breast, his voice, when she broke the kiss, was a husky plea. 'I want to make love to you, Ginny.'

'And I want you to,' Ginny murmured in sensual response. Her gaze held his as his hand moved down the outline of her body to her thigh. She tilted her head to drain the last of the port, then placed the empty glass on the floor.

With hands which were not completely steady he unfastened her robe and released the buttons of her nightgown. Almost reverently, he pushed the garments aside to expose the firm beauty of her breasts to his wondering gaze. He cupped them with tender hands, bending to kiss the rosy aureola of first one, then the other.

To Ginny's immense surprise the touch of his hands and lips on her bare flesh left her totally unaroused. What was the matter with her? There was a time when just the expression in a man's eyes was sufficient to precipitate the warm flow of anticipatory juices. Perhaps

81

Harold was simply inexperienced. Ginny guided his hand back to her hips.

This time he lifted the hem of her gown to slide a caressing palm slowly up her leg. It travelled along the outside of her thigh to her hip, then swept across the firm plane of her stomach and down to her mound. There it rested with the thumb extended to press against the line of her slit.

Ginny sighed. Better, much better. Her vulva pulsed in response and she moved her hips to encourage him further. A soft moan of pleasure was intended to excite him, as was her husky query as to whether he would like her to remove her nightgown. Her own hands were already at work on the buttons of his shirt.

When they were both naked Ginny lay back on the sofa, enjoying the caress of Harold's hands as they moved adoringly over her body. His expression was one of wonder, his words whispered with awe. 'You are truly beautiful, Ginny. Your body is the supreme perfection of womanhood. How could any man not want to possess you?'

Ginny wished he had not used the word 'possess', it conjured up images of Logan, especially as the movement of Harold's finger, once it sought and found her opening, was soothing rather than stimulating. Only mildly aroused, she relaxed and allowed him to stroke along the creases and folds of her vagina. Perhaps, once he mounted her, she would feel more satisfied. When he rolled on top of her and pressed the end of his rod against her moist sex lips she lifted her hips to meet him, encouraging his entry.

His prolonged 'aaah' of satisfaction when he pushed in, pulled back then pushed in a second time, found no response within herself. The thin spear of Harold's manhood barely stirred the needs of Ginny's womanhood.

It was, Ginny decided, terribly disappointing; so much so there was no inclination to work her body against his to magnify the pleasure. Smiling up at her unsatisfactory lover in pretence of enjoyment, she lay perfectly motionless and allowed him to slide his unexciting shaft back and forth in her canal.

If Ginny was light years away from achieving an orgasm, it soon became apparent Harold was also going to take a long time. In fact, it was taking so long Ginny was beginning to find it all rather boring. Seriously considering telling him she wanted no more, and wondering how to do so without hurting his feelings overmuch, her attention was caught by a sound near the door.

Francis stood just inside the room watching them, the degree of excitement in his expression increasing by the second. When he began to discard his clothing, Ginny's unaroused senses came partly to life. Both Harold and Francis! Yes, two of them would be much more exciting. She became aware of a tingling anticipation deep within, precipitating a more copious flow of her love juices.

For the first time Ginny began to work herself against Harold while continuing to watch Francis. Now completely disrobed, he was heading for the sofa with his pale manhood projecting before him like a banner. When he positioned himself behind Harold with one foot on the sofa, Ginny frowned in perplexity as to his intention. Then Harold let forth with a cry of pure ecstasy. His whole body jerked forward so that his shaft was driven into Ginny to its deepest degree.

Ginny's gasp was one of disbelieving shock.

Francis was driving his shaft in and out of Harold's rear passage while Harold, an expression of total bliss on his face, was thrusting into Ginny far more strenuously than before. It was bizarre; it was ridiculous, like the combined thrust of two shafts invading her body; it was a sudden unexpected orgasm.

Ginny stood in the hall, watching the manservant carry the last of her bags out to the waiting carriage. At the sound of her name, she looked around to where Francis was descending the staircase. With a rueful smile on his face, he crossed the distance between them and took her hands in his.

'You know you are still welcome to stay if you want to change your mind.'

'Yes,' smiled Ginny, 'I know, but I will not change my mind. You have been a good friend, Francis, and I will always remember you as such. However, I cannot marry you now.'

'A pity,' said Francis with genuine regret. 'A wife as beautiful and charming as you would be a social asset for any man.'

Ginny flushed slightly at the faint accent he gave to 'any'. 'Please do not think I am condemning you Francis.' A rueful and faintly amused smile touched her lips. 'When you spoke of a shared relationship, I imagined something rather different.'

'That was entirely my fault. I should have realised you were unaware of what Harold and I meant to each other when you suggested marriage.' His clasp on her hands tightened. 'I know how much Everleigh means to you, Ginny. Don't leave. Marry me. You will be giving me social respectability and you may take as many lovers as you like. After all that would only be fair.'

Ginny shook her head. 'I will miss Everleigh, and I will miss you too, but the time has come for me to start another phase of my life.'

'Then I wish you well.'

'You too, Francis.'

He took her in his arms and held her close, pressing a light kiss on her forehead. She returned his embrace. When he released her with a final goodbye, Ginny turned quickly and walked out to the waiting carriage. Her eyes were bright with unexpected tears.

Chapter Six

'The staging inn is just around the next bend. Another ten minutes and we'll be there.'

Ginny smiled in relieved acknowledgement at her informant. After three days of mostly uncomfortable travel she was beginning to wonder just why she had made what seemed, in retrospect, to have been a quite ridiculous decision. She had literally picked Wattle Creek out of a hat – bowl to be precise – and possessed no idea of why she was going there, nor what she expected to find when she eventually arrived.

On leaving Everleigh she had booked a suite of rooms in one of Melbourne's classier hotels. There she resided for two totally boring weeks. Few of her former friends visited or invited her out, and Ginny began to realise William Leigh's widow was less acceptable socially than William Leigh's wife. And at the back of her mind there persisted the stubborn conviction that one day she would meet Logan again. In a restless, disconsolate mood she had written the names of every place she could think of on small pieces of paper and stirred them around in a bowl. She then decided her future by reaching in, with her eyes shut, to pull one out.

This next stage was the last before Wattle Creek. Only

another fifteen miles of discomfort and she would, for better or worse, have reached her destination.

Initially thankful simply to be able to stretch her legs and enjoy a refreshing cup of tea, Ginny took little notice of the inn. Such establishments were all much alike; rough slab structures surrounded by horse yards and a miscellany of other primitive buildings.

'I wonder if Smithy has found a buyer for this place yet?' It was a remark which really needed no response but a prick of interest made Ginny turn to her fellow traveller.

'Did you say this inn is for sale?'

'That's right. Smithy's missus died a few months back and he reckons he wants to go back to the city.'

'I see.' A totally unexpected idea flashed into Ginny's mind and she subsided into deep thought. Could she buy the inn? Should she buy the inn? Her mind worked rapidly, assessing the possibilities. 'Should she' was the first decision to make. The 'could' would depend on the probability of being able to obtain a bank loan. At the first opportunity she spoke with the owner.

'Mr Smith, I have heard that you are desirous of selling this establishment and I am interested to know what price you were wanting.'

'I reckon around 400 quid would see me right. Do you know someone who might be interested?'

'I might be interested.'

'You?' The disbelieving snort accompanied a dismissive shake of the head. 'Begging your pardon, ma'am, but I don't think a lady like yerself could run a staging inn. How would you handle the horses for starters?'

The man's negative attitude succeeded only in making Ginny view the prospect as an exciting challenge. 'I would obviously need to employ help and as yet I have only said I might be interested. I will need to know considerably more about the place before I make up my mind. When does the next stage go through to Wattle Creek?'

'Not till Thursday. Goes up Mondays and Thursdays and comes back Tuesdays and Fridays.'

'Then I think I will stay here those few days – that is, if you can accommodate a guest – which should give me sufficient time to see just how everything is managed. By Thursday I would know enough be able to decide whether or not I could run the place.'

Ginny's luggage was unloaded from the coach, the other passengers reboarded, and the stage thundered out onto the road to eventually disappear through the trees in a cloud of dust.

'Right,' said Smithy, picking up Ginny's two bags, 'I'll show you to your room then me son, Drew, can take you around and tell you what everything is.'

In the small, plain, but not uncomfortable room to which Ginny was shown, she unpacked the few necessities and changed her heavy travelling gown for a simple skirt and blouse. All of her more fashionable gowns had been left in Melbourne until she had need of them. The few dresses she brought with her on this impulsive journey were of plain and simple design.

After washing her face, Ginny brushed the dust from her hair, recoiled it neatly, and thus refreshed ventured forth to meet Drew. The inn keeper's son was a lad of about eighteen years with a strong physique and boyish good looks. Ginny smiled at him and noted with amusement how his blue-eyed gaze rested on the swell of her breasts, then roved very deliberately down the length of her body.

'Where would you like to start?' he asked in an innocuous tone, though the bold expression in his eyes gave the words a meaning which put dancing lights into Ginny's eyes.

'Wherever you think Drew. I am certain there is much for me to see.'

'OK. We'll go across to the horse yards first, then work our way around.'

Drew was a pleasant and informative guide, ably

answering Ginny's numerous questions. In addition to staging the teams for the Cobbs coaches they provided meals and accommodation for other travellers moving up and down from the gold fields. Few evenings went by without at least one overnight guest.

'My Ma did all the cooking and it's not been easy for my Dad and me. We had a woman helping us for a while but she up and left with one of the miners who came through.'

They were strolling along the bank of the wide river which ran along the rear boundary of the property. The banks were scattered with huge, gnarled river gums, the grass soft and green beneath. A gentle breeze rippled the surface of the water and the only sounds were the calls of different birds.

'How beautiful this is,' sighed Ginny, 'peaceful and relaxing. Why, we cannot even see the inn from here.'

'No. We could almost be alone in the world.'

Ginny glanced sideways at Drew, smiled faintly, and continued to walk. 'If I do decide I want to buy the inn, would you stay here in my employ?'

'That would depend on what conditions you offered.'

'I would pay you a good wage and you would receive your board and lodging.' She stopped to face him when he did not answer. 'Is there anything else?'

'You, Mrs Leigh. I want to screw you good and hard.'

Ginny's lips quirked and her brow arched up in amused query. The lad was certainly full of self-confidence. With a speculative expression on her face she allowed her own gaze to travel slowly over his body. He was solid and muscular with strong arms and thighs; powerful thighs which were undoubtedly capable of driving that other bulging muscle deeply into a woman. The thought induced a moist, tingling anticipation between her legs.

'Is there any reason I should not take offence and retract my offer to employ you?' asked Ginny in a cool voice which held a hint of her amusement.

'This reason,' responded Drew with a wide smile and unbuttoned the flap of his trousers to display his engorged penis. It was a credible size indeed. Ginny was becoming sopping wet simply looking at the hard, veined shaft with its smooth, shiny head, but she was not about to let the young man have it all his own way.

'You are very sure of yourself, Drew. Do you really think you could use such an asset to your advantage?'

'To your advantage and mine, Mrs Leigh.'

'Do you mean now? Here?' asked Ginny, glancing back along the river bank.

'Why not? No one can see us.'

'There is just one thing,' warned Ginny, beginning to unbutton her blouse. 'The condition of your employment is not that I allow you to screw me, but that you please me when you do.'

And please her he did.

They lay naked, side by side on the soft grass. Ginny had no idea how Drew had learnt so many tricks of arousal at such a youthful age, for without doubt he was an expert. He played her body with his hands, lips and tongue. As a harpist might coax music from the strings of his instrument, he brought her alive to pleasure, drawing her deliciously towards the pinnacle of desire. Then when he finally straddled her, she sucked in her breath with the joy of taking his hard shaft into her moist receptacle.

He thrust sharply a few times, then pleasured her with a slow rotating movement. 'Is it good?'

'Oh yes!' It was more than good, it was pleasure – pure sexual pleasure; nothing like the cruel passion of her couplings with Logan, nor the pathetic strokings of Harold.

Drew pulled out of her and guided her hand to his shaft, slippery now with her love juices. 'Tease yourself,' he commanded. 'Rub my head against your clit and tease yourself until you come.' He bent to kiss her, captured her mouth with lust, then supported himself on his arms with his weight just off her body.

Ginny stroked her fingers down to his balls, rolled the heavy sacks in her hand and slid back up his shaft to take the tip between her forefinger and thumb. She rubbed his head along her creamy slit a few times to lubricate it thoroughly. On finding the hard peaked nodule of her desire she tickled it quickly, masturbating with her lover's penis. Her small cries told Drew how quickly her internal fires were building and when she was on the brink she rapidly removed her hand, and he thrust deeply into her to release the burning flood of her orgasm.

Lifting her hips Ginny met him thrust for lustful thrust. It was the most wonderful, pleasurable, uncomplicated sex she had enjoyed for a very long time. There was no passion, no violent emotion, just a man and a woman using their bodies for mutual, concupiscent gratification.

Long before Thursday came Ginny decided she wanted to buy the inn. Drew's sexual expertise alone made it worth the price and with the many travellers passing through she foresaw numerous opportunities for other interesting encounters. First, however, she needed to obtain the money. When the next Cobbs coach came through, Ginny boarded it for the final leg of her journey.

The bank manager and his wife sat across the table from each other partaking of a silent midday meal. Although the sun blazed down on the dusty street outside, the atmosphere in the room was as chill as an arctic winter. Mrs Townsend completely avoided looking at her husband, while he cast an occasional surreptitious glance at the cold, unforgiving expression on her face.

It was with the greatest of difficulty he suppressed a sigh. Some women enjoyed sex. Why did his wife have to be one of those to whom it was a distasteful duty? A sudden, unbidden, recollection of his daughter engaged in abandoned fornication atop the accountant's desk brought a dull flush to his neck. He hastily pushed the uncomfortable image aside. Such thoughts were to be considered almost incestuous.

On that embarrassing evening he had been every bit as horrified as Mrs Townsend, yet ever since he had become increasingly dissatisfied with the joyless, infrequent couplings in the marriage bed. Licentious desires he thought buried with the wild days of his youth began to resurface with gut aching intensity. He was uncomfortably aware his wife's assertion that their daughter's wantonness of character was inherited from her father was undoubtedly correct.

From the time he lost his virginity at the age of sixteen until he married ten years later, there was hardly a night went by he was not dipping his wick into some moist and willing receptacle. On stating his marriage vows, he determined to remain faithful to his wife – which became a trial of both will power and righteousness as Mrs Townsend considered the act to be purely for the purpose of procreation, and distasteful in the extreme.

With great difficulty he managed to convince her it was her duty to allow her husband access to her body, then wondered if it had been worth the effort. She would lie so rigid and tense he sometimes believed he would obtain better satisfaction from his own hand. A few times, when frustration became overwhelming, he sought the services of a whore. It was something he found both embarrassing and demeaning, never in his life having needed to pay for his sexual gratification. Since that disastrous night when they discovered Jenny and Mr Alexander in the final throes of orgasmic carnality, he found himself longing to experience again the salacious pleasures of his youth.

Unfortunately the catalyst in arousing his own latent sexual urges had precisely the opposite effect on his wife. Horrifed to discover her sweet daughter behaving like a whore, she placed the blame on some character flaw inherited from her father. From that night the door of her bedroom was firmly shut against her husband.

Months of enforced abstinence had finally taken its toll. Last evening, before his wife could retreat to her room and lock her door, Townsend had pushed her down on the sofa and taken his husbandly rights. Ashamed afterwards of having acted like an animal, he had offered an abject apology; an apology which was not accepted. Just how long she would continue to treat him with cold, affronted disdain was anybody's guess, but he imagined it would be for a long, long time. Perhaps he should leave her in peace and reconcile himself to using one of the town's whores.

With a faint sigh, he dabbed his mouth with his napkin and glanced at the clock. Five minutes to one. At one o'clock he had an appointment with a Mrs Leigh. The woman was a newcomer to town; a business woman in need of a financial loan. Townsend knew nothing else about her, but suspected she was probably some straight-laced old biddy as sour faced as the woman seated opposite. Heavens, yes! She was sour faced; sour faced and plain. It was certain Jenny's beauty had not come from her mother either.

Excusing himself he scraped back the chair and rose from the table. What he really desired was to find a warm and sensual woman who knew how to both give and take pleasure; who could abandon herself in a man's arms for no other reason than to satisfy the appetites of the flesh.

Ginny was early for her appointment. Shown into the manager's office by a bashful young clerk, she glanced around the drab room and wondered if the man was as dull as his office. Whatever it took, Ginny was determined to secure the loan. Her experiences with both William and Francis convinced her that while marriage could provide a pleasant lifestyle, it gave no guarantee of personal financial security. Although inexperienced,

Ginny instinctively believed she possessed a head for business and saw the staging inn as the first step along the road to independent wealth.

Informed his client was awaiting him, Townsend schooled his features into an expression of polite wariness – always useful when people wanted money – pushed thoughts of beautiful, sensual women out of his mind, and entered his office. However, the moment Mrs Leigh rose to greet him every single licentious thought rushed back into his head. This woman was no dried out matron. She was young, very beautiful, and the aura of her sexuality floated around her like the essence of some exotic perfume.

Townsend swallowed his excitement. 'Sorry to keep you waiting, Mrs Leigh.'

'Not at all, Mr Townsend, I arrived early.' Ginny smiled in her most seductive manner and the man's heartbeat increased so greatly it was difficult to remain formal.

'Please be seated.' He indicated the chair and took his place behind his desk where he could press his hands unseen against the sudden ache in his groin. 'Now, how can I be of assistance.'

'I wish to apply for a loan, Mr Townsend.'

'Yes, I understand that. I need to know for what purpose you need the money and exactly how much you require.'

'I wish to buy Smithy's inn.'

'You mean you and your husband wish to buy the inn,' he hazarded a correction.

'No, Mr Townsend, I wish to buy the inn. I am a widow and eager to venture into business.'

Townsend swallowed again, could feel the sweat beading his brow. Not only beautiful, a widow as well. 'A staging inn would appear to be an unusual business for a young woman to undertake. Surely a dress shop or something of that nature would be more suitable.'

'That may be so, but I have never been one to undertake what is dull and ordinary. Drew Smith is willing to stay on to look after the horses.'

'Mmm. Well I must admit you do give the impression of confidence and capability, Mrs Leigh, in spite of your inexperience in business matters. I imagine you are well experienced in other – er – areas.'

Ginny's shapely brow arched upward in the mannerism which always betrayed her amused recognition of a man's sexual interest. 'Perhaps,' she replied in a noncommittal tone. 'Do I understand, then, that you are willing to grant me the loan?'

'Just how large a loan do you require, Mrs Leigh?' Townsend was far more concerned with how to arrange a more intimate meeting with this beautiful, sexy woman.

'I need £400.'

Townsend's thoughts rapidly reverted to business. 'That is a substantial amount, the equivalent of several years wages in fact. Are you putting any money of your own into this venture?'

'I have £100 of my own. Smithy is asking £500 for the inn.'

'You must understand, Mrs Leigh, that without any collateral it will be impossible for me to authorise so large a loan.'

'Surely the bank would hold a mortgage over the inn?'

'Naturally, but the bank would require some other security as well. What if the inn should burn down?' Townsend paused. The tiny frown lines between his customer's brows and the glimpse of sharp white teeth biting her lower lip rendered her even more desirable. 'Do you have anything of value which could be used as security?'

'Nothing which could be deposited in the bank's vaults, Mr Townsend.' Ginny regarded the man with a steady gaze. From the moment he walked through the door she was aware of the nature of his thoughts. And she wanted that loan. 'My only assets are – well covered.

If you would care to inspect them, you should perhaps lock your door.'

The speed with which he hastened to do just that almost made Ginny laugh out loud. Poor man. She had caught a glimpse of his wife earlier in the day and knew just how little satisfaction that woman would give her husband in bed. Townsend might be balding and a trifle overweight, but such physical imperfections could be easily overlooked if he granted her loan – at low interest!

He was gazing at her now in nervous anticipation. Ginny stood up and began, one by one, to release the buttons of her high-necked jacket. With tantalising slow-ness, she slid it from her shoulders and upper arms to reveal the creamy skin of her throat and soft swell of her breasts beneath the fine lawn of her camisole. 'Do you wish to see more, Mr Townsend?'

'Yes, yes.' He was almost drooling at the mouth, his penis throbbing with eagerness. 'I think I should inspect more thoroughly.'

Ginny slid the jacket completely from her arms and released the ribbon tie of her camisole to expose the firm beauty of her breasts to the man's eager gaze. 'More,' he croaked, 'I need to see more.'

'Do I qualify for the loan, Mr Townsend?'

'Perhaps, perhaps.'

'Will this decide you?' Ginny moved close to him, lifted his hand to her breast and placed her own on the hard bulge in his trousers.

Townsend almost came on the spot.

'When?' he panted.

'When I have my money,' replied Ginny, calmly walking away and restoring her clothing to its former respectability. She was not going to prostitute herself for nothing. Ever since that night with Johnny and his friends on the ship – albeit she enjoyed every moment of it – Ginny always decided the when, where and with whom she would engage in sex. Except for Logan, a tiny

95

voice said. Hastily she pushed it aside. Townsend was speaking.

'It may take a few days to organise the loan.' Could he wait that long? 'Perhaps we could discuss the details more fully this evening?'

Ginny smiled and shook her head. Poor man, he was just about ready to rape her there and then. 'I will await your notification when the money is available. Thank you for your time, Mr Townsend.' And she walked serenely towards the door which he opened with a stammered, 'My pleasure, my pleasure.'

When a letter was delivered to her hotel the following evening informing her everything was arranged, Ginny was not surprised to learn her loan had been approved so quickly. Nor was she perturbed by the bank manager's insistence on personally escorting both her and the money back to Smithy's in his private coach. The man was obviously anticipating a night spent in her bed at the inn as his repayment for pulling the necessary strings to obtain her loan.

Ginny briefly wondered what Drew might think of such an arrangement before deciding his opinions were unimportant. Drew and she understood each other. Her body was hers to do with as she pleased and she had vowed never again to become slave to such savage possession as Logan's. An all too familiar quiver tore at her gut and she hastily pushed the disturbing memories aside.

Townsend's letter requested Ginny meet him at the bank at two o'clock the following afternoon, and a little before that time she left her hotel to walk the two blocks to the bank. There were a number of people in the street, some of whom nodded a friendly greeting. Many of the men gazed at her with open admiration, attracted not only by her beauty, but also by her unmistakable aura of sensuality and hint of an earthy sexuality beneath the respectable exterior. The lustful stares of men were something to which she was accustomed; why, then, did she have the uneasy feeling of being watched?

Pausing in front of the general store, she made a pretence of studying the goods on display in the window. Instead she studied the reflected images of the other people in the street. With what she hoped was a casual movement, she turned to look back the way she had come. No one appeared to be watching her with any uncommon degree of interest. Not entirely reassured, she continued the few hundred yards to the bank.

Townsend ushered her into his office with nervous ceremony. 'There are some papers for you to sign, Mrs Leigh. I have sent my driver to the hotel for your bags and as soon as he returns we can be on our way.'

'May I see the money?' asked Ginny.

'Of course.' He opened a small leather case. 'It is all here, along with the necessary documents for purchase of the inn.'

Ginny smiled, her eyes holding a glint of provocation. 'I see I am going to be in capable hands, Mr Townsend.'

'You may be assured of that, Mrs Leigh.' Townsend's manhood was already swelling with anticipation. He had no intention of waiting until evening to collect the promised 'collateral'. If his driver kept the horses to an easy walk as instructed, they would have close on three uninterrupted hours enclosed in his carriage. The prospect made him feel young and virile again. In the wild days of his youth he had engaged in numerous sexual indulgences within the confines of a moving carriage.

With Ginny's signature on the necessary papers, Townsend placed them in his safe, and escorted her out to the waiting carriage. Smiling at him as he gallantly handed her in, Ginny was once again assailed by the certainty someone was watching her. This time when she looked around she caught a glimpse of a black-haired woman disappearing into one of the shops.

It was only a glimpse and she could not be certain, but a sickened sensation settled in the pit of her stomach.

Tessa! Could it have been Tessa? And if it was her former maid, did that mean Logan was also somewhere in the vicinity?

The idea was so disturbing she lapsed into a sombre introspection which caused Townsend to fear she might be regretting her promise. His concern was only momentary. He was not certain what serious thoughts were in her mind but he was confident that once they got down to the business in hand the beautiful Mrs Leigh would fulfil his highest expectations. From a wicker hamper on the carriage floor he extracted a bottle of wine and two glasses.

'Shall we toast to the success of your venture, Mrs Leigh?'

Ginny turned away from her unseeing contemplation of the straggling buildings on the outskirts of the town and thrust discomposing memories of Logan from her mind. 'Why not?'

The alcohol eased her tension and she reclined back against the plush upholstery with a languid smile. 'Your coach is far superior in comfort to the stages, Mr Townsend.'

'I have always appreciated quality and beauty, Mrs Leigh, and you possess both. Ever since you allowed me to look upon part of your womanly beauty I have been filled with the greatest longing to see more.'

'And so you shall.' Ginny was beginning to enjoy herself. This would be the first time she had ever done it in a coach and anything different always added a spice of titillation.

In the manner of a provocative strip tease artist she carefully removed her hat and gloves and placed them neatly on the opposite seat beside her companion. He was watching her every move with eyes which were hot with lustful anticipation and an imp of mischief entered Ginny's own eyes.

Very, very slowly she began to release the buttons of her jacket. When she reached a stage low enough for a

98

tantalising degree of cleavage to be visible, she paused with her fingers on the next button and ran the tip of her tongue slowly around her lips. 'I feel a little thirsty, Mr Townsend.'

The man blinked, managed to drag his gaze away from the glimpse of deep shadow between milky mounds, and poured another glass of wine.

Ginny sipped a little and smiled. 'The buttons are difficult to manage with one hand. Perhaps you would like to release them for me.'

While Townsend's cautious fingers fumbled with the tiny buttons, Ginny sipped at her wine in thorough enjoyment of the entire situation. If the man was amusingly nervous in his eagerness, there was certainly nothing hesitant about the bulge within his trousers. When the last button was released, the garment was pushed aside and her breasts cupped in adoring hands.

A frisson ran through Ginny; from the sensitive tips of the breasts he so expertly massaged through to the innermost seat of her desire. Even if his wife was a sour-faced old biddy, it was apparent the bank manager had not forgotten how to arouse a woman. Ginny was soon as eager as he to free her body of her bulky outer garments. Not without a certain degree of difficult manoeuvring, they managed to remove her skirt and petticoats to leave her clad only in her camisole, pantaloons, stockings and laced ankle boots.

Townsend's mouth and hands were all over her body. He kissed her lustily and slipped a finger into the moist crevice which promised so much pleasure. Anxious as he was to slide his throbbing penis into that receptacle of delight, he knew that to do so immediately would give him an instant orgasm. Instead he held himself in check, knowing from his youthful experiences that the longer he denied himself, the longer he would last once coition was finally achieved. And when his rock hard shaft was eventually encased within the sex canal of the beautiful and willing Mrs Leigh, he wanted it to last a long, long time.

Dan, Josh and Charlie were reconnoitring the southern road. Rumour was about that a gold shipment would be leaving Wattle Creek within the next couple of weeks and they were searching for a suitable location to stage an ambush – if they decided to hold up the escort. Josh and Charlie were eager, Dan more cautious. He held an uneasy conviction such an attempt would end in bloodshed, for the escort could not be expected to docilely lay aside their rifles and allow the gold to be taken.

When Dan's acute hearing detected the sound of an approaching carriage the three men urged their horses off the road and out of site behind a convenient jumble of massive boulders. From there they watched it pass. A lone driver was seated in a relaxed posture on the driving seat and drawn blinds hid the vehicle's occupants from view.

'Isn't that Townsend's carriage?' asked Charlie.

'Yes,' agreed Dan, 'it is. I wonder where he is going? That is if he is in it.'

'Do you think maybe the gold commissioner is being a mite cunning?'

Dan glanced sharply at Charlie. 'You don't think the gold's in there?'

'Might be. It's been a pretty open secret the gold's going out within the next week or so. The rumour could have been deliberately set up as a blind.'

'Mmm. You could be right.'

'There aren't any guards,' offered Josh.

Dan's eyes narrowed thoughtfully, his gaze following the coach. 'The blinds are drawn. They could be inside.'

'Well there wouldn't be more than two, maybe three. I reckon we could take them.'

For several moments Dan said nothing. His lips were pursed and a frown creased his handsome brow. If indeed the gold was being transported within that coach, it presented a far different proposition from the heavily armed escort he had anticipated. And if it should only be Townsend engaged on some journey, then it would afford Dan the greatest of pleasures to relieve him of whatever valuables he was carrying.

'Right. We'll cut across country to get in front of them and bail them up at the river.'

Inside the coach Ginny was lying along the seat with one foot on the floor and the other propped on the window sill to part her thighs as wide as possible. Townsend knelt on the floor with one hand twisting and pushing inside her love hole and the other squeezing and massaging her breasts. She was panting in eager response to the stimulation of his fingers within her sex wet canal. The man had aroused her with far greater expertise than she had imagined he would possess. No longer did she consider she was favouring him with her body in payment for the loan; she was a lusty woman engaged in very enjoyable sexual foreplay with a man who knew what it was all about.

With a gasp she reached for his arousing hand to still his movement. Any moment now she would come and she wanted it to be either with his shaft inside her or his mouth sucking hard against her sex lips. A jolt of the coach momentarily fractured her quickening, then shattered it completely by coming to a dramatic standstill which upset Townsend's balance and set him on his backside on the floor.

'What the – ?!'

'Bushrangers?' Ginny heard the shouted commands and hurriedly struggled to a sitting position. Fear rapidly replaced desire. Townsend was fumbling to his feet.

'Throw out your guns, then open the door and come out slowly with your hands up.'

'Oh, please do as he says,' whispered Ginny.

Townsend extracted a heavy revolver from a pocket in

the side of the coach and threw it out. The splash it made when it hit the water caused Ginny to start nervously.

'Is that all?' demanded the voice.

'Yes.'

'Then come out; one at a time.'

'I can't go out like this.' Ginny appealed to her would-be lover.

'I am afraid we have no choice.' Townsend was himself in considerable disarray of clothing and highly embarrassed by the situation. However he valued his life and knew better than to argue with desperate criminals.

'If you don't hurry there'll be a bullet to help you along.' The voice was becoming impatient.

Townsend opened the door and peered out. At first he could see only two then realised a third kept his driver well covered. Hastily he jumped down, wincing when he landed in six inches of water which splashed up his legs.

'Good afternoon, sir,' mocked a deep voice and Townsend looked up into a pair of dark brown eyes which held amusement yet little mercy.

'You!' he spat. 'Why you – ' Words failed him but Dan was taking no notice of him anyway. His attention was directed at the door of the carriage and a low whistle hissed through his teeth. 'Well, well.'

Townsend was gentleman enough to turn around and assist Ginny to alight. When she was standing beside him in the water he appealed to the bushranger. 'Now look here, Berrigan. I want you to forget the past – know now you were not entirely to blame.'

'So I heard,' responded Dan without even glancing at the man. He was far too occupied with taking in every luscious detail of the beauty whose scant attire clearly indicated just what they had interrupted.

'Yes, well.' Townsend was becoming increasingly alarmed. Heaven knew the man had a right to hold a grudge. 'You don't intend to do anything foolish I hope.'

'Foolish?' Dan stared down at him in derision. 'Do you think I might shoot you in cold blood, Townsend?' he asked and laughed outright at the man's undisguised fear. 'If I was a violent man I might, since I have you and your slut of a daughter to thank for ruining my life.' His gaze returned to Ginny who stood shivering and silent unable to make sense of what was being said. 'I wonder what the most respectable Mrs Townsend would have to say if she knew you were having it off inside the carriage with your floosie.'

Ginny's gasp was one of outrage. Sparks of anger flashed in her eyes and Dan's interest was heightened. 'Search the coach, Charlie, we'll see what else our estimable bank manager has got worth taking.'

'Like hell!' declared Ginny, who immediately understood the innuendo.

Dan laughed; this time in genuine mirth. 'A spitfire, Townsend. How could you handle someone like her?'

The barely veiled slight on his sexual prowess brought a dull flush creeping up Townsend's neck. Of all the things which could have happened, being held up by Berrigan just when he was about to achieve the ultimate pleasure with the sexiest woman he had been with in many years, was worse than his worst nightmare. The red-bearded Charlie was emerging from the coach with the leather case.

'Look at this, Dan. I reckon there's a few hundred quid in here.'

'That's mine!' shouted Ginny, seeing all hope of buying the inn rapidly disappearing.

'Oh?' Dan quirked an amused eyebrow. 'For services rendered? You must be good.'

Ginny almost choked on her chagrin. Her clenched fists itched to wipe the amused smirk off his handsome face, however he had turned back to Townsend to bark, 'Anything else?'

'No, no, that is all. You can take it.'

'I intend to. And I'm taking her as well.'

'Like hell!' declared Ginny a second time only to take an unsteady step backwards when the man walked his horse closer. His brown eyes were laughing down at her, inciting her to greater fury.

Suddenly he leaned over, curved a muscled arm around her back, and scooped her off her feet. In spite of her struggles and the sideways stepping of his horse, she found herself dragged up in front of him. There she hammered at him with angry fists.

Dan evaded the blows with ease and pulled out a piece of rope to tie her hands securely in front of her. 'That should keep you manageable until we get back to camp.'

Ginny glared into the bushranger's face. 'You'll pay for this,' she threatened. 'Kidnapping is an offence.'

'Really?' taunted Dan with that maddening smile. 'Do you think someone might want to pay to get you back? Easy women come cheap. Though £400 is a lot of money.'

If Ginny could have slapped his face she would have. Instead she turned her head angrily aside. Strong arms hauled her back against a firmly muscled chest and with a mocking salute for Townsend, Dan cantered his horse out of the river.

Chapter Seven

*F*or some time Ginny held herself as rigidly as possible, her captor's soft chuckle of amusement increasing her anger. It was obvious the bushranger had taken
her for his own pleasure and what would become of her
once he was satisfied she could not begin to imagine.
Fear, however, played no part in her emotions. In spite
of the deadly looking pistols levelled at Townsend, she
did not believe he was a man of violence.

'Why don't you relax.' His voice laughed in her ear.

Ginny ignored him – until a strong brown hand slid
inside her camisole to cup her breast. The pad of his
thumb teased her nipple to hardness and an erotic shiver
ran through Ginny's body. Considering the state of
arousal she was in when the coach was held up, it was
little wonder she should immediately feel an aching
need, understandable that her vulva should begin to
throb with eagerness. The hard pressure of purely male
muscle against her thigh increased her excited anticipation and she wondered how far they were going to
ride.

They were well clear of the road and heading up into
the hills. Dan's hand left Ginny's breast and worked its
way inside the opening of her pantaloons to find her

moist love hole. A shudder of desire ran through his own body. On first sighting this woman he had felt the stirring in his loins. Her state of undress and tousled sexual beauty were sufficient to arouse any man. And Dan had been too long without a woman.

A desire to mock Townsend was only part of his decision to take her captive. He wanted this woman more than he had ever wanted any woman before. And he wanted her now, not in two hours time when they arrived back at their hideout. The temptation to stop, lift her to the ground and take her immediately was almost overwhelming. Caution barely overrode lust. They were not yet far enough away to consider themselves safe from pursuit.

When he brought his horse to a halt, Ginny glanced up at him for the first time since leaving the river. There was a mischievous gleam in his eyes, his grin a flash of even white teeth. 'I can't wait any longer but I dare not stop here.' One hand was holding the reins and supporting Ginny; the other was undoing his belt and opening the flap of his trousers to release his iron-hard rod of manhood. He lifted Ginny's leg and turned her to face him, telling her to place her arms around his neck.

Totally bemused, Ginny did as she was bid, lifting her bound wrists over his head. Dan's hands grasped her buttocks and shifted her into position. She sucked in her breath at the first touch of his shaft against her wet sex lips, then exhaled on a drawn out gasp when he eased her down.

For Ginny the pleasure was in the magnificent size of him; for Dan it was in the discovery she could encompass all of him with ease. For a moment they remained thus, each revelling in the feel of the other, of sex-salved skin against satiny skin. A hoot of laughter from Josh and a shouted, 'Hey Charlie, I think we'd better leave Dan to his own devices,' was completely ignored. Dan supported Ginny with an arm around her back, caught up the reins and urged his horse to a slow jog.

'Dear Lord!' gasped Ginny, clinging to Dan for all she was worth. The gait of the animal established the motion of their bodies. Without either needing to move, Dan's massive rod stroked to the very depths of Ginny's womanhood. It was the most erotic coupling Ginny had ever experienced, but for Dan his abstinence had been too long and her sheath was deliciously moist and receptive. With a loud grunt he shot his load and the almost simultaneous flood of warm juices over his shaft told him that she, too, had climaxed.

The muscles of Ginny's womanhood clenched in spasms around his shaft as wave after fabulous wave of orgasmic delight wrenched through her body. When the ecstasy abated she raised her head from his shoulder to look up at him. There was a gleam of satisfaction in his eyes and a smile curving his lips. Ginny smiled in response and rested her cheek against the comfortable strength of his shoulder once more.

Dan slowed his horse to a walk but they remained joined, enjoying the pleasurable movement of one within the other. The horse splashed through a clear, fern-fringed stream and Dan turned the animal to follow the sparkling watercourse higher into the hills. Man and woman exchanged no words until they reached a place where a small waterfall tumbled into a deep, rocky pool.

When Dan hauled back on the reins Ginny lifted her head only to have her mouth captured by warm lips. 'I want to make love to you properly. Do you mind?'

Surprised and strangely moved that he should even ask, Ginny shook her head. He could not want it more than she did. Dan lifted her free from his semi-relaxed shaft and eased her down until her feet were on the ground. Then he dismounted and freed her wrists. 'Let's bathe,' be suggested, starting to strip off his shirt.

Ginny glanced towards the crystal clear water, where the sun danced rainbows from the froth at the base of the falls. 'The water looks awfully cold.'

'It will be, but think of the fun we will have warming

each other up afterwards.' His expression held such amused devilry that Ginny laughed in response and sat on the ground to unlace her boots.

She soon discovered 'cold' was a gross understatement. The water was icy. Immediately she placed a foot in the pool she gasped with shock. Very gingerly she waded knee deep then stopped. Dan, who had dived in and surfaced some distance away, was laughing at her. 'You have to wet yourself all over,' he called, swiping his open hand across the surface of the water to splash icy spray onto her body.

Ginny recoiled with a yelp of protest. 'That's not fair.'

'Yes it is. It's not so cold if you get right in.'

Before she could retreat, Dan lunged at her and pulled her down, holding her tightly in his arms to prevent her escape while he fully immersed them both. When he pulled them upright, waist deep in the water, he maintained the embrace. His mouth came down on hers, tasting her, savouring her, gentle at first then increasing in passion. It was a passion which found a shaking response in herself.

'I want to wash you,' he said, when at last he broke the kiss. With gentle hands he scooped the water and sluiced it over her body. There was not an inch of her he missed. Starting at her forehead he smoothed the moisture from her face, then washed his palms slowly down over her shoulders and arms, her breasts, her hips and stomach, then down under the surface of the water to between her thighs. Very thoroughly he washed the creases and folds of her love lips, washing away the lingering juices of their coupling.

All the time his gaze held hers and Ginny began to tremble, the expression in her eyes telling him of her awakening need.

'Now you wash me,' he said.

Ginny did as he had done, reaching up to wipe wet hands across his face. She sluiced the water and washed it over his body, admiring his muscled leanness and the fine, brown hairs which now clung in tiny, damp tendrils to his chest. When her hand curved gently around the heavy sacks of his balls, his sudden intake of breath heightened her own arousal. Very gently she slid her hand up his rapidly stiffening shaft to swill the water in delicate touches around the head.

'Enough,' groaned Dan. He scooped her in his arms and carried her out of the pool to the blanket he had spread in readiness in the sun. There he set her carefully down, stretched alongside her and took her in his arms to kiss her deeply. His manhood was throbbing with eagerness to take her, but he wanted to extend the pleasure for them both.

With her arms wound around his neck Ginny returned his kiss with equal fervour. She arched her body against his, enjoying the sensation of the drying hairs of his chest scratching against her hard peaked nipples. One of his hands trailed a leisurely path down to the soft curls of her mound. His fingers toyed with the hairs, teasing her with anticipation of a more intimate caress.

Ginny's own hand stroked down his back to the firm curve of his buttocks with their soft, downy covering of hair. 'Touch me,' he groaned and she moved her hand around to embrace his huge swollen penis. Only then did Dan cease his teasing to part her folds with his fingers and seek the moist entrance to her love canal.

They pleasured each other with their hands, eager for the ultimate satisfaction yet in no hurry. The anticipation of fulfilment acted as an aphrodisiac bringing their bodies vibrantly alive. Dan kissed the sculptured perfection of her breasts, then nibbled gently at the sensitive peaks with his teeth. He eased his body lower, spreading her thighs with his hands and parting her sex lips with his fingers to enable him to taste the sweetness of her desire.

Ginny's hands were entwined in his hair, her little shivers of ecstasy trembling their impatient message. Dan heaved himself along the length of her torso. The hot tip of his manhood kissed the moist and eager lips of her vagina, then he was within her, revelling in the knowledge there was no need to be cautious in his entry. Her body accepted him joyously, her warm sheath taking and embracing the full extension of his shaft.

The pleasure was doubly intense for having been so long delayed. Dan drove hard into her and Ginny lifted her legs to curl them around his waist, opening herself to the fullest. Her fingers clutched at the firm flesh of his buttocks; her own were lifted to meet each thrust to extract every fragment of delicious sensation.

For each, the intense orgasm was an exquisite pleasure, so close to pain it was almost beyond endurance. Spasm after spasm of unbelievable ecstasy racked Ginny's body as Dan reached his own cataclysmic pinnacle.

Sated, the sun warm on their bodies, they lay in each others arms. After a while Ginny must have slept, for when she opened her eyes the shadows were touching the edge of the blanket and Dan was propped on an elbow watching her. Ginny noted how dark his eyes were – almost as dark as Logan's. Yet there the similarity ended. The one pair was as hard and dark as onyx, glittering with a cruel possessiveness; the other was as warm and soft as brown velvet and held an expression remarkably like regret.

'Do you want me to take you back?' he asked.

'Do you want to take me back?'

'No. I want you to stay with me.'

Ginny did not immediately reply, taking time to examine her feelings. She was content, almost happy. Perhaps with Dan she had found the man with whom she could exorcise all memories of Logan. And, after all, what was there to go back for? Even if she asked it was highly unlikely Dan would give her back the money; the possibility of obtaining a second loan even more unlikely. She became aware he was watching her carefully, almost as if endeavouring to read her thoughts. Ginny smiled.

Her bushranging captor was really rather nice and he certainly knew how to satisfy a woman's sexual needs.

'I will stay, for a while. Though there is the small matter of my clothes.'

The enormity of Dan's relief surprised him, for he did not realise there were reasons other than sexual ones for wanting her to remain with him. He kissed her softly, the mischievous gleam she was coming to know lighting his eyes. 'I would prefer to keep you exactly as you are without a stitch hiding any part of that beautiful body. However I am certain we can arrange some way of collecting your luggage without alerting the police.'

In the weeks which followed Ginny discovered a happiness unknown at any stage in her life before. Where once she coveted all the trappings of wealth and fine living, she found herself content to live under the same primitive conditions as the bushrangers. That Dan was the main reason for her contentment she was willing to admit.

On that first evening it was almost dark by the time they reached the rough slab and bark hut high in the hills. The other two men eyed her with lascivious interest when she entered the hut. For the first time in her life Ginny felt uncomfortable under their avaricious gazes, for normally she enjoyed the appraisal of men. Now she wished she was clad in more than her undergarments.

'So you brought her back,' the red beard leered. 'Do we get our turn with her now?'

'Shut up, Charlie!' The angry snarl brought three startled gazes to Dan's face. If Charlie and Josh were surprised the question could incite such anger, Ginny was seeing for the first time the harsh, unforgiving streak in his nature which set him on his unlawful career.

Charlie held up a placating hand. 'OK Dan, simmer down. How long is she going to stay?'

'For as long as she wants to stay.'

'Is that so? And where do you reckon we're all going

to sleep? Do you expect Josh and me simply to shut our eyes and ears while you and she are panting and humping in the corner?'

The man's enmity was so apparent Ginny felt a stirring of unease. Was he resentful of Dan's exclusive claim on her, or was it simply because he did not want a woman at the hut? That Dan was experiencing great difficulty in controlling his temper was patently obvious. His voice was harsh, his eyes no longer soft as velvet but as hard as the rocks in the cliff behind the hut.

'You're pushing it, Charlie. Ginny stays here and that is all there is to be said on the subject. And don't worry, I'm not going to toss you out of your beds – yet. We'll use the cave tonight.'

No more was said but Ginny realised the man, Charlie, would never be her friend.

The cave of which Dan spoke was set in the cliff, about 100 yards above the small level area on which the hut stood. The tiny entrance gave no indication of the spaciousness of the cavern. When Dan lit a lamp, Ginny saw that it was equipped with the basic necessities, including a straw mattress against one wall. There was also, she noted with a degree of misgiving, a large supply of ammunition within the cave.

'This is our retreat,' explained Dan. 'If the police ever manage to find the hut, we can come up here and there is no way they will ever be able to take us. Not alive anyway.'

A shudder ran through Ginny. The possibility of Dan being shot and killed was too terrible to contemplate. 'Why did you become a bushranger?'

Dan glanced at her, wondering what caused the faint tremor in her voice. 'It's a long story.' He held up a tin plate on which he had placed some damper and cold meat. 'Come and have something to eat. You'll need your strength,' he added with a grin, 'for I have plans for far better things tonight than telling you the tale of my misfortunes.'

'Your friend Charlie doesn't like me,' announced Ginny a short time later.

A faint frown creased Dan's brow before he gave a dismissive shrug. 'Don't worry too much about Charlie. You see it has been just the three of us for so long. He'll get used to the idea of having you around.'

Would he, wondered Ginny.

The mattress on the cave floor was far more comfortable than it appeared. Ginny lay on her side gazing at the small, rock-framed patch of sky. Outside the cave entrance the sky was gradually changing from grey to gold with the start of a new day.

Long into the night they had given each other full joy of their bodies many times over. Then they had slept, wrapped in each other's arms. It was the raucous laugh of a kookaburra somewhere nearby which had woken Ginny with the dawn. She felt Dan stir behind her and his hand came over to cup her breast. With a smile Ginny placed her hand over his to hold it against her body.

'Awake already?' he murmured, with his lips against her hair.

'Yes.'

'Didn't you sleep well?'

'I slept soundly.'

'Mmm, so did I. It must have been all that sex.' His hand was gently kneading her breast and she could feel the hard rod of his manhood pressing against her buttocks. 'Ah, Ginny. I wonder where you have been all my life?'

The caressing hand skated down the plane of her stomach and over her hip to her buttocks, then down between them to find her slit. The response of Ginny's nerve ends was dramatic. She rolled half on her stomach, crooking her knee to free her opening to his probing fingers. He slid his other hand beneath her hips, bringing it around to the front to tease her love bud while the

113

middle finger of his other hand stroked in and out of her canal.

To have both of Dan's hands stimulating her was so absolutely wonderful Ginny remained with her cheek pillowed on her hand moaning her approval. Her protest when the exquisite innervation ceased soon changed to a sigh of anticipation. Dan knelt across her extended leg almost sitting back on his heels. Lifting her other leg high he opened her wide, guided the head of his shaft with his other hand and slid it into her moist and throbbing love hole.

He pushed and twisted, driving in to touch every internal part of her. When his fingers returned to her special spot Ginny shuddered with delight, crying out aloud at the indescribable explosion of her senses. Not wanting the perfection ever to cease she worked herself against Dan, rotating her sheath around his thrusting shaft. But eventually the flooding of her love juices eased and she lay quietly, simply enjoying the feel of Dan still moving within her.

Without breaking the joining of their bodies, he shifted her legs to roll her onto her back. In that position he rested his weight on his hands, the expression in his soft, dark eyes serious. 'I hope you intend to stay for a long, long time, Ginny, for I don't think I ever want to let you go.'

He kissed her then, claiming her lips in tender passion. Ginny's reaction was immediate. She clung to him, kissing him with an emotion different from any she had ever felt with any other man. Mouths and genitals joined, they rolled over so that Ginny was lying on top of Dan. In that position she moved her pelvis to work her love wet sheath around Dan's shaft, pressing down to the hilt and driving them both into a renewed frenzy of desire.

They slept in the cave for almost a week until a rough, lean-to extension had been built at the rear of the hut to provide sleeping quarters for Charlie and Josh. How those two managed to retrieve her bags and clothing on the first day she had no idea. Neither would any of the men enlighten her, except to say there were many in the district who were still their friends. And if Charlie showed no more sign of liking Ginny, he at least appeared prepared to accept her presence.

Ginny began to feel very much like a wife. She cleaned the little hut, cooked the meals and washed their clothes. That water needed to be carried from the stream and heated on the open fire over which she cooked was an inconvenience barely to be considered. And learning how to make the scone-like damper and create a tasty stew from the meat of a wallaby were skills she learned with ease. Dan's presence made everything worthwhile.

It seemed they understood each other on every level of awareness. Thoughts were communicated with a smile or particular expression and they knew all the little tricks which delighted and aroused the other's body. When they made love it was in perfect harmony.

The only time they came close to fighting was when Ginny heard the three men discussing plans to rob the gold escort. Even a person not as attuned to Dan's feelings as she could have seen he was being persuaded against his will. Having missed the escort which went out the day after they held up Townsend's coach, both Charlie and Josh were determined not to allow the next opportunity to go by.

'You don't have to go,' interrupted Ginny, with heat in her voice. 'If Charlie and Josh want to risk their lives let them do so on their own.'

All three looked at her; Dan with frowning concern and Charlie with undisguised contempt. 'It's none of your business,' he snarled. 'You just stick to doing what you were brought here for.'

An angry flush stained Ginny's cheeks for at that time she was engaged in mending one of Dan's shirts. She appealed to him again. 'You could be shot. I don't want you to get hurt.'

'Why? Afraid if he does you might miss out on some good screwing?'

'Charlie!' There was a warning in Dan's voice and in the frown he directed at his mate. He turned back to Ginny, noting her flushed cheeks and anger-bright eyes. They rendered her more beautiful and desirable than ever and his always eager manhood began swelling in response. However – 'In a way he is right Ginny. This is nothing to do with you.'

'Oh, you are all mad fools.' She jumped to her feet and set her mending aside with a glare for her lover before storming out of the hut. 'Well don't let my feelings stop you.'

Ginny walked down to the creek and began to wander along the bank following its course downstream. Such was her anger, she forgot Dan's injunction never to roam far from the hut. The causes of her anger were many, the underlying emotion fear; fear for Dan's life.

Absorbed as she was in her thoughts, she did not realise just how far she had wandered until she reached a place where an outcrop of rocks impeded her progress. With a sigh she sat down on one of the rocks, rested her chin in her hands, and stared broodingly into the water.

The rays of sunlight filtering through the trees caught the rippling stream in a sparkle of light. Rainbow colours danced off its surface and the water shimmered silver and gold.

Gold?

Ginny peered more intently, her heart thudding loudly in her breast. A sudden breeze rippled the surface of the water, scattering the refracted light. The golden colour remained unmoved.

She had never seen a gold nugget before, nor held one in her hand. It was about the size of her thumbnail. Not worth a fortune, though large enough to become excited about. Ginny was excited beyond belief. A more detailed search along the edge of the stream produced another half dozen smaller nuggets. Her joyous laughter rang

116

through the trees to be answered by a voice calling her name.

'Oh Dan, you'll never guess.' Ginny turned a sparkling countenance towards her approaching lover.

'I don't suppose I will,' he agreed. 'Why are you so happy now when you were so angry when you left the hut?'

'I am happy because I can present you with a very good reason for not holding up the gold escort – or any one else.'

'What are you talking about?'

'These,' laughed Ginny, and held out her hand.

Dan could not speak. He simply stared at the cluster of nuggets resting in her palm.

'It is gold, isn't it?' Ginny was suddenly anxious.

'It's gold all right,' agreed Dan, finding a hoarse fraction of his voice. 'Where did you find it?'

'Here.' Ginny indicated the stream. 'I was sitting on that rock looking at the water and there it was.'

Dan gave a great shout of laughter, caught her in an embrace and swung her around. 'Woman you're a marvel. I knew you would be good for me.' He kissed her passionately and the gold was immediately forgotten with the urgency of desire.

Their clothes were soon discarded, tossed on the ground to create a soft palliasse for their entwined bodies. Dan took her quickly, both of them impatient to reach a climax, thrusting with wild urgency against each other.

Ginny's erotic pelvic gyrations drove Dan into a sexual frenzy. He had known many women who enjoyed sex but never one who used her body with such erotism as Ginny. She matched her movements with his taking all of his enormous size deeply and satisfyingly, without need for caution.

Much later he lay on his back, hands pillowed beneath his head. He was smiling up at Ginny who knelt over him, riding up and down on his shaft. The hot rays of the sun were falling directly on them, its heat and their physical exertions polishing their bodies with sweat. Ginny pushed as far down on Dan as she could go; down until her swollen sex lips were nestling against the dark pubic hair at the base of his shaft. There she rested, raising her arms to lift the hot, heavy weight of her hair from her neck.

The action stretched her breasts into taut cones of perfection, tightened her stomach muscles and contracted her luscious womanhood more tightly around his stalking manhood. Dan groaned, a spasm of ecstasy crossing his face.

'Did you like that?' asked Ginny, conciously contracting and relaxing those same muscles. A deeper groan was her only answer.

With a sensual smile parting her lips, Ginny began to rotate her hips. Her intention was to give Dan pleasure. Not only did she succeed in that aim, she created the most wonderful sensations deep within her own body. Panting now, she pressed even harder against his groin so that his wiry pubic hairs stimulated her clitoris. Faster and harder she twisted. Dan's eyes were closed, her own glazed with knowledge of her approaching orgasm.

'Oh Dan! Dan!' It was flooding from her, saturating them both.

'God! Ginny!' he yelled, grabbing her waist and thumping her up and down a half dozen times to complete his own body wrenching release.

Ginny's suggestion they keep the discovery of the gold to themselves was quickly overridden. The others were his mates, Dan informed her. They had always done everything – well, almost everything – together, and he saw no reason to change now. What gold they found would be shared equally between them.

And that soon became a quite considerable amount. As their fortune accumulated even Charlie appeared to regard Ginny in a more friendly manner.

'When I have sufficient gold,' Dan said one night when they lay in each other's arms sexually replete, 'I am going to go as far away from here as possible. I want to start a new life.'

'Does that mean you are going to put bushranging behind you?'

'I never did enjoy it all that much. It's only because of Charlie and Josh that I've stayed around this long. But then again, if I hadn't I would never have met you.' He turned his head slightly so that his lips brushed against her forehead. 'Will you stay with me, Ginny? Wherever I go.'

'You know I will,' she responded, snuggling more comfortably into his arms.

'Good,' he smiled, and was soon fast asleep.

Thus the weeks passed, settling into a dreary, cold winter. Yet their physical discomfort was of minor consideration. Ginny was happier than she had ever been in her entire life and knew Dan felt the same. So complete was their absorption in each other that at times they appeared almost to forget that Charlie and Josh existed. Together they made plans, some sensible, some ludicrous, of what they would do when they had gathered all the gold they wanted.

Late one August afternoon, Ginny ventured along the track which led to their latrine. Instead of returning immediately to the hut she wandered down to the creek. Close to dusk the wallabies would come down to drink. The strange little animals with their long tails, short front legs, upright ears and limpid dark eyes fascinated Ginny. She could sit and watch them for hours and two nights earlier had been delighted to discover one carried a baby joey in its pouch.

Selecting a secluded rock from where she could see but not be seen, Ginny sat down to wait. As usual she was not disappointed and she watched the timid creatures until the last of the sunset's colour was fading from the sky. Then she rose and hurried back along the creek bank to the clearing, not wanting to be away from the hut after dark.

When she reached the path which led from the stream, an impression something was not quite right slowed her pace. With a faint frown she studied their little home. There were saddled horses hitched to a tree – unfamiliar horses. Her heart began to beat a little faster in fear. Although the men claimed to have many friends in the town, no one ever ventured up into the hills to their remote hideout. Not even the police with their native trackers had ever been able to find them. Or had they?

Moving cautiously and quietly, Ginny made her way across the clearing to the door. There she could hear Dan's voice; perfectly controlled; perfectly normal. With a sigh of relief she pushed open the door and stepped into the hut.

Every drop of colour drained from her face.

The five who were seated at the table looked up at her and a sardonic smile curved the thin, cruel mouth of one.

'Hello, Ginny,' said Logan.

Chapter Eight

Dan glanced from Ginny's colourless face to the dark, enigmatic countenance of the stranger who had arrived with his sister half an hour earlier. There was something here which he decided he did not like one little bit. 'Do you know each other?' he demanded.

'You could say that,' Logan agreed.

Ginny turned a shocked face towards Dan. Her question came as a hoarse whisper. 'What are they doing here?'

That particular question was still worrying Dan. It bothered him that anyone, even a couple supposedly on the run from the law, could have found the hut. 'They want to stay here awhile.'

'No!' Ginny's denial was so vehement Dan's frown deepened.

'What is the matter, Ginny? Do you think they will betray us to the police?'

Ginny shook her head. Unwilling to look directly at either Logan or Tessa and, disturbed by Dan's frowning appraisal, she gazed instead at a spot on the floor. 'No, they won't turn you in to the police,' she admitted.

'No – we won't,' agreed Logan, with unmistakable emphasis on the pronoun, 'but what about you, Ginny? Do you still dispose of your lovers so mercilessly?'

It was impossible not to raise her head, to be trapped in sexual awareness by those glittering black eyes; inevitable that there should be a moist tingling within her love place.

'Were you two lovers?' Dan's question held a jealous belligerence.

Logan was watching her; holding her with that mesmeric gaze. 'We are more than lovers, aren't we, Ginny?'

Ginny's limbs were trembling so much she could barely stand and when Logan rose and came towards her there was no way she could have moved even if she had wanted to. And she did not want to move for already her body was remembering – responding. It did not require the force of his fingers in her hair, nor the pressure of his hand on her buttocks to mould her in desire against the hard length of his maleness.

As he bent his head downwards flames of retribution and desire flickered in the onyx depths of his eyes. Then his mouth was on hers; hard, possessive. Passion flared. The others in the room ceased to exist. There was only Logan – holding her – kissing her – claiming her body for his own. And it seemed to Ginny they had never been apart.

Josh glanced uneasily from the embracing couple to Dan's thunderous face. 'I reckon it might be a good time to go and visit Molly, eh Charlie.'

'Yeah.'

Ginny neither heard them nor knew when they left the hut. Only when Logan released her did a semblance of reality return. She became aware of Dan's anger and the way Tessa's hand rested on his thigh. Momentarily she shut her eyes, knowing he was awaiting her next move. Dan and Logan. Two men, both capable of arousing her to violent sexual desires, yet so vastly different in every other way. How could she explain Logan to Dan when she was unable herself to understand his power? How could she make Dan understand she wanted to go to him but was incapable of moving, even though Logan was no longer holding her?

In the end the choice was not hers to make. Dan rose abruptly and grabbed Tessa's hand. 'Come on. We'll leave them to their tender reunion. I'm sure we can keep each other company for the night.'

'Dan?' It was a bewildered plea, which faded into silence at the bitter look Dan flashed at Ginny before almost dragging Tessa out of the hut.

'Why did you come here, Logan?' she whispered in anguish. 'I was happy with Dan.'

'But you do not belong to him, Ginny. You are mine, you always have been; from the beginning until the end of time. Did you really think, when you forced us to leave Everleigh, that you were free of me?'

Ginny lifted her shoulders in a hopeless admission. 'I thought I saw Tessa in Wattle Creek.'

'I was close to you then, but you were kidnapped. Your bushranger has chosen his hideout well. It has taken me all this time to find you.'

'How did you find us? No one ever comes here.'

Logan smiled; the thin, cruel, enigmatic smile she had come to know so well. 'Do you doubt my powers, Ginny?'

His fingers were combing through her hair, twisting the strands to hold her head motionless. The dark, piercing eyes stared down into hers. 'You know you cannot wait for our bodies to meld. You want me to take you, don't you, Ginny?'

A violent shudder of awareness coursed through Ginny's body. 'Damn you to hell, Logan – ' she husked, 'you know that I do.'

Dan scrambled up the ill-formed path to the cave, giving little thought to the woman who clambered in his wake. He was angry – very angry, and there was an uncomfortable sensation in his gut which was disturbingly akin to jealousy. And that made him even angrier. No woman had a right to make a man feel that way. What did Ginny have to make her more important than any other woman? When all was said and done sex was sex and the black-haired Tessa certainly gave the impression she knew a thing or two.

Immediately they were within the cave he pulled her into his arms and kissed her hard, one hand squeezing over her breast. One of Tessa's hands slid between their bodies to curve under his crutch, test the weight of his balls and measure the thickness of his shaft. So suddenly that her actions took him by surprise, she knelt before him, released his trouser fastenings and took his hardened rod into her hands and then her mouth.

Dan sucked in his breath at the wonderful sensations created by her lips pressing around his shaft. His one disappointment in Ginny was her unwillingness to suck him. The few times he persuaded her to please him in that manner, he sensed it was with a degree of reluctance. But there was nothing reluctant about Tessa's hungry mouth.

To his amazement she was able to take him in deep, sliding her lips up and down and licking with her tongue while her hands caressed his balls and stroked around to the tightness of his anus. The woman was a marvel. Lord but it was good – too good! He tried to pull out but she held him there. He shot into her mouth and she greedily gulped down the warm sperm juices, drawing out every last drop. Gazing up at him with satisfaction in her dark eyes, she ran her tongue around her lips to take up the globules which had dribbled out of her mouth.

It was an action designed to incite lust. Dan almost tore her clothes in his impatience to strip her naked. He wanted to suck her juices as thoroughly as she had sucked his then drive his shaft deep into her body.

Tessa's breasts were big and heavy, crowned with large brown nipples. The size of those breasts fascinated Dan and he knew that before the night was over he would squeeze them around his shaft and thrust between them until his semen spurted all over her throat. But that particular pleasure was for later. His fingers parted the jungle of black hairs between her thighs to locate her wet slit. Using both hands, he spread her sex lips wide and used the hard tip of his tongue to find her rigid nodule.

He teased her love bud and licked along her slit until she was almost at the point of an orgasm. Then he rested, rubbing her slippery cleft to spread her love juices around to the puckered entrance to her rear passage. His lubricated finger slid easily into her anus, her cry of delight proving him correct in thinking she would like such an intimacy. Tessa was not a silent lover, her cries and gasps arousing him even more. Once again he began to lick her slit and tease her love bud with his tongue. While he sucked on the flood of her juices, his finger twisted and frigged her rear passage sending her into a screaming, lustful frenzy.

When he heaved his body on top of hers Dan forgot, accustomed as he had become to Ginny, to enter her carefully. At Tessa's gasp of pain he paused to look down at her. 'Did I hurt you?'

'God, yes,' she gasped, 'but it felt so good. Don't stop. I want it all.'

Dan withdrew before pushing in more slowly, easing his entire shaft into the very depths of her womanhood. Tessa writhed and moaned beneath him, begging him to move faster – harder.

'Yes, yes. Fill me, hurt me. Slam it deep inside.' She had bent her legs, lifting her feet from the floor and hooking her arms under her knees to open herself as wide as possible. Dan thrust into her, his shaft sliding easily along her slippery canal, the head banging hard against her womb. Over and over he thrust, knew when she had an orgasm and continued to slam into her so that she experienced another before he came.

* * *

Ginny's cheeks were wet with tears; tears precipitated by the exquisite agony of being united to Logan. The orgasmic inferno which consumed her body spun her into space and carried her along to that strange nether-world where she existed only in completeness with him. His lips were hard and possessive upon hers, his hands beneath her buttocks lifting her against the thrust of his hips while the weight of his body pinned her to the mattress.

Ginny had not expected Logan would forgive her for sending him away. Nor did he. He had skilfully pun-ished her until she was driven almost to the edge of endurance, her body aflame with pain and savage long-ing. It was as it had always been between them. Logan drove her into a sexual frenzy and sent her into a vortex of torment and passion, from which relief came only when the hard shaft of his manhood thrust into the innermost sanctum of her womanhood. That was when her tears spilled over.

Suddenly Logan moved, rolling onto his back and taking her with him so she lay on top. Strong hands grasped her hips, hard fingers bruising her flesh as he manipulated her love-wet sheath around his rigid shaft. Her initial orgasm had barely ceased, the onset of the second almost too much to bear. Ginny entwined her fingers in the crisp blackness of his hair and cried his name, the sound wrenched from her when he gave a final thrust, so violent that her entire body jerked upwards.

'Oh God, Logan!' she sobbed. She collapsed upon him, moving her hands and clinging to him so fiercely her fingernails were digging into the hard flesh of his shoulders. The increased pressure of his grip was hurting her hips as he held her down with her swollen sex lips pressed against his groin while he used his thighs and hips to push his shaft even deeper.

When finally he was satisfied, his hands moved to grip her hair. Twisting the strands until it hurt, he lifted her head to stare with harsh intensity into her eyes which burned with lust. 'This is how it is always going to be Ginny; our bodies as one, driven to ecstasy by pain and pleasure. Nothing has changed – nor will it ever change. You could have sex with 100 other men but the moment I looked at you, you would know that your body can only ever belong to me.'

He rolled them over again, pressing her back against the mattress, rotating and thrusting inside her. 'Isn't that true, Ginny?'

Ginny shook her head – would not answer. Her mind reasoned that if she refused to admit it, then it would not be so. Her body told her otherwise and before the night was out she had satisfied Logan with an admission wrenched from her during a turbulent storm of sexual passion.

Much later Logan lay asleep with the weight of his arm across her breasts pinning her to his side. Sleep eluded Ginny and for the first time in several hours she thought of Dan – with Tessa. A sickened sensation assailed the pit of her stomach. She wondered what was going to happen in the morning. Surely Dan would send Logan and Tessa away for he would not want anyone to learn of their gold find. Perhaps Dan would want to send her away as well. The expression on his face when he stormed out of the hut suggested their carefree plans for the future were all to be forgotten. But even if Dan did still want her, she knew that Logan would never let her go. A shiver of something near to despair ran through her body and fresh tears spilled down her cheeks. She had known Dan – loved Dan, yet she had allowed Logan to take possession of her again.

Ginny was alone in the hut when Dan walked in the next morning. For a long moment they stared at each other. 'I trust you had an enjoyable night,' Dan said eventually. 'I know I did.'

Ginny bit her lip and fought down the flare of jealousy. 'Please, Dan, try to understand.'

'Understand what? This man turns up laying claim to you and you fall into his arms. Who is he, Ginny? Your husband?'

'No!'

'Well it makes no difference, you made your choice.'

'Doesn't everything we had between us mean anything?'

'Obviously not. It was fun while it lasted but Tessa pleases me very well; and in a way you never would,' he added with malicious intent. 'Go with your Logan, Ginny. I won't miss you.'

Thus Dan unknowingly answered every one of Ginny's nocturnal self-questions. Her heart beat heavily within her breast. If that was how he felt then she would go – but not with Logan.

Wanting to be gone before Logan returned from his ablutions in the creek, Ginny hastily bundled a few things together and hurried across to the bough shed which served as a stable. To her relief she found Charlie there, and it was hardly a surprise that he should be eager to saddle a horse for her when she told him she was leaving.

Ginny was mounted and beginning to ride across the clearing when Logan came back up the path through the bush. When he saw her he called her name and sprinted the remaining distance to grasp her horse's bridle. Flames of anger burned in the black depths of his eyes and Ginny knew a moment of fear. His voice was deceptively soft, hypnotically seductive, his dark gaze holding her with mesmeric intensity.

'You're not leaving are you, Ginny?'

'Yes she is,' declared Charlie.

Logan ignored him, concentrating all his attention on Ginny. His strange power was reaching out to her, ensnaring her. Charlie saw her hesitation and decided to take matters into his own hands. He wanted to be rid of all three of them, but Ginny most of all. The butt of his pistol hit the back of Logan's skull before either man or woman realised his intention.

As Logan's senseless body sprawled in the dirt an agonised cry tore itself from somewhere deep within Ginny's being. She would have dismounted, except Charlie now held the business end of the pistol pointed at her. There was no attempt to hide his hatred. 'You said you were going, so go. And if you know what's good for you, don't ever come back.'

Ginny cast a last stricken look at Logan's motionless body and urged her horse forward. With her tears wet upon her cheeks, she rode down from the hills and through the scented eucalyptus in the direction of Wattle Creek. Tormenting thoughts and feelings she strove to put aside. Surely life would be simpler with the Johnny Salters and Drew Smiths of the world. Men to whom sex was merely a pleasurable pastime with no devastating involvement of emotions.

There was someone else who rode through the bush that August morning giving more attention to inner thoughts than the untamed surroundings. Sergeant Malcolm Ferguson, as he frequently did of late, was wondering if he would ever receive a promotion or be transferred somewhere more civilised than Wattle Creek. He had been in charge of maintaining law and order ever since the police station was first established in the boom town and he was becoming heartily sick of drunks and horse thieves, not to mention the numerous other petty crimes with which he dealt almost daily.

On this particular morning he was feeling rather more disgruntled than usual after having his latest application for transfer rejected. If only he could capture Dan Berrigan, his superiors might look upon him with more favour. That he had not yet succeeded in taking the bushranger captive was not from want of trying. Although Berrigan had been quiet of late and the stage coaches passed through unmolested, Ferguson remained convinced the man was somewhere in the district. And he was damned certain his hideout was up in the rugged, blue misted hills which loomed ahead of them.

Unfortunately Ferguson's training in the constabulary of his native Scotland had not equipped him with the skills necessary for tracking a criminal through the Australian bush. And for some reason, which he had never been fully able to discover, his assigned trackers were reluctant to venture beyond the stream which cut across the base of those formidable hills.

Dan Berrigan had become very much a thorn in the sergeant's side. The initial annoyance because the man had escaped before he could be arrested on the rape charge had developed into something close to a personal vendetta. Sergeant Ferguson was not very well liked in the town and it was humiliating to know the outlaw held more of the miners' sympathies.

When he saw the woman riding towards him, almost at the instant she became aware of his approach, it was difficult to say which of them was the more surprised. Ferguson deduced her identity immediately, for there were many rumours about the mystery woman snatched from Townsend's coach.

Ginny's heart lurched with fear when she recognised the police uniforms and the fear was not for herself. She knew with certainty she would be closely interrogated; knew every effort would be made to force her to divulge the location of Dan's hideout. But no matter how jealous and hurt she might be feeling, betray him was something she silently vowed she would never do.

They reined in facing one another, Ginny's expression a mixture of defiance and wariness. The sergeant had heard many stories of this woman's beauty. He now saw that not a single one had been exaggerated. She was indeed a woman of rare loveliness; a woman a man need only look upon once to want to lay her on her back and savour the pleasures of her sex. He wondered if the three bushrangers had shared her body. Did they take it in turns to sleep with her or did all three have her at once?

That last ribald thought jerked so erotically from his mind to his hardening shaft that he debated sending his trackers ahead. He wanted to take this woman there and then. However there was the matter of Dan Berrigan's apprehension. First he would persuade her to take them to the hideout, then he would have his leisurely way with her.

Although hardly surprised she should be uncooperative, Ferguson experienced an increasing annoyance. He did not for a moment believe her assertion she neither knew from where she had come nor would be able to find her way back.

'Very well, ma'am. You either cannot, or will not, guide us to Berrigan, but you have already assisted us more than you realise. Your horse will have left very clear tracks. We will simply follow those tracks until we find our man. And you, ma'am, will come with us.'

Tessa, who had been asleep when Dan left the hut, was lying awake, leisurely pleasuring herself, when he returned to the cave following his confrontation with Ginny. With deliberate motions she removed her finger from her secret place, popped it in her mouth then very slowly drew it out again with her dark-eyed gaze fastened on Dan's face. She spread her legs wider, revealing more of her sex to emphasise the invitation in her eyes.

This time he took her impatiently, using her body as an outlet for his inner turmoil. It had been easy to say those things to Ginny – harder to convince himself he meant every word. While he worked his rod in and out of Tessa's eager, wet canal, he was not thinking of the woman who gasped and bucked beneath him. His thoughts were with Ginny. Unsettling thoughts of how perfect she had been for him, he forced aside. To refuel his anger with her he made himself dwell on the fact she had gone eagerly into Logan's arms.

Physical release brought no lessening of his mental anguish. For a time he remained lying heavily on top of the woman he had used. When he pushed himself up on his hands he gazed in derision at her lust sated features; the glazed eyes, slack mouth and huge breasts which rose and fell with the heaviness of her breathing.

With an oath of self-contempt he pulled free and began to dress. A woman was just a woman when all was said and done. All a man needed was a wet, accommodating sheath to take his shaft. Why the hell should it matter whether golden-brown hair and seductive brown eyes went with it or not?

Just the same, as he fastened his belt, he found himself wondering what Ginny was doing – and the man, Logan. Were they already preparing to leave together, or were they waiting for Tessa? The temptation to go back down to the hut and ask Ginny to stay was almost too great to ignore. But Dan Berrigan possessed a fierce pride as well as an unforgiving temper, and he was damned if he was going to allow a woman to make a fool out of him again. Not after Jenny Townsend.

Oh, no, he had not forgotten that malicious, lying little bitch. Even if her parents had bundled her away from Wattle Creek, his determination to gain his revenge had not been discarded. It had merely been set aside until such time as their paths crossed again. And that time would come. Of that Dan was certain.

He glanced down at Tessa who remained on her back with her legs spread, one hand pressed against her swollen vulva and the other fondling a breast. Heavens above, wasn't the woman satisfied yet? Well Dan was certainly in no mood to give her any more.

He spoke to her in tones of contemptuous harshness. 'You can get yourself dressed. I agreed that you could stay last night but today I want you gone. And tell your brother to take the other whoring bitch with him.'

With that, he stalked out of the cave and turned to climb higher into the hills. His intention was to go for a good stiff hike. By the time he returned he hoped Charlie and Josh would be the only ones at the hut. From now on there would be just the three of them; the way it had been before that fateful day they held up Townsend's coach.

Ginny was becoming frantic, although she was careful to display no outward sign of her inner turmoil. The sergeant had attached a leading rein to her horse, ensuring she could not escape. Now, slowly but surely, they were retracing her tracks back towards the hideout. She must do something – soon – for the thought of Dan being taken captive was far too horrible to be borne.

The two aboriginal trackers rode a short distance ahead, bending over their horses' necks to study the ground. Every now and then they would stop and dismount for a closer inspection. Each time they did, hope flared in Ginny's heart. Each time they remounted to continue in the right direction, that hope shrivelled to nothing.

When they reached the creek, they glanced uneasily from the water which gurgled around the exposed rocks of the crossing to the dense bush on the opposite bank. Their superstitious fear was stamped all over their features when the sergeant and Ginny drew alongside them.

'Well, what are you waiting for?' demanded Ferguson. 'Get across and find the tracks on the other side.'

'That debil-debil country.'

'Heathen rot!' snorted the sergeant.

The two shook their heads. Not even the distinct probability of receiving a flogging for disobeying orders would make them step foot on the other side of that creek. 'Him bad fella country.'

Ferguson's patience was wearing thin. 'Damned savages,' he muttered so that only Ginny could hear. His hand touched the revolver at his belt. He was seriously contemplating using it to force the men to continue.

133

Carefully watching all three and making a rapid and accurate assessment of the situation, Ginny spoke – keeping just the right degree of petulant reluctance in her voice.

'It won't be necessary to use force, sergeant.'

'What do you mean?' Ferguson studied her with narrowed eyes.

Ginny gave a deep sigh. 'I see that there is no hope for Dan Berrigan. You are determined to capture him and while we have been riding I have had time to think. There is no need to threaten your men. I will show you the way across the stream.'

It was just a mite too glib. Ferguson was not certain whether to trust her or not, but there were ways of bringing a woman to heel. Ordering the trackers to remain where they were, he led Ginny's horse across the creek then removed the leading rein with a curt warning. 'Just don't try any tricks.'

Which was exactly what Ginny did intend to try. She veered right, away from the direction of the camp. Knowing how easy it was to become lost in the bush, she brought all the knowledge Dan had imparted into practice. She took careful note of the things which would help her find her way back again; the bird's nest in a tree; the dead sapling which lay across the forked branch of another.

For close on half an hour they rode, Ginny saying nothing and watching the country, Ferguson saying nothing and watching Ginny. He was finding it exceedingly difficult to concentrate on the matter in hand – namely the capture of Dan Berrigan.

It was much, much easier to fantasise about the type of sexual activities this beauty had indulged in with the bushrangers. He was convinced they would have been many and varied for the woman exuded a heady sexual scent which reached out to a man to make his rod rise regally in response. And Ferguson's rod was responding with increasing stiffness with each minute that ticked by.

Quite suddenly Ginny drew her mount to a stop. Ferguson glanced at her with suspicion. 'Why have you stopped?'

For answer Ginny pressed her hand to her forehead with a deep sigh. 'I feel a little faint, sergeant. Could we please rest in the shade awhile?'

'Of course,' agreed Ferguson, his eyes gleaming with a lecherous eagerness which almost made Ginny laugh in scornful triumph. What fools men were! Maintaining her act, she allowed him to assist her to dismount, swaying against him so that her breasts were pressed against his chest and her hand against the bulge of his rampant manhood.

The sergeant settled her in the shade of a tree and returned to his horse to fetch a blanket. He was no longer contemptuous of the superstitions of the trackers. It was going to be to his advantage that they had stayed behind. He could wait no longer to discover just how good this woman was at pleasing a man. After all these months what were another hour or two before he took Dan Berrigan captive. By then he was certain he would have this beautiful creature in such a state of sexual gratification she would be more than willing to give her assistance.

He spread the blanket on the ground and seated himself beside Ginny. 'Perhaps, while you are resting, you could tell me about the bushrangers,' he suggested.

'Oh, no!' declared Ginny. 'I feel too faint and it disturbs me so to recall such things. They are brutal men.'

'Do not distress yourself,' soothed Ferguson, even though he was bursting with voyeuristic curiosity. 'You, ah – did not enjoy being with the men?'

'Not with those men, sergeant,' responded Ginny with precisely placed emphasis.

'Of course not. A woman as beautiful as you would appreciate a man with more finesse than rough outlaws.' His hand reached out to stroke the thrust of her breast

135

and he was rewarded with the shuddering sigh of delight which left her lips.

'Your touch is so gentle, sergeant. I believe you know how to pleasure a woman instead of merely using her body for your own needs.'

'I do pride myself in it being so,' responded the sergeant with a degree of smugness. 'I promise I will give you all the pleasure your body desires.'

He was rapidly unbuttoning her blouse to expose her breasts to his eager hands. They were twin mounds of unparalleled beauty, the finest breasts he had fondled in many a year. He was impatient to strip her naked – to gaze upon the most intimate place of her womanhood.

But there was too much at stake, so he caressed her gently, teasing her nipples into hardness before easing her back on the blanket. His mouth covered hers in a kiss which was intended to be seductive. Ginny was too clever to let him know it affected her not at all.

She allowed his hand to move down over her skirt and press between her thighs. She even allowed him to fumble beneath her skirts to find the opening of her pantaloons. Then when his hand reached her mound and began to search for her slit, she stayed him with her own. 'Wait,' she said.

Ferguson's eyes narrowed. 'You're not going to start playing the tease, are you?'

'Oh, no,' Ginny assured. 'I want to keep going. It's just that – you see – I have a need to pass water before we go any further.'

'Oh.' Ferguson removed his hand from beneath her garments and sat up. 'Well don't be long. I'll be waiting to undress you when you come back.' He smiled at her in what he imagined was an irresistibly seductive manner. 'When I make love to you I want all your body naked against mine.'

He stood up and began stripping off his jacket, then his shirt. Ginny wandered a short distance away to relieve herself – for she truly had that need – and as soon as she saw that her would-be lover had shed his trousers and was naked, she ran.

Almost before Ferguson realised her intention she was astride her horse, urging it back in the direction they had come.

With a shout he started after her until he recalled his state of undress. Swearing savagely he dashed back to the blanket and began to hastily re-don the recently discarded garments.

Two hours of tramping over rugged, difficult terrain had done little to improve Dan's disposition. Having found it impossible not to keep thinking of all he believed he and Ginny meant to each other, he decided the only solution was to become blind, rotten drunk; so drunk that he would be incapable of coherent thought for a long, long time.

Such was his intention when he turned back to the hideout, for he fully expected the unwelcome guests to have left by then. But he discovered, as he began his descent, that it was not so. Down near the creek, he could see Tessa and Josh. Though he was still some distance away, their actions were clearly visible.

Dan observed them with unfeigned indifference. Albeit he had spent the previous night enjoying wild and torrid sex with the black-haired temptress, it bothered him not to discover her engaged in the same activities with his mate. She knelt before Josh sucking hard on his rod until he, as Dan had the night before, spurted into his mouth.

When she had licked up the last drop, she divested herself of her skirt and blouse to reveal that she wore nothing underneath. In naked abandon she settled herself on a low, smooth rock and spread her legs wide to enable Josh to suck her to her own orgasm.

Dan turned his eyes away from the couple, his gaze roving instead across the huts and the clearing in which they stood. Both horses were still outside the hut, which

137

meant that Logan had not yet left either. Indecision kept him from continuing on. He had not expected to have to face Ginny again. Should he go down and ask her to stay, or should he simply go back up the hill and wait until they all left.

His gaze went back to the couple on the creek bank. Tessa now knelt on all fours while Josh pumped into her from behind. From their positions and the fact that Tessa slipped a hand under her body as though she was stimulating herself, he gathered Josh was stroking in her rear passage. The woman's lusty cries rose up to him to bring a derisive twist to his lips. Lord, but she was an insatiable slut. Idly curious, he wondered if she had been with Charlie as well.

On that thought he made up his mind. He would send brother and sister on their way and ask Ginny to stay. If she showed any reluctance, he might even humble himself sufficiently to beg.

Certainly he did not expect the sight which greeted him on entering the hut. The man, Logan, sat at the table with his head in his hands, while Charlie sat opposite with the lethal end of his revolver pointed at the man.

'What's going on?' Dan demanded.

Charlie's lips quirked in a grin which twisted into something closer to a sneer. 'Reckon he's got a bit of a sore head, and I'm just keeping an eye on him until that whoring sister of his gets back. Then I'll send them both on their way.'

'Where's Ginny?'

Before Charlie could respond to that sharp query, Logan raised his aching head to pierce Dan with his black gaze. 'Gone. It would seem she does not want you either.'

'What do you mean – either?'

'She was leaving,' Charlie explained with smug satisfaction, 'and he tried to stop her. I could see she was wavering, so I put him out of action and let her go.'

'You let her go alone?'

138

'Sure did,' responded Charlie, not at all disturbed by the dangerous glint in Dan's eyes.

'God almighty! Anything could happen to her. I'm going after her to bring her back.'

Heedless of Charlie's oathful protestations that she was well able to take care of herself and to let her go, Dan sprinted the short distance to the stables and wasted no time in saddling his horse. His heart beat with painful anxiety against his ribs. For better or worse he wanted Ginny back. He hoped she had not gone too far; prayed she had not become lost.

Ginny's triumph lasted only until she crossed back over the creek, where she found her way barred by the trackers. Even if their fear of evil spirits was strong enough for them to refuse to cross the creek, they knew better than to allow the woman to escape. One held the bridle of her horse and the other pointed his rifle at her heart. Before long she discovered just how close behind her Ferguson had been.

Quailing before the vindictive anger of his expression Ginny knew, with a sinking heart, there was nothing she could do now to save Dan. The sergeant drew his horse abreast of hers, leaning forward until their faces were only inches apart. Retribution flared in the highland blue of his eyes.

'No woman makes a fool of me,' he rasped. 'I want you and I intend to have you.' He gave a short, cruel laugh, his glance flicking momentarily towards the trackers. 'I've a mind to take you right now while they're watching. Then I'll let them have their turn with you. How would you like that, my beauty? Have you ever done it with a black man before?'

He reached a hand to the front of her blouse with the intention of ripping it open to expose her body to the interested gaze of the trackers. Then, suddenly, one of the men held up a hand. 'One fella horse come.'

Ferguson's hand dropped to his rifle. He accepted the

man's statement without question, even though he could detect neither sight nor sound of an approaching rider. There was no doubt in his mind it was Berrigan, coming after his woman. A quiet command sent the trackers into hiding, then he brought his attention back to Ginny. The hand which had fondled her breast now pointed the rifle at the same part of her anatomy.

'You will wait here and when he comes in sight you will ride slowly towards him. If you do or say anything to warn him you will both be dead.'

Ferguson walked his horse out of sight of the crossing to leave Ginny alone, quaking with fear and anguish. Dan was riding into a trap and there was nothing she could do to save him, for she did not doubt the sergeant's threat to kill them both.

When Dan saw Ginny waiting on the opposite side of the creek he was filled with elation. Calling her name he cantered his horse across, reining in when he was almost upon her. A broad smile spread across his face. 'You changed your mind. You were coming back.'

Only then did he become aware of the strange tension of her expression. It was too late. Ferguson and the trackers rode out of concealment with their guns levelled at him.

Ginny did not even have a chance to say she was sorry.

Chapter Nine

The iron-barred cell door clanged shut with a finality which sent a shudder of despair through Ginny and locked a steel band of bitterness around Dan's heart.

He had not spoken a word to her – not even when he realised he was trapped. There had been no need. He had merely looked at her with his lips twisted in bitter cynicism, the expression in his eyes telling her plainly what he thought.

Now, as Ferguson grasped her arm to lead her away from the cells, she chanced a quick glance at Dan's face. She wanted to run to him, beg his forgiveness. For a moment their gazes locked, Ginny's eyes mutely pleading for understanding, Dan's condemning without question.

Pain stabbed through Ginny's heart. No matter that she been riding away from Dan. It was one thing to leave him a free man, quite another to turn her back on him when he was imprisoned. Regardless of what he now thought of her, she must do all she could to secure his release.

The sergeant desired her. Ginny had used her sex before to get what she wanted and she would do so again. The glimpse she had of Ferguson's rampant manhood before she leapt on her horse showed it to be a tool of admirable dimensions. It would be no hardship to give him what he wanted – for a price.

Once she secured his promise, Dan would be freed and she would go far away from Wattle Creek and start her life anew. These months with Dan would be tucked into the recesses of her memory as a pleasant interlude which was never meant to last. And Logan. She would forget, if possible, that Logan had ever held her in sexual thrall. This time she would escape him. On that she was determined.

'Come, Mrs Leigh.' Ferguson's voice disrupted her thoughts. 'We have a little unfinished business to attend to. I am eager to collect on your promise to show me more of your womanly charms.'

'Whoring bitch!' The savage snarl from the prisoner curled a smirk of satisfaction across Ferguson's mouth.

'It would appear, my dear, that your outlaw lover does not like the idea of you giving yourself to other, worthier, men. Shall we do it here, in front of him, and make him squirm?'

That suggestion appealed immensely to Ferguson. How amusing it would be to screw the bushranger's woman right under his nose. The sergeant knew men well enough to know that Berrigan's tool would soon be rampant. And there would not be a damn thing he could do about it. The potential to inflict such torment was enticing in the extreme.

The prospect so horrified Ginny she was quick to demur. 'But, sergeant, you said you wanted me to explain in detail exactly what happened to me after I was kidnapped. I will be able to do that so much better in the comfort of a hotel room.'

While her fingers toyed with the buttons of her blouse, the pink tip of her tongue circled slowly around her lips. Her attitude was one of deliberate provocation. Neither man realised how sickly her stomach churned with the

142

knowledge her actions would only serve to enforce Dan's belief in her treachery.

The hotel to which Ferguson escorted her was a dingy establishment in a back street of the town. The publican was an overweight, unkempt individual with more of the appearance of a man who should be behind bars than the one recently imprisoned. A knowing leer, as he handed a key to the sergeant, displayed decaying, yellow teeth and sent a blast of fetid breath drifting across their faces.

Feeling very much like a common prostitute, Ginny realised the man and the sergeant held a mutually satisfactory agreement. The publican would remain mute on the sergeant's illicit sexual activities and in return his own more questionable undertakings would be ignored.

To Ginny's surprise, for she was fully prepared for him to demand immediate gratification, Ferguson halted at the door of the room. 'Unfortunately I cannot neglect my duties for the length of time I need to "interrogate" you thoroughly, Mrs Leigh. This evening will be far more convenient. I suggest you rest. You may find my method of interrogation physically tiring. And if you have any notion you will be able to escape, then I assure you that your room will be guarded.'

'I have no intention of attempting to escape, sergeant. You may find, at the end of the night, that it is yourself who is physically exhausted. My sexual needs can be quite demanding.'

'Would that be a promise, Mrs Leigh?'

'On one condition.'

'Condition? Ha! What makes you imagine you are in any position to dictate conditions?'

'You want sex with me, sergeant – which you will have no matter what I say. Either I lay unresponsive on my back and let you do what you will, or I use my considerable talents to give you a night far beyond your wildest sexual dreams.'

'Hmm. Exactly what is your condition for such a night?'

'That you allow Dan Berrigan to go free.'

'Ha! I knew he was not keeping you against your will. Does he mean so much to you?'

'Yes, he does.'

Ferguson pursed his lips in thought. His speculative gaze travelled from Ginny's face, over the luscious curves of her body to the place, hidden beneath her skirt, which promised so much pleasure. He could take this tantalising woman any time he wanted. She was in his power. Yet the thought of having her responsive and willing to engage in whatever sexual activities he desired set his manhood straining against his trousers in eager anticipation.

Berrigan's capture would almost certainly bring the sergeant promotion, not to mention the £500 reward. An escape would ensure Ferguson spent the rest of his days as a policeman in Wattle Creek. Still, if the woman was so anxious to have her criminal lover set free, it should be easy to persuade her to make her delectable body available for longer than just one night.

'I'll think about it,' he said. 'Until tonight, Mrs Leigh.'

Ginny was waiting for him. During the intervening hours she had bathed and scented her body. Her gold-brown hair cascaded over her shoulders to conceal the rosy nipples which would otherwise have been visible through the semi-transparent material of her robe.

When the key grated in the door lock, she hastily swallowed the last of the wine the publican had brought with her dinner and adjusted the drape of the robe to reveal the shadowy valley between her breasts.

Ferguson wasted no time on preliminaries. He locked the door behind him then dragged Ginny roughly against his body. His hot, lustful mouth pressed upon hers; his hand slid inside her robe to squeeze her breast.

144

'Tell me if he did this to you – and this.' His other hand pressed between her thighs.

'Of course he did,' agreed Ginny. 'He wanted me willing so he would massage my breasts and finger me down there until I was begging him to take me.'

The sergeant's finger rapidly found the desired opening and slipped into its warmth. 'It doesn't take much to make you willing. You're already wet with anticipation. Ah, yes. I do like to frig a woman with a hole that's all afire and slippery. Now tell me, Mrs Leigh,' he continued, working his finger so expertly within Ginny's love canal that she was finding it impossible to concentrate, 'when Berrigan stuck his cock into you did he do it from the front or the back?'

'Well – the first – ah – time – ' she gasped, for the twisting, stroking finger was bringing her ever nearer a climax, ' – we did – it – on his – horse – while we were – ooh – riding – to – the – hideout.'

The erotic action of the finger ceased as Ferguson's mouth gaped open. 'How did you manage that?'

Ginny breathed more evenly. 'Shall I show you how?'

'I insist. Do not forget that this is an official interrogation. I need to know every detail of your time with the outlaws.'

'Very well,' agreed Ginny. 'But in order that you understand perfectly, I believe it would be better if I dressed as I was then.' The robe slid down to the floor, giving Ferguson a tantalising view of her nakedness before she slipped behind the screen.

His perplexity showed on his face when she emerged clad in her undergarments and lace up boots. He had naturally expected her to be robed in a travelling gown.

Ginny gave a provocative smile. 'Poor Mr Townsend was most upset, having managed to undress me to this stage just before the coach was waylaid.'

She handed him a short piece of rope and held out her arms. 'Now you must tie my hands in front of me, for that is how they were. Unfortunately we do not have a horse so we will just have to imagine that chair is one. If you sit on that, sergeant, and release that magnificent shaft of yours from the confines of your trousers, I will show you how it was done.'

Ferguson hastened to obey. The novelty of this sex game was sending a pulsing ache from his balls to the glistening tip of his engorged shaft. He would have been gratified to know Ginny felt an equally pulsing need to have that throbbing shaft embedded deep within the burning passage of her womanhood.

Slipping her bound wrists over the sergeant's head she straddled the chair and eased herself over the hot purple rod of manly muscle. On an exhalation of ecstatic satisfaction, Ferguson grasped her hips to begin working her up and down. 'Was it as good as this?' he gasped.

'Better,' cried Ginny, with deliberate provocation. 'Imagine the horse going faster and the way that made me bounce on his cock.'

'Hell!' gasped Ferguson, increasing the speed with which he manipulated Ginny's movements. 'Faster, eh? Faster.'

The strength in the hands which gripped her hips was incredible. Ginny was no longer in control. Like a rag doll with no bones, her breasts bounced and her head shook as Ferguson thumped her up and down with such speed that it seemed the burning flow of her love juices would never end.

'Good, Mrs Leigh, very good,' he approved when finally he ceased his manipulations and her head slumped in exhaustion upon his shoulder. 'You have really been most helpful. For that you deserve a little rest. Then I want to take you from behind.'

Before Ginny was halfway recovered he was eager for her again. Totally naked she went down on all fours in readiness. He did not, as she expected he would, kneel behind her. With his knees slightly bent he reached down, grasped and spread her thighs to open her folds and lifted her buttocks high in the air.

Ginny was forced to balance herself on her outstretched arms while her legs were hooked around the sergeant's waist. Then the head of his raging rod pressed against her vulva until it found the opening it sought. His thrusting was deep and vigorous. Ginny's head dropped forward between her arms, the flow of her hair sweeping down to the floor. From that angle she was able to look back along the length of her body; was able to watch his heavy balls swinging like pendulums and note, each time he withdrew for another thrust, how the base of his shaft glistened with the creamy excretions of her sex glands. It was difficult to figure which of them was receiving the greater enjoyment. If this was what it took to set Dan free, it was no hard task.

Only, much later, when her partner moved to enter her rear passage did she object. 'Not like that. I've never done it that way.'

'Do you want Berrigan released?'

'Yes.'

'Then I'm sure you'll soon decide to enjoy a man this way.'

To his credit he took his time to work her anal passage, using the plentiful residue of her juices to lubricate it in readiness for his entry. Yet when he did the painfulness of it brought tears to her eyes and a cry of protest to her lips.

'Just think of Berrigan swinging on the end of a rope,' advised Ferguson. But even that image could not erase Ginny's pain. Bravely swallowing her tears, she bit her lip and endured in silence. Had she realised that Ferguson would declare he needed to interrogate her further before he could agree to Berrigan's release, she would not have submitted so docilely.

The grating of the key turning in the lock woke her the next morning. After the sergeant left she had fallen into an exhausted slumber, disturbed by nightmarish dreams of Dan in prison. She was still rubbing sleep from her eyes when the door swung open to admit the publican. In his hands was a tray holding what Ginny presumed was meant to be her breakfast though neither the tray nor its unappealing contents appeared any cleaner than the dirty individual who carried them.

The man's lecherous eyes gleamed at the glimpse of smooth, bare shoulder visible above the blankets. More awake than she appeared to be, Ginny's mind was working with crystal-clear rapidity. Filthy and uncouth, the publican filled her with the greatest revulsion but the bulge in his grubby trousers told her exactly what he had in mind. Stretching languidly so that the blanket slipped away to reveal her naked breasts Ginny smiled invitingly up at him. This time she would make no mistakes.

Ginny's heart beat with nervous fear as she opened the door of her room to peer cautiously into the passageway. There was no one in sight, the only sound the rattle of pans from the kitchen. She closed the door, locked it, then moved as quietly as she was able towards the rear exit.

A snuffling sound brought her to a trembling halt. The bitter smell which assailed her nostrils was one of stale beer and she realised the strange noise came from a drunk who was sleeping off the night's excesses draped across the bar.

Luck remained with her, for when she reached the dusty yard moments later it, too, was deserted – except for the saddled horse hitched to a post. Horse stealing was a crime. So, too, was murder.

Ginny did not bother to ascertain whether or not she had killed the publican when she hit him over the head with the heavy brass candlestick. Quite frankly she didn't care. The man was a lecherous, brutal animal who handled her body with rough insensitivity. Only her determination to escape enabled her to endure the pawing of his calloused, grubby hands. Just when he positioned himself ready to drive his filthy rod into her, she had reached for the candlestick and brought it crashing on to the back of his skull.

He had collapsed heavily on top of her and for a few terrible moments she feared she did not have the strength to push him off. Her fear gave her the strength, the thud of his body hitting the floor seemingly loud enough to raise all the inn's occupants. Taking time only to pull a skirt and blouse over her nakedness, Ginny had grabbed her bag and made her escape.

Even as she rode a circuitous route through the outskirts of the town, she constantly expected to hear a shout as somebody recognised the horse; or else the terrible sounds of the police in pursuit. Not until she was well beyond the outer dwellings did she allow herself to release a little of her tension.

Only then did she begin to wonder just what she was going to do. Other than escaping Ferguson and the inn, she had made no plans. All that was clear in her mind was that she must do something to rescue Dan.

As a woman she had only one weapon. She had used that on Ferguson and failed. Her only option, she realised, was to return to the hut to inform Dan's mates of his capture. Charlie's threat she must simply ignore.

When Dan had not returned the previous evening neither Charlie nor Josh was overly concerned. They naturally assumed he had found Ginny. Charlie, however, was not reticent in expressing his hope Dan would return alone. If anyone had dared suggest his hatred of Ginny stemmed from the fact he wanted her for himself and resented her preference for his more dashing mate, he would have laid that person out with an iron-hard fist to the jaw. For such a suggestion would have been indicative of disloyalty to Dan.

As fate would have it he was alone in the hut when Ginny rode up to it late the next afternoon. By that time both men were experiencing a degree of uneasiness over their mate's prolonged absence.

Assuming, at first, that it would be Dan returning, Charlie was more than mildly surprised to discover the rider was Ginny.

'Where's Dan?' he rasped.

'The police have captured him. I've come for your help.'

'Dan's been taken? How? When?'

'Yesterday, when he came after me.'

A sneer of malignancy twisted Charlie's features. 'So you betrayed him, did you?'

'No!' Ginny, having dismounted, stared up at the red-bearded man in shock. 'You can't believe that.'

'I can believe anything of you,' declared Charlie, grabbing her arm and hustling her across the yard. With unnecessary force he thrust her into the hut and kicked the door shut.

Recovering from her stumbling precipitation across the room, Ginny turned to face him. 'Please, Charlie. I know you don't like me but I did not betray Dan. If I did, do you think I would have come back here?'

'You're a woman, and a conniving one at that. I've no doubt you've got your reasons.'

'Of course I've got my reasons. I came to fetch you both so we can plan how to get Dan freed.'

'You're not fooling anyone, Ginny. If you really cared anything for Dan you would not have spent a night humping about with that stranger. Seems a good screwing is the only thing that matters with you.'

Ginny lifted her shoulders helplessly. She wasn't even going to begin to try to explain. 'I thought Dan was your mate? Aren't you going to do anything to help him?'

'Oh, we'll think of some way to get him out but we won't be needing you around.' He advanced towards her with menacing intent. 'Reckon I might teach you a lesson or two before we do, though. If it's a screwing you want then it's a screwing you're going to get.'

He lunged towards her and Ginny hastily side-stepped to put the table between them. 'Don't you dare,' she warned.

Charlie responded with a menacing laugh as he proceeded to stalk her around the table. 'I told you not to come back. You should have listened to me Ginny. But seeing as you didn't, I'm taking what I always wanted.'

Like a cat with a helpless mouse, he advanced slowly until she was backed against the wall. Again he lunged, ripping her blouse as she twisted free. She managed to reach the door before he caught her the second time, his hands tearing the remnants of her blouse from her body as he flung her down to the floor.

He dived after her, clawing at her breasts. Ginny attempted to crawl free, kicking back with her foot. There was a moment's respite before her skirt was yanked down over her hips causing her to lose her balance and collapse face down on the floor.

'Bastard!' she gasped, bringing her elbow sharply back when Charlie flung himself on top of her. Whatever part of his anatomy she caught, the unexpectedness of the jab was sufficient to enable her to scramble out of reach.

Once on her feet she was more easily able to evade him in their lunging, ducking struggle around the hut. Predator and prey they fought a desperate, determined battle. Eventually Charlie's superior strength triumphed. Ginny was trapped against the table with Charlie's arms imprisoning her on either side and his body pressing hers backwards. Both were panting heavily. They glared at each other in silent, mutual hatred. The man's eyes were aflame with lust and Ginny, her face covered in sweat and contorted with exhaustion, drew on what little reserves of energy she had to let loose a stream of insults. Her fury was exacerbated by the hardness of male muscle now pressing against the flat plane of her abdomen.

'You're an animal,' she hissed. 'Dan will kill you for this.'

'Yeah?' sneered Charlie. 'I don't really think Dan's going to care too much what I do to you seeing how you betrayed him.'

He spun around to push her face down across the table. One big hand held both of hers behind her back.

'I was right about you,' he snarled. 'You're nothing but a common slut who'll come for any man. I'll bet you're as wet and willing as any whore who's panting for a cock.'

Ginny, her cheek flattened against the rough timber of the table, cursed him in language that would have done the foulest mouthed, most blasphemous whore, proud. She might just as well have saved her breath. Charlie merely laughed at her and thrust his free hand between her legs.

Just as Charlie was about to replace his hand with his aching member, Josh entered the hut to be pulled up short by the incredible spectacle of his mate savagely manhandling a screaming, abusive Ginny.

Goggle-eyed, he stared at them both. 'Shit!' he gasped. 'Dan'll be having your hide for this, mate.'

'Hardly,' responded Charlie, tightening his grip on Ginny's arm. 'She betrayed him to the coppers so I reckon we can do just whatever we like with her. You can have your turn afterwards, mate. I guarantee she won't be unwilling for long,' he added at Ginny's vehement protest.

Josh's gaze roved over the perfection of Ginny's body. Jesus! She was like a golden-skinned goddess. The sight of her agile body bent over the rough wooden table immediately inflamed his desire. He had always wondered what it would be like to have her. But the fear of what Dan may do to him if he ever followed his animal instincts had been enough to make him see reason. And now, Josh's loyalty to his friend was once again being put to the test. Dan was in trouble. To use his absence as a reason to sate his own lust would be an insult to his mate's honour. He didn't want to jump to conclusions.

As much as he desired Ginny, he wanted to hear from Dan's own mouth the truth about her betrayal. Josh was determined that the temptation to which Charlie had succumbed would not claim him. At least not until he knew the full story. He averted his eyes from the lustful tableau in front of him.

'I reckon you might be making a mistake, Charlie. I know what you think of her but you're letting your anger get the better of you. Dan won't like it. He'll never forgive you.'

Taken aback by Josh's unexpected championing of the struggling Ginny, Charlie – for a fleeting moment – relaxed his hold. Only a moment, but time enough for her to wrestle free from her ignominious position and place some distance between them. Her voice was shrill, her breathing ragged.

'Josh is right. Dan will never forgive what you have just done to me. I never betrayed him. You just want an excuse to justify your vile behaviour. You're scum and nothing more, Charlie. You'd screw a dingo if it stayed still long enough. You can't possibly imagine I'd ever enjoy having sex with the likes of you.'

Ginny stood panting and dishevelled with tears burning her eyes, wondering how she could have been foolish enough to become embroiled in such an intolerable situation. She wished Dan would somehow appear. Her emotions were in tatters, her thoughts in turmoil. She was thankful Josh had intervened. If she had not been certain he, in reality, regarded her with feelings not unlike those of his more volatile mate, she would have moved to his side for protection.

If rape had been Charlie's earlier motive he now looked as if he was ready to punch her unconscious. The tension in the small, stifling room had reached a barely tolerable pitch. Something had to give. Josh's glance slid to the dusty bottles which stood, almost out of sight, in the corner. 'I reckon we could all do with a drink,' he

153

growled. While Ginny reassembled the remnants of her tattered clothing, Charlie, to her immense relief, and after an acrimonious glare in her direction, grabbed one of the bottles and stormed out of the hut. Josh downed a generous draft of Molly's evil brew before reluctantly passing the bottle to Ginny. She took it gratefully and drank recklessly of its contents.

'You have got to believe me, Josh,' she pleaded, looking him straight in the eye. 'The sergeant had captured me, had me in his power, before he captured Dan.' Her voice deepened with the earnest desire to be believed. 'I never wanted him taken, Josh. I care for him too much to want to see him hurt.'

'Yeah, so I noticed,' sneered Josh. 'That's why you screwed the stranger the other night.'

'You don't understand. And I do not intend to explain.'

'I understand all right. I know what you're like, Ginny. You're no good for Dan and bad luck for us. I've often wished we'd never held up Townsend's bloody coach that day. Things were good before you turned up.' Josh reached out to relieve Ginny of the bottle and took another gulp.

Ginny lapsed into silence. She was tired and fed up. The thought of having to set out on another long journey made her feel even more fatigued. But fighting against her exhaustion was the dramatic effect Molly's brew had on all who drank it – an uncontrollable inflammation of lust. Despite having escaped the evil intentions of Charlie not twenty minutes ago, Ginny began to feel aware of her own arousal – the strongest arousal she had known in a long time.

Her thoughts were in a muddle. How could she now be feeling desirous of Josh when he had never before appealed to her in that way.

Though, if she was to be honest with herself, what she desired was any man hard and willing enough to satisfy what was becoming an increasingly urgent need. She would take her satisfaction and, in doing so, turn the tables on the men. They could have their way with her but they would have to live with the knowledge that they had betrayed their friend and broken his trust. There was no point in denying that what she wanted now was to impale herself in the rigid flesh of the nearest male – whoever he might be. That it was Dan's mate, Josh, mattered not in the least. The drink had taken control.

'I saw the way you looked at me before,' she said suddenly. 'You want me too. Well, if it must be either of you then I rather it was you. I don't believe you're as brutal as Charlie. You do want me, don't you Josh?' she added, staggering to her feet.

Once there, she swayed slightly and took another swig from the bottle to fortify herself. The perspiration from her earlier struggle had left her body covered in a thin film which glistened and accentuated the golden colour of her skin. The full mounds of her breasts strained against the muslin of her ripped blouse and Josh knew that he would be powerless to resist once she touched him. To illustrate her intentions she began to caress herself, rubbing her hand between her dew-soaked legs and laughing, enjoying the power of tantalising the partly inebriated, prostrate Josh with her gyrations. Who is in control now? she thought, as she observed him scrabbling to release the fleshy beast that lived inside the dusty material of his trousers. Who is going to decide when he shall have his pleasure; when he will know the satisfaction of sexual release? Me, she answered to herself, and slowly lowered her body onto the drunken and grateful man. All reason vanquished, all good intentions forgotten, Josh could only grunt his lustful satisfaction as he lunged into her. She had held him spellbound. And once entranced, all attempts at rational thought were useless. He was too far gone to stop now. Dan need never know, he justified himself. He need never know that his best friend had taken the woman he cared about so deeply.

Outside it was getting dark and Charlie lay slumped against a tree cradling the now empty bottle. He'd downed the entire contents and dealt with its side-effects in the time-honoured tradition all men used when female company was not available. But he'd cursed. He'd cursed and swore his hatred for Ginny; hatred fuelled by a loathing for his own lustful weakness. It was her image that was imprinted onto his mind at the moment of his crisis. An image of her pressed beneath him and struggling as he was about to take what was rightly his; his and any other man's who cared to dip his wick. Damn Josh, he mumbled. If only he'd returned two minutes later. Damn him and his stupid sense of honour to his mate. Where were they, anyway? Why hadn't Ginny fled the hut? he wondered. She couldn't possibly be talking his mate round to her way of think-ing, could she? After a couple of feeble attempts to regain a vertical position, Charlie finally hauled himself to his feet and traced a circuitous route back to the hut, his vision somewhat impaired by the evil brew. But the sight which greeted him was not a hallucination or one for which Charlie was prepared. In the middle of the room, on the floor, Ginny and Josh were locked into their desperate coupling, oblivious to Charlie's presence. So that's why Josh had stopped him from taking her, thought Charlie. He wanted to be the first, or have her to himself. Well of all the conniving tricks. Anger, lust and drunkenness formed a lethal combination in his already addled brain and, letting forth a stream of obscenities, Charlie lunged at his rutting mate, grabbed him by the scruff of his shirt and pulled him backwards onto the floor.

'You two-faced bastard, Josh,' said Charlie. 'That was a bloody quick turnaround of events. What hap-pened to "Dan won't like it"?' he continued. 'Well if you're going to have what you want, there's no way I'm going to be left out.'

Josh wasn't quite as far gone as Charlie and when the incensed outlaw took a swipe at him, it wasn't difficult for Josh to parry the blow and push him over onto his back. From this point, the two men rolled around in drunken combat for a while, taking haphazard swipes at each other until Ginny shouted at them to stop. She had scant regard for Josh and nothing short of hatred for Charlie, but she simply couldn't bear the scene becoming any more ugly than it already was. In her inebriated state, she hatched a plan of revenge. She would allow Charlie his moment of filthy pleasure with her. She would let them both take her. One thing was certain. She was determined that they would live to regret their weakness more than she.

Several hours later, Ginny opened her eyes and, with a groan of true agony, pressed a hand to her aching head. Very gingerly, feeling as fragile as if she was made of bone china, she sat up. The room spun and when she struggled to her feet her stomach heaved. Staggering outside the hut, she retched helplessly, feeling only slightly better when her stomach had rid itself of the residual alcohol.

Cloudy and chill though the morning was, she walked down to the creek where she plunged into the icy water. The shock of that immersion had the desired sobering effect. Even if she did not feel entirely well, she was at least capable of coherent thought. Shivering with the cold she hurried back to the hut to dress in her warmest clothes.

The two men lay asleep on the floor; Charlie on his back with loud snores emanating from his open mouth and Josh curled on his side like a baby. They were naked, and the rigid shafts of muscle which had given her no rest during the night were reduced to insignificant little appendages in their relaxed state.

157

Once she was warmly dressed and her shivering had ceased, Ginny left the hut to climb up to the cave. Though it was close on midday, the pale, feeble light of the overcast sun had not yet penetrated its interior and it was with trembling hands she located both candle and matches.

Just as the wick caught light, a scuffling outside the entrance brought a jerk of fear to her heart. For a terrified moment she held her breath until reason told her it was only a lizard or small animal moving through the ground cover of dead leaves.

With the candle held high, Ginny looked around the cave. At sight of the mattress where Dan and she had spent that first wonderful night of loving passion she almost changed her mind. But it was also where he had lain with Tessa and, after all, it was Ginny who had discovered the gold in the first place.

Their cache was secreted in a crevice high in one of the walls, its opening barely visible to the casual observer. For Ginny, who knew its location, it took only a few minutes to clamber onto a box and extract the bags of nuggets. Initially she intended to take only the gold, but at the last moment she gathered up the stolen jewels and money as well.

All the while the fear that Charlie, Josh, or both, would awaken and come after her kept her nerves taut. Only when she had crossed the stream at the base of the mountain and was riding through the valley did she begin to relax.

With the easing of her tension there came an awareness of the burning discomfort between her thighs. Lord, what a night it had been. Charlie and Josh had been insatiable – but so too had she. Heaven alone knew what was in that stuff they drank. Whatever it was so heightened their sexual urges and capabilities that they clawed, explored, thrust and banged at each other for hours on end.

The men did not have it all their own way. Frequently

Ginny was the one who actuated their couplings, driven almost mad by the drink crazed need for coition.

Just thinking about it was sufficient to precipitate a desire to have a man's shaft ease the tingling of her deepest love point. Ginny wriggled, uncomfortable in the saddle. How long, she wondered, was it going to take for the effects of that heathenish brew to work out of her system. Heavens above! If a man – any man – was to come along just now, she would just about tear his trousers off, so great was her need for sex. She knew she would have to find a place to stop so that she could give herself relief, or she would surely go mad.

It was later, when she rested back against a tree with her knees crooked and her fingers pressed into her wet and only partially satisfied sex, that she reasoned she had been a fool to go back to the hut in the first place. Charlie had warned her. Well Charlie, Josh – and Dan – could all go to hell as far as she was concerned. Wattle Creek would soon be far behind her. From now on she would live her life by her rules. The gold in her bag was assurance of that.

Molly Jones and her husband stood behind the bar of their inn making a pretence at cleaning glasses while they darted furtive glances at the dark stranger who sat at one of the tables. He had arrived at the inn two nights ago and apart from asking for accommodation had spoken not one word since. In spite of that aloof attitude, it peeved Mr Jones somewhat that his wife had not yet taken the man to her bed. Mr Jones was certain the stranger's sexual prowess would be quite magnificent to watch.

He said as much to Molly for perhaps the tenth time, suggesting that she should serve their guest some of her special brew.

'Lordy no,' she gasped. 'He's not for the likes of me, Mr Jones. Have you seen them eyes of his. It ain't natural, eyes as black as them. Cor! The way he looks

159

at you. Fair sends a shiver down my spine, it does. I reckon he be the devil himself, Mr Jones. Aye, the devil himself.'

Ginny found it necessary to stop frequently during the course of the day, either to rest until an unpleasant wave of nausea passed, or to alleviate that other sickening need. By late afternoon when she caught her first glimpse through the trees of the little bush inn, she was feeling both tired and dispirited. Heavy, black clouds now blanketed the sky to settle a gloomy darkness over the land. A chill wind set up an eerie, sibilant moaning through the high branches of the densely clustered trees. When she looked up a few errant spots of rain fell on her icy cheeks.

Yet the dismal change in the weather could not be held totally responsible for her mood. A terrible sense of fatalism had taken her in its grip. She told herself she was simply both emotionally and physically drained by all the events of the past few days – and nights. Though the ill feeling remained in her stomach, the residual sexual hunger had finally eased away. A good night's sleep was probably all she needed to restore her to her usual brave spirits. And this drab little slab-walled inn would, she supposed, be as good a place as any in which to rest.

A threatening rumble of thunder found a responsive thudding within her chest. Ginny hastily hitched her horse to the rail, cast an anxious glance to where distant jagged shafts of lightning rent the heavens, and hurried into the inn.

For a moment she paused, adjusting her vision to the dim interior light. The scraping of a chair being pushed back brought her gaze to the inn's only other occupant. Ginny felt not even the faintest flicker of shock. Somehow she had known he would be there.

Dark, powerful, he drew her slowly towards him with

160

the magnetism of his presence. 'I have been waiting for you,' he said.

Iron-hard hands gripped her shoulders, onyx eyes gleamed down into her own and firm lips took hers in savage possession. Time was as nothing. Past, present and future blended into one. With a sob in her throat Ginny wound her arms about his neck and surrendered to the strange forces which bound her to Logan.

'Cor!' whispered Molly Jones, peering from behind the door. 'Do you see that, Mr Jones. Now that be true passion.'

Chapter Ten

*T*hose next days were the worst of Dan's life. To be taken captive was bad enough. To have been betrayed by the woman whom he had so recently acknowledged he loved was far, far worse. Not even when forced to become an outlaw had he experienced an iota of the anguish which now held him in its grip. As soon as he was left on his own, the walls of the tiny cell closed in on him, encasing him in claustrophobic gloom.

Escape appeared impossible. There were no windows fitted into those thick walls of rough stone; walls which rose twelve feet high to the roof. Even the floor was made from crudely hewn slabs of rock cemented together. Through the iron bars of his cell door all that was visible was another stone wall; the outer wall of the gaol. Dan stared at that wall for hours, frustrated by the knowledge that freedom lay on the other side.

A hard iron bed with a blanket, but no mattress, and a slop bucket, were all the cell contained. There was not even a candle or light of any kind. A faint lessening of the gloom was the only way he could tell the difference between day and night. That, plus the fact it was during the daylight hours Ferguson came to taunt him.

Dan was told nothing of how close Ginny had come to

being a murderess. Forty-eight hours after the candlestick crashed against the base of his skull, the publican remained in a semi-comatose state. There were those who thought he might yet die, and rumours of the who and how of the assault were rife throughout the town. It was with great satisfaction that Ferguson wrote the warrant for Ginny's arrest on a charge of attempted murder.

For the time being, however, the sergeant planned to keep that warrant to himself. He did not want the police from any other town to take the elusive, yet wonderfully sexy, Mrs Leigh prisoner. Ferguson intended that particular satisfaction to be his alone. When she was locked in a cell of the Wattle Creek gaol – from which there would be no escape – he would collect, with interest, on all the sexual delights he had expected to enjoy for several nights. If Berrigan was thus forced to listen to their grunts and pantings, then so much the better.

Not only had Ferguson been anticipating the pleasure of 'interrogating' Ginny again and having her sit astride him with her warm, wet sheath encasing his shaft, but he had also greatly looked forward to regaling her bushranger lover with explicit daily accounts of how willing she was to assist the police.

Wickedly devious, Ferguson soon realised there was no need for Berrigan to be told that the woman had managed to get away. There was no way the man could learn the truth. Even if he was temporarily denied the one pleasure, the lewdly sadistic sergeant had no intention of foregoing the other. When it came to ways and means of engaging in intercourse, Ferguson possessed an inventive imagination. His descriptions of Ginny's charms and sexual proclivities were both lurid and graphic.

Though he raged inwardly, Dan maintained a pose of stony-faced indifference. Only a sudden flaring of his nostrils or spark of anger in his eyes betrayed when the malicious shafts found their target. When his tormentor was thus satisfied Dan was left to seethe in the semi-dark loneliness of his cell. Not for a moment did he doubt the sergeant's tales. Only a man who had known Ginny intimately could describe her body in such accurate detail.

After the first time Dan had howled his rage and slammed his fist against the cell wall. The resultant pain was almost welcome for it distracted slightly from the other, agonisingly unbearable, one. That agony was a canker in his breast which festered and grew to coalesce into a hard black core of bitterness. Every single one of Dan's feelings and emotions became centred in an all consuming hatred for the woman who had dared to take his love then callously throw it away. Tormented thoughts of how to effect an escape and how to gain his revenge occupied his mind through all of his waking hours.

When, on the third day, he heard the sound of the outer door being opened, he steeled himself to endure more of the sergeant's mental torture. He heard Ferguson speak, then the light tones of a woman's voice propelled him to a sitting position with a jerk of murderous anger. The bitch! Was she come to add her taunts to those of her new lover? Such a terrible shaking assailed Dan that he was forced to thrust his clenched hands between his knees in an effort to regain control. If Ginny came within reach he would surely curl those hands around her neck and throttle the life out of her beautiful, traitorous body.

The sergeant's gruff words became audible. 'I really don't know why you are so insistent on seeing the prisoner.'

'Because I know how anxious you were to capture him. I do wish I had been here to congratulate you, my brave husband, when you brought him in.'

It was not Ginny! Dan's shaking eased. Cursing himself for a fool he lay back on the bunk with his hands under his head. With his gaze fixed on the high ceiling, he ignored the couple who had now reached his cell.

'Do light the lantern, Malcolm. I really must see what he looks like.'

'He is just a man, like any other.'

'Oh, but the tales that are told about him. They say he is very handsome and so dashing he can have any woman he wants.'

'Why should that interest you?' There was unmistakable jealous suspicion in the query.

'Mere curiosity. I would see what it is that reputedly makes women lie panting in their beds with thoughts of being taken by him.'

'I trust,' said Ferguson in tones of chill disapproval, 'that you, my dear, are not one of them.'

'But of course not. Why should I be when I have such a wonderfully virile husband?'

The answer apparently satisfied the sergeant for a sudden flare of light indicated the lantern had been lit as requested. A moment later a beam of light shafted into the cell to illumine Dan's prone figure.

'Oh, Malcolm, I cannot see him properly while he is lying down.'

'On your feet, Berrigan. Now!' snapped Ferguson when Dan did not immediately obey the command.

Dan rose with deliberate slowness, planted his feet wide and folded his arms across his chest. Pasting an insolent smirk on his face, he stared directly at the woman, studying her as closely as she was studying him. She was sharp featured and plain, dressed in a prim, unbecoming gown of grey serge which disguised whatever feminine attributes she might have possessed. Her gaze travelled from his head to his feet and halfway up again. There it paused while she ran her tongue over her lips.

'Do I pass inspection?' Dan taunted.

The woman looked up, caught the derision in his eyes and cast a nervous sideways glance at her husband.

Ferguson glared at the prisoner. 'That's enough Berrigan. Come along, my dear. You have satisfied your curiosity.' The lamp was extinguished and the sergeant's wife was hurried back down the passageway.

Dan's bitter, mocking laugh followed them. So Ferguson did not like his wife to take an interest in other men, eh? And the prim, plain-faced Mrs Ferguson had most definitely been interested. That was a little item of information Dan intended to keep stored in his mind. If he ever did escape, he knew just how he would even up the score in that particular quarter.

There was no way he could have anticipated just how soon he was to be given the opportunity. His next encounter with Mrs Ferguson came that very night.

Since his imprisonment, Dan slept very little either day or night, dozing only spasmodically. Thus it was he was awake and pacing his tiny cell when the outer door opened and a glow of light seeped into the darkness of the passageway. Dan moved to the door, curious to know who entered the gaol at that time of night. He presumed another prisoner was being brought in and wondered who the man might be. If he was at all halfway decent they could probably engage in the occasional shouted conversation to alleviate the mind destroying boredom brought on by secluded incarceration in a space hardly big enough to satisfy a dog.

Peering into the shadowed passage, Dan certainly never expected to see Ferguson's wife come to a halt in front of his cell.

She was dressed in the same unbecoming grey serge, her face sallow and even more unattractive in the yellow light cast by the lantern she carried. Dan was not left too long to puzzle over the reason for her presence. One hand held the lantern high to shine on his face; the other felt for the crotch of his trousers.

Dan's gasp of astonishment was unfeigned, his response to the caress unavoidable. Yet even as his manhood swelled his eyes held a wary question.

The woman smiled, a sensual smile oddly at contrast with the primness of her features. 'You have been here three nights and I am certain you must be feeling in need of relief. It is something at which I am very good.'

Almost before he had time to wonder how she intended to supply that relief she placed the lantern on the floor and knelt in front of him. She was then the one to gasp in astonishment when the magnificence of Dan's fully engorged shaft was exposed. For long moments she simply gazed at it in admiration, running her fingers gently along its length as though committing its shape and feel to memory.

Her tongue flicked out to tickle the tiny crack at the tip, then circle slowly around the crease. Warm lips closed over the head, her hand guiding as she gradually drew it deep into her throat. With a low growl of acceptance, Dan clung to the iron bars of the door, pressing his pelvis hard against them to assist her to take in all of his shaft. Head tilted back he closed his eyes, savouring the pleasure imparted by her mouth.

Her declaration she was an expert had been no idle boast. Dan suspected, quite correctly, he was not the first prisoner to have benefited from her oral talents. She took him deep, eased him out to tease with the tip of her tongue, then sucked him in again. Her mouth worked avidly up and down his shaft until the semen pulsed along its tract and he gave a convulsive groan. Immediately she slid her lips right to the base so that the warm, salty liquid spurted deep into her throat and not a drop was lost.

Dan was breathing raggedly, still clutching the bars, when she stood and moved to pick up the lantern. 'Wait,' he said. Even while she worked so expertly on his shaft his mind had been figuring how to turn her unexpected appearance to his greater advantage. He favoured her with the lazy smile which turned so many feminine hearts. 'It seems hardly fair that you should give me so much pleasure when I am unable to do the same for you. Wouldn't you like to learn just how well I can please a woman?'

The lips which had so recently delighted his manhood pursed in consideration. 'I really don't see how you could.'

He sensed her hesitation, saw her cast an almost longing glance at his half-masted rod. Determined not to lose the advantage, he reached through the bars to pull her close with a hand at the back of her waist. His other hand pressed against the thick material of her skirt to cover her mound, his fingers curving against the place below.

'You claim women lie panting in their beds wondering what it would be like to be taken by me. You have the opportunity to find out. You have pleasured me with your mouth – I can pleasure you with mine. By then I will be hard again, ready to stroke deep inside you and fill you as you have never been filled before. I can feel your trembling as you try to imagine what that would be like. You do want it, don't you?'

She was the one who now breathed raggedly. 'It's not possible,' she gasped, while wondering desperately if it was. Even through the folds of her skirt the touch of his fingers was highly arousing. To have them against her skin, feel them stroke inside would be – ooh, she could hardly begin to imagine how exciting it would be.

'Anything is possible, if you want it badly enough,' coaxed Dan. 'Admit that you do want it.'

'Oh, yes, yes! But how?'

'Very simply. You have the keys, and no one need ever know.

'I – I cannot.'

'Has your courage failed you? You took a great risk to come here in the first place. Why leave now, without satisfying all your desires?'

Within a few minutes she was lying naked on the rough blanket on the cell floor, moaning with delight as Dan expertly tongued her clitoris and stroked a tantalising finger along her eager slit. He played with her, bringing her close to an orgasm only to leave her suspended on the very edge. When she begged him to continue the stimulation he declined; told her he wanted the enjoyment to last.

For a while he stroked her breasts, tweaking her rosy nipples into hard peaks. The voluptuousness of her body had come as a pleasant surprise. Her breasts were full, her hips lusciously rounded, the tight black curls of her mound a dramatic contrast against the fairness of her skin. With her hair loose and the bloom of sexual desire softening her features she was almost pretty.

He suckled her breasts and slipped a finger into the warmth of her love hole, frigging her until she was ready to come. Again he denied her and moved to kneel across her chest with his shaft close to her face. His fingers slid through her hair, lifting her head to bring her mouth forward so that she could suck him again.

Before long he had swelled to his maximum size and she was desperate to have him penetrate her, peeved when he said, 'Not yet.'

When his tongue returned to her aching love place to tease and frustrate, she cried her need, sobbing and begging to be given release. Only then did he oblige, clasping her buttocks to suck and tickle while fierce orgasmic spasms wrenched her body.

Before those spasms had fully eased he turned to mount her, intentionally driving fully into her with the first thrust. She was stretched and filled, the head of his shaft banging against her womb with such force she cried out loud and almost fainted.

There was no mercy shown. She had been anxious to know what sex with Dan Berrigan was like and she was now finding out in a manner she would never forget. Before he came he tipped her over to take her from behind, then again with her astride his pelvis. The penetrating thrusts jerked her entire body, each one forcing an accompanying 'aah, aah', from her lips. She was once more on her back, helplessly weak from an almost continuous orgasm, when Dan gave the last few necessary thrusts.

For a time he remained pressed deep within, then he slowly eased out. When that giant rod, which had given her both pain and pleasure, was completely withdrawn her breath exhaled on a long sigh and she lay with her eyes closed, totally spent.

Such was the near swooning state of her sexual satiation she was unaware of Dan dressing and gathering up her clothes. Only when the cell door clanged did she open her eyes. By the time she realised what was happening it was far too late. She was naked, locked in the cell, and her clothes were outside.

'Give my regards to the sergeant, Mrs Ferguson,' Dan mocked. 'And don't forget to tell him just how much you enjoyed your sexual encounter with the "dashing" bushranger.'

In a sky of black unalleviated by any lunar glow, the stars twinkled with startling brightness. There was not the faintest whisper of a breeze to ruffle even the highest branches of the trees, yet the night was not still. From here and there, throughout the bush, came the rustlings of the creatures which hunted only during the cool hours of darkness.

The haunting 'who-who' of an owl took Ginny's gaze from the glowing coals of the fire to a nearby tree. Even when the bird called again, Ginny was unable to define its position for its mottled grey feathers blended so perfectly with the branch on which it perched.

Ginny hugged her arms around her legs and rested her chin on her knees to resume her contemplation of the fire. A short distance away Logan attended to the horses. Soon he would join her. A deep ache of longing twisted in Ginny's gut and she hugged herself more closely.

A night and a day had passed since she walked into Molly Jones's inn, and in all that time Logan had not taken her, nor even held her in his arms. At first they had eaten; a tasteless stew accompanied by heavy damper which, for all it had been unappetising, succeeded in banishing the last of the queasiness from Ginny's stomach.

While they were eating the storm had broken with frightening violence. The spears of lightning darted earthward with deadly menace, loud thunder cracked to jar the nerves and the heavy rain ran in sheets off the shingle roof and seeped through gaps to drip noisily onto the floor.

Logan led Ginny to the room he had been using but to her surprise had left her at the door. 'We cannot stay here, nor can we leave until the storm eases. You are tired and we have a long journey ahead of us. I will waken you when I am ready to leave.'

Perplexity and disappointment puckered her face. 'You do not want to –' her voice trailed off at the gleam in his eyes.

'Always, in all ways. However you are not entirely yourself. Nor is it my intention to provide a sexual spectacle for our voyeuristic landlord and his slattern of a wife.'

Ginny's eyes widened. 'Do you mean they would watch?'

'Most certainly. There are conveniently placed peepholes in the walls. You will see them if you look. Go to sleep, Ginny. The storm will last some time yet.'

Not until the chill hours of early morning did he wake her. The heavy storm clouds had finally rumbled away and they rode from the inn with their horses splashing to their fetlocks in the mud and the trees shaking heavy drops of moisture over them.

For the remainder of that night and all of the next day they had ridden, changing horses twice at different homesteads. Ginny never questioned, obedient to Logan's commands, anxious herself to put as much distance as possible between them and Wattle Creek.

Only as the sun sank beyond the western horizon to paint a fiery glow across the sky did he declare they could stop.

Even when they found a suitable sheltered place near a small waterhole, he built the fire, heated the stew they had been given at one of the homesteads, then spread the blanket for Ginny before he went to ensure the horses were settled for the night. All the while they exchanged the barest of conversation though his dark gaze rested frequently on Ginny's face. Mixed emotions of puzzlement then acceptance flitted like shadows across her mobile features. Desire filled her eyes. Logan's own gleamed with triumph.

When he joined her on the blanket she turned eagerly into his arms, needing the feel of them holding her, aching for the unique fulfilment she found only in Logan's possession. Passion flared, the heat of desire which coursed through their bodies far greater than that which emanated from the fire.

Soon they were naked, skin against skin, hands and lips caressing, stimulating. Then Logan's tongue was teasing the bud of her desire to carry her away to that netherworld of erotism where only they two existed. When he guided the rigid shaft of his manhood towards her mouth she took it willingly, without thought, aware only of the heightening of their ardour.

They came at the same instant, drinking deeply of each other's love juices. Then Logan turned; bent his head towards hers. Their mouths met, with the taste of each other on their lips, and their kiss became one of drugging passion.

When Logan lifted his head, red flames burned in the coal-black depths of his eyes. 'Now you are forever mine. No other man will ever have your body, nor will you want to give yourself to another. We are one Ginny, you and I, your body is of mine and mine of yours. Only death can ever tear us apart.'

* * *

Constable Smith unlocked the gaol door at precisely six o'clock to carry in the prisoner's breakfast. Not believing the sight which greeted his eyes he closed them rapidly, wondering if he had drunk a few too many glasses of rum the night before. Very cautiously opening them again he found nothing had changed. Instead of the outlaw, the sergeant's wife sat on the bunk, huddled in the blanket. The recognition of the fact she was entirely naked under that blanket momentarily deprived him of speech.

To even begin to surmise how such a transposition of occupancy had occurred stretched the young constable's imagination beyond the limits of credulity. Aware such imaginings were having a stimulating effect on his manhood, he executed a hasty red-faced retreat, muttering his intention of fetching the sergeant. This he did with a great degree of nervous trepidation, terrified of what assumptions his superior might make if he noticed his highly uncomfortable state of arousal.

The sergeant's wrath was every degree as great as he feared. The fact that he would not, at first, believe the constable's story was perhaps understandable. But when he went so far as to blame the constable for somehow being responsible for Berrigan's escape, plus the presence of some unknown floosy in the cell, the young man drew himself stiffly to attention, his face a study of righteous indignation.

'I am sorry you do not believe me, sergeant. I assumed you would prefer that I reported the matter to you directly instead of to the senior constable. However I am certain he will be able to confirm the identity of the woman in the cell.'

'The devil take you, constable. If you wait a moment I will prove that my wife is asleep in her room.'

Ferguson's face was livid with rage and embarrassment when he slid the spare key into the lock of the cell door. Without a word he hustled his petrified wife out of the gaol and across the yard to their house.

Hell! He would be the laughing stock of the Victorian Police if this fiasco ever became known. What, he wondered, would it take to ensure the constable kept his mouth shut. Quick promotion perhaps? Transfer to a better town? Not a man to take lightly to being made a fool of, Ferguson ground his teeth with rage.

Just when he thought everything was going his way it was suddenly all going horribly wrong. First of all Berrigan's woman eluded him, now Berrigan himself had escaped. And it was the manner of that escape which caused the greatest chagrin. He pushed his wife into the room, locked the door, and began to remove his belt.

'Now, my dear, before I give you the beating you most assuredly deserve, you will tell me, in the greatest detail, exactly what happened last night.'

As soon as Dan was beyond the precincts of the police station and gaol his escape became much easier. There were many friends and sympathisers in the town who were only too willing to assist. His first intention was to find Ginny, to exact some terrible form of retribution for her betrayal. Revenge had been the uppermost thought in his mind during all the hours of his imprisonment.

It was not long before he heard the rumours which were circulating; easy enough to ascertain a certain uncouth publican was indeed barely clinging to life.

So Ferguson had lied when he claimed Ginny was his mistress. Not that it mattered, for it was only an exaggeration of facts. What difference did it make whether he had enjoyed her body for one night or one month? That she had given it freely at all was treachery enough for Dan.

Rife though the speculation was, no one knew for certain just where Ginny had gone. All anyone could say definitely was that she was no longer in Wattle Creek. Deprived for the time being of his revenge, Dan headed back to the hideout. No one had seen or heard anything of Charlie and Josh either. Though he would not want either of them to place their own lives in jeopardy, he wanted to know why the hell they had done nothing to assist his escape.

Immediately he rode up to the hut, Dan sensed something was amiss. Delighted and relieved though they expressed themselves to be, both Charlie and Josh appeared ill at ease.

They relaxed slightly when he recounted the events leading up to his escape, agreeing it was almost worth being locked up to have been able to inflict such embarrassment on the detested sergeant. Dan's mocking grin twisted into one of bitterness. 'I guess it was tit-for-tat. I screwed his wife and he screwed Ginny. Ah, that bitch!' His clenched fist banged against the table. 'It's as well for her she left Wattle Creek, though I'd like to know where she's gone.'

The exchange of nervous glances did not pass unnoticed. 'Just what is the matter with you two? You've been acting strange ever since I got here. Is it Ginny? Is she here?'

'Not now,' confessed Charlie.

'But she was,' Dan accurately deduced. 'And there's something you don't want to tell me.' He glared from one to the other. 'Josh?'

'Well, you ain't gonna like it, Dan.'

'I'm not going to like what?' His voice held the deadly calm both men knew spelt trouble.

'Hell, it wasn't our fault Dan,' Charlie defended. 'She stole all the bloody gold.'

'What!?'

Charlie shifted uncomfortably, for Dan had sprung to his feet and towered menacingly over him. 'You heard, mate. She came back here and cleared out with the whole lot.'

Dan slumped back in his chair, succumbed to a momentary despair and dropped his head into his hands. 'So that was her plan.' When he lifted his head his expression was as hard as if his features were carved in granite. His mates realised they would never see Dan's carefree grin again. 'There is just one thing I'd like to know. Where the hell were the pair of you when this happened?'

There was another exchange of hesitant glances. Neither man wished to be on the receiving end of Dan's temper, yet they knew him well enough to know he would badger them until he learned the truth. When they decided to have their night of fun with Ginny, neither expected it to end with her the winner.

Josh was the first to speak. 'Well, she came back here three days ago just as we were thinking something must have happened to you.'

'Did she tell you I had been arrested.'

'Yeah. She told us – '

'Exactly what did she tell you?'

'Bloody hell, mate, stop interrupting will you,' exploded Josh. 'We don't feel too good about things as it is.'

Charlie took up the explanation, glossing over the more lurid details. The sexual activities of that night they blamed entirely on Molly Jones's wicked brew. Charlie did not admit that he had tried to rape Ginny initially. Not that it would have mattered if he had. He had been right about that. Dan wouldn't have given a damn.

His bitterness seared the desire for vengeance deep into his heart. If it was necessary to search to the ends of the earth he would find her. And when he did she would pay. God, how she would pay.

Chapter Eleven

*L*ogan and Ginny spent over a week travelling slowly south-east to Melbourne. They avoided the main roads, patronised none but the loneliest of inns and frequently slept in the open with only the bush creatures for company. During the course of their journey, Logan's domination became supreme. Ginny was his and his alone. Wherever Logan went she was bound to him for all time by the invisible threads of their sexual passion.

There were a few days spent in a dingy dwelling house not far from the wharf while they awaited the arrival of the coastal schooner. It came under full canvas, fleeing into the shelter of the bay in the teeth of a violent storm. When it departed on a grey and grumbling sea, with bad-weathered clouds scudding above and a powerful wind swelling the sails, it carried them around the southern curve of the continent and north to Sydney. Tessa sailed with them.

Ginny resented the other woman's presence for she could not feel comfortable with her former maid; there were too many things from the past to build distrust between them. To the greatest degree possible, Ginny avoided Logan's sister. As Tessa appeared to have no desire to communicate with Ginny either, they spoke little with each other throughout the journey.

Once, when circumstances found them alone, Tessa reached a hand to finger the cheap material of Ginny's simple gown. 'How the mighty are fallen. Where is the fine madam now?' she mocked. 'You thought you were so clever, thought you could resist my brother's power. But now he has you, and he will use you until he decides he has had enough of you. By then you will be fit for no other. Never again will you play the grand whoring lady. Ah, bitch,' she laughed softly, 'you don't know how much such knowledge pleases me.'

From that day on Ginny ignored her totally. Logan's desire found its antithesis in Tessa's dislike.

To Ginny's immense relief they parted company shortly after their arrival in Sydney, Tessa to remain in the city, Logan and Ginny to travel out into the grazing districts. As always, Ginny followed where Logan commanded, yet her curiosity would not be quelled. The voices of brother and sister had been raised in angry altercation the night before, and Ginny wished to know why.

Logan's lips curled in a sardonic line. 'We have always been close, Tessa and I. She thought it would always be so; thought I would tire of your body once I possessed you totally. She wanted to come with me, could not understand that we two are one and need no one else.'

He glanced down at her, seated beside him, and there was an expression in the thoughtfulness of her eyes which made him draw the waggon to a halt. His arm was strong around her shoulders, his lips savage upon hers. 'No one else, Ginny, only each other.' He took her immediately, on the high seat of the waggon, cruelly emphasising the truth of his statement as her body responded wildly to the driving ruthlessness of their union.

Ever northward they travelled until they reached the rich pastures of the New England District. Over several thousand acres of that rolling green country, Richard Cumberland grazed sheep which produced so fine a wool he had soon become an extremely wealthy man. With sufficient money to be able to indulge his every whim he raised, for a hobby, thoroughbred horses which were almost as valuable as his annual wool clip.

Richard Cumberland's portly physique and the soft plumpness of his wife attested to their enjoyment of the good things in life. Cumberland Downs was the finest sheep station in all of New South Wales. Not only did Richard Cumberland enjoy sitting down to a well laden table, he approved the physical display of wealth. The floors of the grand stone mansion were covered with the richest carpets, the walls adorned with priceless treasures of art and the furnishings of the most luxurious materials.

A long, tree-lined drive curved up the gentle slope to the grand entrance porch with a branch leading off, in a circuit around the side of the house, to the cluster of buildings at the rear. The lesser drive was the one Logan and Ginny took.

Though the Cumberlands lived in affluent splendour, they were not indifferent to the needs of their employees. The house servants lived in semi-detached quarters, the farm hands in small stone cottages. Dairy, meat house, laundry, storeroom and various other buildings stretched back over the acres behind the main house. Dominating them all were the magnificent stables where Cumberland's valuable horses accepted as their due the quality of their care.

Beyond the stables, some distance away from the other buildings, was the tiny, shingle-roofed, stone cottage assigned to Logan and Ginny. It consisted only of one room, with a fireplace to cook upon, a bed against one wall and a table and cupboard against the other. It had been empty for some time and dusty cobwebs hung from the unmilled timber rafters.

Standing in the centre of that dismal abode, Ginny

found it difficult to believe she had ever lived in as fine a house as the Cumberlands. When she first saw it, rising above manicured lawns and colourful gardens with its stonework reflecting the warm colours of the afternoon sun, Ginny was strongly reminded of Everleigh. Was it really little more than a year since she bade goodbye to Francis? All that part of her life was as a distant memory – an unreal dream. Yet it was at Everleigh Logan first claimed her for his own. And if Ginny had sufficient gold hidden among her possessions to buy a house almost as grand as Everleigh, then that was her secret, and hers alone.

Richard Cumberland had initially been reluctant to take Logan on trial, for he distrusted a man with no references. But few days passed before he realised this man possessed a rare skill with horses and innate ability to understand their needs. Such was his pleasure and his eagerness to retain the man's services, he quickly suggested moving the couple into a far more comfortable cottage closer to the main house.

He was somewhat taken aback when the offer was declined with cool hauteur. 'The cottage we have suits us well enough. We have no need of anything more.'

'Damned strange fellow,' Cumberland remarked to his wife that evening when relating the surprising response. 'Can't help but feel there's a mystery there somewhere. Both the way he speaks and that supreme self-assurance make him appear more the master than the servant.'

'I know what you mean, dear. Certainly there is some mystery, though I believe if one was to delve into the backgrounds of half the men and women in the colonies one would be very surprised at what secrets might be divulged.'

'True enough, I suppose. How do you find his wife?'

'A mystery there, too, I believe. She speaks so little and appears so totally indifferent to all that goes on around her that at first I believed she must be a trifle simple. But when I did manage to draw her into conversation one day, I realised she has a fine intellect and apparent good education.'

'Is she a good worker?'

'I have discovered she is very skilled with a needle, so I have set her to work doing the mending and remodelling some of my gowns. You do not mind?'

'As long as she is earning her keep I do not mind in what capacity she works.'

Neither did Ginny care very much what work she was asked to do. Her mistress was kind and the sewing, which was in no way arduous, something with which to fill the days. She existed solely for the nights when Logan joined his body with hers in passionate, primitive possession. That was the only reality. The ordinary, everyday acts of living were simply what went between.

On a cool winter's afternoon Ginny sat beside the fire in their cottage, stitching carefully around the hem of a tiny gown. The cottage was considerably cleaner than when they first arrived and, even if it still only contained the most basic of requirements, rather more comfortable. Golden rays of the late afternoon sun slanted through the crystal-clear glass of the window to brighten the colours of a rag rug on the floor. Those same rays also cast light on Ginny's sewing.

A too familiar wave of nausea made Ginny lower the work on to her lap. With one hand pressed lightly against the slight mound of her abdomen she rested her head back and closed her eyes.

For six months she had endured this misery and there were times, like this, when she wondered how she could possibly endure another three. Each day, it seemed, both the awful feeling of sickness and the terrible lethargy, became worse. At least the mistress was both compassionate and understanding. Deprived herself of the joys of having children, she looked forward to the birth of Ginny's baby, sympathising because the young woman was having such a difficult time with her pregnancy. Mrs Cumberland insisted Ginny sewed only when she was able and rested when she was not.

Ginny felt nothing for the coming child other than an acceptance it was growing inside her womb. For Logan it appeared to represent some special triumph, almost as though it's conception was ordained; the supreme proof of his power. Ginny fully recalled the details of the steamy January night when Logan made her pregnant.

On that summer night, the coming of darkness only slightly alleviated the enervating heat of the day. Ginny lay naked and sweating on the bed, wishing for a cooling breeze to stir the stillness of the air. Logan was somewhere outside, checking the horses.

When he burst back into the cottage his eyes burned with a strange excitement. Because of the heat, he too was naked to the waist, clad only in a pair of cut-off trousers. He grasped her hand to lead her out into the night. 'Come,' he commanded.

'Wait!' she protested. 'I must at least put on a robe.'

'You must come as you are. It is time.'

'Time for what?'

He did not answer, leading her out into the night and over to the small horse paddock. There, silhouetted in the light of the full moon, a proud, black stallion flung its head with a loud challenging call.

'Watch,' said Logan.

The stallion preened and called, performing for his small harem of mares. Ginny watched entranced when a young mare was singled out for his mating needs. She saw the stallion's long penis extend and felt herself pulled back against Logan's body, the rigidity of his manhood pressing against her buttocks. His lips were close to her ear, nuzzling gently. One hand curved over her naked breasts while the other slid down between her thighs to find the moisture of her erotic awakening.

The young filly shied nervously, giving a plaintive neigh when the stallion attempted to mount her. Logan's finger slipped deep into Ginny's warmth and she leant back against him, relishing the intimate caress. His voice was husky, almost hypnotic.

'See how she shies away, yet does not go far. She is afraid for she has never mated before. She tries to evade him but cannot – her own instincts are too strong. Look, now. This time he will mount her. See how strong and powerful his organ is and how she trembles with her need. You tremble too, Ginny, for you know what must come. Hear her scream with pain. She knows she must endure the stallion's mastery, but not why. A new life will grow inside her and only when her foal is born will she understand.'

The stallion was fully mounted, thrusting his organ into the screaming mare. Ginny's entire body was burning with sexual awareness, almost as if she was one with the filly and could feel her pain. She was panting her own need when Logan pushed her forward on to her hands and knees. Her own cry rent the night air at the depth of his thrust. His proud manhood filled and satisfied her aching womanhood, moving strongly and rythmically with an action as old as life itself. Responding with her own primitive need, Ginny knew that, even while the stallion was planting his seed within the young mare, Logan's seed was taking root in her own body.

Almost at the moment the stallion screamed his triumph, Logan gave his final thrust with a great cry of satisfaction. 'It is done, Ginny, it is done!'

He withdrew and turned her onto her back to reinsert his still hard shaft, his lips fierce and possessive on hers. Ginny curled her legs around his waist and reached her hands down to clasp the firm flesh of his buttocks, bucking against him in a frenzy of sexual need, wanting all he could give and more.

The opening of the cottage door brought Ginny out of her reverie. Logan paused just inside, to cast his dark gaze over Ginny's forlorn figure. Involuntary tears of misery and self-pity welled in her eyes. Why was it that, the more ill she felt, the more vibrant Logan appeared to become.

He stood there now, black haired, black eyed, an aquiline nose above thin, cruel lips; proud, powerful, enigmatic. Ginny knew him no better after all these months than on the first night he took possession of her body. Everything about Logan, including the strange forces that bound her to him, remained a mystery.

Standing there, with the light of the setting sun bronzing the deep olive of his skin, he appeared as the personification of a dark, sensual Lucifer. Hysterical laughter bubbled in Ginny's throat. Logan, Prince of Darkness. There had once been nights when she consigned him to the devil with passionate frequency. Each time he had merely mocked her with a cruel laugh, knowing it was only a matter of time until he possessed her totally.

The rising laughter died abruptly as the tears spilled in a slow trickle down Ginny's cheeks. Logan moved further into the room to stand over her, gazing down at her with nothing of compassion in his expression. 'You are unwell?'

Ginny wiped a tired hand across her wet cheeks, regaining control with a weary sigh. 'You know I am always unwell.'

'It is unavoidable, Ginny. My child grows within your womb, his strength draining yours.' He reached down to take her hands and draw her to her feet. 'You have need of me, Ginny. Just as my son weakens you, I, alone, can restore your strength.'

'Oh yes, Logan, yes.' Ginny clung to his shoulders, lifting her lips for his kiss. As always, the demanding pressure of his mouth upon hers ignited passion, her pregnancy having in no way affected their mutual sexual hunger. Ginny ached for him with an intensity far greater than before. Only when Logan joined his body with hers did she feel relief from the draining illness, as though he indeed gave her some of his strength.

'I don't understand,' she whispered, for already the nausea was easing away.

'There is no need for you to understand, Ginny. You must simply accept that it is so. Our bodies are of each other, united in a manner that far transcends the purely physical.'

His hands were at work unfastening her gown. One by one he removed her garments until she stood naked. He knelt before her, his hands smoothing over her rounded abdomen, then sank back on his heels. His lips pressed against the skin his hands had caressed before trailing a sensual touch downwards to seek the intimate sweetness in the lips of her womanhood.

Ginny entwined her fingers in the crisp blackness of Logan's hair, easing her hips forward at the guiding of his hands to make easier the task of his seeking tongue. Heat, vibrant and stimulating, began coursing through her body.

She cried his name again. This time there was no perplexity, only the acknowledgement of her need. 'Take me, take me,' she begged. 'I must feel you inside me, stroking the illness out of my body.'

They lay naked on the rug in front of the fire, the orange light of the flames flickering over their sweating bodies. Their coupling had been savagely passionate, pain and pleasure mingling with erotism to carry them out of the world to that other plane of awareness, where they existed when their bodies were one.

Exhausted, they remained wrapped in each others' arms, holding to themselves the residual pleasure of their sexual union. After a time, Logan rose and fetched a blanket to drape over her, encasing her body in its warmth. Ginny slept, wakening to the dark of night and the appetising aroma of hot soup.

The latter came from a pot Logan had suspended over the fire, prompting a realisation she was hungry. On turning her head, she could see him at the table, cutting thick slices of bread for their supper.

Ginny watched him through half-closed eyes and, not for the first time, attempted to assess her feelings. She did not love Logan – of that she was certain. Even though they had been together for almost a year, there had been no lessening of the sadistic cruelty of his lovemaking. Yet her feelings were both deep and strong. Whatever was between them went far beyond love. She knew, as he knew, she could never leave him. She had fought so hard to defy Logan's domination that, from the moment of her surrender, her subjugation to his will became absolute.

Beneath the cover of the blanket her hand curved over the mound of her stomach. If Ginny was finding it difficult to visualise herself as a mother, it was impossible to imagine Logan as a father. What would it be like when they were three instead of two?

On seeing she was awake, Logan carried bowls and the bread over to the hearth. He ladled the nourishing broth into the bowls and they ate in silence seated in front of the fire. Though Ginny had only the blanket to cover her nakedness, Logan was already dressed.

'The new foal is weak,' he told her when he took away her empty bowl. 'I must return to the stables to see how it is. Go to bed, Ginny, and sleep. I will come to you later.'

Shortly before midnight he stretched out behind her on the bed, the hard shaft of his manhood pressing against the smooth flesh of her buttocks. The warm contact brought her partly awake, the action of his fingers spreading her folds to seek the moist passage between, evoking a moan of desire.

He shifted his position to lift her uppermost leg and thus open her vagina. Kneeling astride her other leg, he pressed the hot head of his shaft against the sensitive bud of her desire. He tantalised her, teased her sensitive nerve ends. With his hand guiding its action he rubbed the tip of his shaft against her hard-peaked nodule, fingering her with the other hand until she cried aloud,

'Now, now!' as the burning flood of her orgasm started deep within.

Logan thrust into her, using both hands to hold her leg high and the strength of his thigh muscles to drive his shaft. Ginny clutched the pillow, clenching the wet sheath of her womanhood around the powerful shaft of his manhood. Deep and satisfying were his thrusts; supreme and long-lasting her orgasm. When he stretched out beside her and took her in his arms Ginny turned her lips to his, seeking his kiss as confirmation of their oneness. Secure in his arms, she fell asleep.

Some hours later, Ginny stirred and rolled over, something outside her consciousness dragging her awake. She puckered her brow in the notion all was not right and in the instant of her horrified realisation, Logan jerked upright beside her. From outside the cottage the shifting glow of orange light played across their small window.

'Fire!' Logan was immediately on his feet, dragging on his trousers even as he hurried to the door. 'It's the stables,' he cried. 'The stables are on fire!'

Then he was gone, running across the yard to join the others who came shouting.

'Get water, get water!'

'Oh, my God!'

'The horses, the horses. We must save the horses.'

Ginny drew a robe over her nakedness and hurried to take her place in the line of men and women who passed buckets of water from the well as rapidly as they could be filled. Others grabbed them, threw their contents in valiant hope on the burning building then passed them back to be refilled again and again.

The flames were gaining in fierceness, the terrible sight and sound of the conflagration magnified tenfold by the shouts and cries of both men and women and the terrified screaming of the trapped horses.

There were renewed shouts to save the animals. Several of the men attempted to enter the burning building.

The intense heat drove all back. 'It's no use. The flames are too hot.'

Nobody realised one man was already inside, freeing the horses from their stalls.

Ginny, working in the bucket line, was no wiser than the others. In futile desperation they continued to pass the water until Cumberland shouted, 'Leave it, leave it! Save your strength. The fire's got too strong a hold.'

'Dear Lord,' prayed his wife as the workers drifted out of their lines to stare silently and helplessly at the burning building.

'Can nobody save the horses?' whispered Ginny.

No one answered, the terrible question finding an echo in every mind. Mrs Cumberland, herself distraught, placed a comforting arm around Ginny's shoulders.

Then, unexpectedly, miraculously, the horses were breaking free, bursting through the flames and smoke. There were cheers of relief and shouts as men ran forward to grab their bridles and lead them to safety. Cumberland rapidly counted them.

'They are all out except the mare and foal.'

'Oh, look!' exclaimed his wife. 'Look there.'

Barely visible in the dense smoke, a man could be seen dragging the stubborn screaming mare clear of the burning building.

'Good grief!' exclaimed Cumberland. 'It's Logan. How did he manage to get in there?'

Ginny swayed and would have fallen except for the support of Mrs Cumberland's arm. More terrified than the mare she pressed her hands to her mouth, fighting back both her screams and the rising nausea.

The mare was safe and Cumberland was shouting, 'Come away, man, come away! Leave the foal.'

Logan either did not hear, or took no notice, ducking and weaving back through the flames.

A fearful hush fell over the watchers. Anxious moments, which seemed to Ginny as long as eternity, ticked by. Above the crackling of the flames could be heard the mare's distraught cries, the awful sound chilling Ginny's heart.

Suddenly, they all became aware there was an answering call. The mare responded, fighting to break free of the men who held her, calling to her foal which came cantering out of the flames. A great cheer went up, then faded to a tense silence.

Everyone expected the man to follow. Some thought they could see his silhouette. One called, 'There he is,' only for the words to be lost in the terrible crashing roar of the collapsing roof. Bright, triumphant, the flames soared high into the night sky.

Ginny screamed Logan's name. Screaming his name and crying her denial of the unacceptable horror, she broke free of the arms which held her and started forward. A crippling pain stabbed through her abdomen to stop her, a second one brought her to her knees. There was the warm stickiness of blood between her thighs, and she realised, in the instant before she lost conciousness, she was losing Logan's child.

The doctor closed his bag with a worried sigh and motioned Mrs Cumberland to precede him out of the room. This she did after casting her own worried gaze over the too white face of the woman in the bed.

'What do you think, doctor?' she asked, the instant they were in the passageway with the bedroom door closed behind them.

'I wish I could say,' he responded with a frown. 'It has been over six weeks now since she lost the child. Even though she lost a great deal of blood with it, I would have expected some improvement in her condition by now.' He paused, decided the woman at his side was eminently sensible, and continued. 'I am not a fanciful man, Mrs Cumberland, and I confess I am perplexed. Always, just when it appears she is beginning to recover she slips back again. She is, I am certain, fighting for her life, yet it seems almost as if something – or someone – is trying to drag her beyond the grave.'

'I fear you may be right, doctor. Poor thing, to have lost both her husband and child on the same terrible night.' She shook her head in as much perplexity as the doctor. 'You never knew him, her husband, did you? There was something of a mystery there. He had a sort of – ' she paused, searched for the right word and shrugged her shoulders in defeat. 'It is impossible to describe just what it was about him that made him seem so different. And the way they were together – that, too, was strange. They did not act like a couple deeply in love, yet it was as though they existed only to be with each other. Such a terrible, unnecessary tragedy. I wish there was more I could do to help her recover.'

'You have done your Christian duty and more by bringing her into your home and nursing her with such care. I am afraid there is little else anyone can do for the poor woman now except pray.'

Being a devout woman, Mrs Cumberland prayed nightly, and also frequently during the day while she was easing drops of nourishing gruel into her patient's mouth. Perhaps it was the power of her prayers, for a little over a week later Ginny opened her eyes.

That first time she was barely aware of her surroundings, drifting almost immediately back into the deep sleep of near unconciousness. Several more days passed before she was sufficiently returned to life to wonder at the elegance of the room in which she lay.

A kind, familiar face bent over her, asking her how she felt. Memory returned with a rush, bringing with it an unbearable pain which caused her to moan, 'No, no,' and brought weak tears to form in her eyes.

'Hush, my dear, do not think about it,' comforted Mrs Cumberland. 'You are going to get better but you must rest and try not to stress yourself.'

Very gradually Ginny's condition improved. Each day she became a little stronger and now there was no slipping back. Only when memory could not be denied would she lie tearful and listless in her bed. Though she never spoke Logan's name, nor made reference to the events of that night, she did, eventually, ask the question Mrs Cumberland had been dreading. 'Where was he buried?'

The good woman fidgeted uncomfortably, making a great deal of plumping up Ginny's pillows. 'Do not worry about it, dear,' she prevaricated. 'Time enough for that when you are fully well.'

Tears, precipitated by her weakness, welled in Ginny's eyes. 'I want to know. Please tell me.'

Mrs Cumberland sighed, left the pillows alone and clasped both of Ginny's hands in hers. There was the sad hint of tears in her own eyes. 'I am so terribly sorry, my dear. The men searched thoroughly. They could not find him. The fire must have been too hot.'

The anguished moan which escaped Ginny's lips tore at the older woman's heart strings and the manner in which the invalid slumped back on the pillows made her fearful of a relapse. Ginny was unaware of Mrs Cumberland's fussing, for behind her closed eyelids she was seeing again the burning stables, the collapsing roof, then the flames soaring triumphantly into the sky.

Nothing! There had been nothing of Logan left. The fire had taken him, consumed him. It was as though he had never existed.

Ginny's convalescence was slow. By the time she was able to leave her bed and move about during the day, the warmth of spring was in the air. On the lawns in front of the house the flower gardens were a blaze of perfumed colour. Behind the house the ruined stables had been pulled down and new ones were being built in their place.

Though she frequently walked in the gardens, Ginny never ventured anywhere near the rear of the house, even avoiding the windows which gave a view of the yard. At her request, Logan's things had been disposed of and her own brought to her at the house. Never again would she step foot inside that tiny cottage.

During that time she developed a gentle rapport with her former mistress. Then eventually there came the day when Mrs Cumberland enquired of her plans for her future.

'I would like you to stay at Cumberland Downs, Ginny. I have become very fond of you and now that you are better, greatly enjoy your company. It would please me very much if you would remain here as my companion.'

Ginny's expression held a sad regret. 'You have been so very kind to me, Mrs Cumberland, that I feel I should in some way repay you. If it were possible I would do as you ask. Please do not think me ungrateful, but I cannot stay here.'

Mrs Cumberland reached over to pat Ginny's hand. 'Do not fret yourself, dear, I understand. I believe I would feel the same if I had lost my husband in like manner.'

Immediately she had spoken she wished she could retract the words. She saw the shutters come down over Ginny's eyes to mask their expression and sensed the cold withdrawal into a hard shell which shut out the rest of the world.

It was the same any time the briefest reference was made to Ginny's loss. Mrs Cumberland thought she understood. Only Ginny knew how terrible was the emptiness inside.

She grieved for Logan with an intensity which devoured all other feeling. Always, when the pain was so great it was almost impossible to bear she could hear his voice, passionate, determined.

'We are one, Ginny, you and I. Your body is of mine and mine of yours. Only death can ever tear us apart.'

Now death had torn them apart, and in taking Logan it had taken part of herself as well. It seemed to Ginny she could never be whole again.

Chapter Twelve

*S*ydney, with its bustling streets and narrow alley-ways, was a town where a man could easily blend in to the crowds. And if that man happened to be desirous of avoiding confrontation with the officers of the law, then it was convenient to be able to fade out of sight whenever prudence deemed necessary.

On seeing the constable turn into the street not more than a dozen yards ahead to begin walking towards him, Dan slipped quietly into a nearby laneway. There was a price on his head and he knew there were many who would not hesitate to turn him in if they suspected his identity.

In an attempt to disguise that identity, his hair now grew almost to his shoulders and a wild, full beard covered the greater part of his face. Dan doubted even Charlie or Josh would recognise him without a second or third look.

Exactly where those two were he did not know. Neither did he particularly care. That friendship had come to an end. Perhaps it had begun to fade from the moment Ginny came into their lives; it most certainly ended with the manner of her departure.

It was not so much what she had done with Charlie

and Josh that came between them, it was the subsequent theft of the gold and Dan's obsessive desire for revenge. Many were the angry words which were passed back and forth. After one heated exchange precipitated a vicious fight between Charlie and Dan that nigh killed both of them, they agreed to go their separate ways.

They divided equally the small amount of gold they had managed to find in that short space of time. Though each share was not great it was sufficient to enable Dan to set out on the trail of vengeance.

The unexpectedness of a hand being placed upon his arm made Dan jump. In that instant he reached for the knife in his belt with the natural instinct of self-preservation, aborting the action on seeing the owner of that hand. From the shadow of a doorway a plump, brassy prostitute smiled up at him in bold invitation.

Dan ran a cursory glance over her body, noting how her fleshy white breasts were barely concealed by the low cut of her bodice. Why not, he thought. Her room would give him somewhere safe to stay out of sight for a while and it had been some time since he last emptied his load. Gone were the days when both the pursuit of sex and indulgence were pastimes of the greatest enjoyment. Such was the single-mindedness of his search for vengeance he now used a woman only when necessary to ease the ache in his balls.

'How much?' he asked.

The prostitute gave a saucy wink. 'That depends. For a strong and handsome cove like yourself it might be less than for some of them what comes looking for a bit.'

'All right. Let's go.' He hustled the woman back inside and was not surprised to find they were in a type of parlour where other women of the same profession awaited their next customers. They all looked him over with interest – too much interest. Dan felt his rod rising, the expansion in his trousers noted by one of the whores with a shrill giggle.

'Looks like you got yourself a big one there, Polly. Sure you can handle him?'

To Dan's immense surprise Polly rounded on the other girl like a spitfire. 'You shut your face, Betty. I can handle any man better than you, you skinny, dried-up bag.'

The insult brought a screech of rage from the other woman who jumped to her feet with a lunge at Polly. Realising a spitting, clawing she-cat fight was imminent Dan hastily propelled Polly through the door leading to the bedrooms. He was anxious to avoid the police, which would not be the case if he became embroiled in a brawl at a brothel.

Within the privacy of one of those rooms, Dan accepted the glass she offered, making only a pretence of drinking the contents while he watched her undress. He was far too cautious to take the risk of the liquor being drugged.

'Aren't you going to undress too?' Polly pouted with practised artifice when she was naked and Dan remained both seated and clothed.

'Why don't you do it for me,' he suggested, rising lazily to his feet.

Polly's hands were eager. First they rapidly removed Dan's coat and shirt, then his boots, leaving till last the revelation of what pushed against his trousers. When that magnificent organ was finally revealed, she sucked in her breath with an avaricious gleam in her eyes.

'Cor, you are a big 'un aren't you?' She curled her fingers around the rigid muscle and the feel of such length and thickness was almost too much. In an instant she was on her back on the bed with her legs spread wide. 'Oh, put it inside me, please. I can't wait to feel it stroking me.'

Dan obliged, his shaft sliding easily into that well-used passage.

'Oh gawd, you're filling me up,' Polly gasped, wriggling her hips and pushing against him in a movement reciprocal to his pumping action. 'Oh, ah, ah. Oh I ain't enjoyed a cock so much in ages. Oooh, bang it into me lover, bang me harder. Ah, yes, yes, ah, yeees!'

Polly's lusty cries could be heard in the parlour where the listeners, each one of them wet between the thighs, exchanged knowing glances and wondered if the bearded stranger could be persuaded to become a regular visitor to their establishment. It was all very well being paid for sex, but their customers rarely gave them such pleasure as Polly was apparently receiving.

As soon as he had satisfied his own need, Dan left the bed and dressed. Still marvelling at the wonderful intensity of her orgasm, Polly shook her head when he reached for his purse. 'Cor, it wouldn't be right to charge you. I reckon with a tool like that women ought to be paying you for the pleasure.'

She raised herself to a half-sitting position, her avid gaze on the now concealed, though greatly desired, portion of his anatomy. 'Will you come back, again?' she begged.

'Maybe,' said Dan, 'maybe not.' He tossed a coin onto the bed. 'You did more for me than you realise. Now is there another way out of here?'

The rear door led to a filthy, cluttered yard behind an inn of questionable respectability. From there Dan found his way back to the street to continue his interrupted journey to the commercial centre of the town.

Although it had taken him several months of following what were often frustratingly false leads, he had traced Ginny as far as Sydney. There he had lost the trail. However he would not, even after three futile months of scouring that bustling town, admit defeat.

With no reason to suspect he was any closer to finding Ginny on this day than on any other day, he was shocked to a standstill on recognising the woman walking along the opposite side of the street. Her attention was directed solely at the man at her side, the topic of their conversation apparent from their mannerisms and expressions.

They were almost abreast of Dan when they turned into a small hotel. Dan permitted himself a small grim smile and settled down to wait until they reappeared. Recalling the black-haired Tessa's insatiable hunger for sex, he imagined he might have to wait for some time.

In that he was not mistaken. So long, in fact, was the wait, he was almost on the point of deciding she must live in the hotel when she emerged, bade goodbye to her lover, and set off at a brisk pace down the street.

Always keeping her in sight, Dan followed at a cautious distance. If Tessa was still in Sydney then it was possible her brother was here as well. Wherever Logan was, Dan was certain he would find Ginny, for he had learnt that the three sailed from Melbourne together.

Tessa's route took them out of the main part of the town into wide residential streets where the more affluent citizens apparently resided. All of the houses were of two or three stories, set in spacious grounds with privacy ensured by high walls and fences. The street they were in wound up a hill and Dan rounded a curve just in time to see Tessa slip through a small gate in one of the walls.

A quick glance up and down the street was sufficient to show Dan there was nowhere he could loiter unobtrusively to see whether or not she came out again. Somehow he doubted she would. Instinct told him this was where Tessa lived. But whose was the house? Had Ginny bought it with the stolen gold?

In one of the bedrooms inside that grand house, Mrs Timothy Wetherby paced angrily up and down her room. Where was her maid? The woman always came to her in the afternoons when the household thought the mistress rested. Jenny never rested – not until after Tessa left her. Her maid gave her what her husband would not, to make bearable the fiasco of her marriage.

Having worked herself into a rage of frustration because her maid had not appeared, Jenny flung herself onto the bed to pummel her pillows with angry fists.

Once that tantrum had satisfied her temper she drew her knees up under her body and reached her own hand down to press it against her aching vulva.

Frantic for satisfaction she slipped her finger into her love hole, rubbing desperately to bring herself to a climax. At the same time she bucked on the bed as though she was in reality banging her wet sheath over a man's hard rod.

When she came, it gave her only a fraction of the pleasure she craved and she curled up on the bed in tearful angry misery. Damn, the woman! Still one to want things to go her way, Jenny had a good mind to have her maid dismissed. That would teach her a lesson in obedience. The trouble was, it would also leave Jenny in a terrible fix.

On the very first night of her marriage Jenny learned her husband had absolutely no interest in women. He told her so, quite bluntly. He also made it very plain that he had married her only to provide him with a facade of respectability. Timothy Wetherby was a vain man and it satisfied his twisted ego to possess a beautiful wife.

He also made it plain there was to be no hint of scandal attached to his name. His own sexual affairs were conducted with the utmost discretion. His wife was to have none at all.

Once Jenny's initial shock wore off, she tossed her blond curls in the privacy of her room with the vow to take, discreetly of course, just as many lovers as she liked. To her intense chagrin and even greater frustration, she soon discovered this would not be so.

Aware of her son's sexual preferences and determined both to protect the family's good name and promote the image of connubial bliss, Jenny's militant mother-in-law chaperoned her as closely as if she were a novice in a convent.

Such was the degree of Jenny's frustration that, the day her new maid set aside the hairbrush to run her hands down over Jenny's breasts, her only reaction was one of pleasure. The woman was watching her reaction in the mirror with a half smile on her lips.

'I know how it is with you, ma'am. Your husband cares only for other men. He takes his lovers as he will and allows you none. He derives a sadistic satisfaction from denying you any sexual pleasure.'

While she spoke, her hands were working over Jenny's breasts, tweaking her nipples into hard peaks of awareness. Within the mirror, her gaze held Jenny's with mesmeric intensity. 'You are enjoying my touch, aren't you, ma'am. I know how to give you almost as much pleasure as you would find with a man. Shall I pleasure you, ma'am.'

A shudder of anticipation shivered through Jenny's body. 'It has been so long and I am desperate for sex.'

'Then come, ma'am. Take off your robe and come to the bed.' If, at first, Jenny felt any strangeness in being undressed and fondled by another woman, it was soon forgotten when she lay naked on the bed with Tessa's tongue licking her intimate parts and teasing her love bud. Jenny came almost immediately for she had been starved of sex too long to be able to withstand such delicately erotic stimulation.

'Was that good?' asked Tessa as she massaged Jenny's love juices into her thighs.

'It was wonderful. Oh, Tessa, suck me some more, please. It has been so long that I want to come again.'

Thus began Jenny's sexual reliance on her maid. No matter how awkward the demands Tessa made, Jenny quickly succumbed. If she prevaricated or refused, Tessa simply withheld herself until Jenny was aching with frustration. Sooner or later Tessa got what she wanted.

Once, when Jenny barely extricated herself from a difficult explanation of how she had come to lose a pearl brooch, she told Tessa she would give her no more. Even before the episode of the brooch, she had needed all her skills in deceit to concoct lies which satisfactorily accounted for overspending her allowance.

On being delivered the ultimatum, Tessa merely smiled and walked out of the room. For days Jenny endured the frustrations of her solitary afternoons, angry because her maid had such power to thwart her. Then, on the night Tessa came to help her dress for a dinner party and spent the time regaling the sulking girl with an account of how she had spent the afternoon with her own lover, Jenny came very close to throwing a tantrum.

'You are talking like that just to upset me. How can I go down and act like a contented wife when I will be looking at every man present and wanting his shaft inside me.'

Tessa shrugged. 'Isn't that what you always do?'

'Well of course I do, but it is not so bad when I know you will help me.'

'I have something which could help you even more.'

The object she produced from a pocket of her dress not only made Jenny gasp in amazement, but it set up a warm tingling in her love place. A feline smile curving her lips, Tessa ran her hand over the carved ivory phallus in a manner which illustrated to Jenny exactly how it could be used.

'Where did you get such a thing,' she gasped.

'I have many interesting acquaintances. Here.' Tessa reached for Jenny's hand to place it on the phallus. 'Feel how perfectly it is shaped, exactly like a man's organ and so very, very hard. Imagine the pleasure you could have with this.'

'Give it to me,' demanded Jenny. 'I would not need you then.'

Tessa shook her head and slipped the fascinating ivory shaft back into her pocket. 'I will not give it to you, ma'am, but I might, for a consideration, allow you to experience its pleasure.'

'What do you want?' sulked Jenny.

'Those diamonds sparkle very prettily in your ears, ma'am.'

Jenny's reaction was one of genuine shock. 'I cannot give you my diamonds.'

'Then I cannot help you. There.' She put the final touches to the dressing of Jenny's hair. 'You look so beautiful, ma'am, that all the men will want you. When they look at you with desire and you feel yourself grow wet in response, think of my ivory shaft.'

How Jenny endured that dinner party she did not know. Her thoughts were totally occupied with the ivory phallus and how it would feel to have it stroking her love passage. True to Tessa's prediction the men did look at her with desire and so great was the degree of her arousal she was certain every one of them could smell the scent of her sex. If not for the watchful eye of her mother-in-law, she would have thrown caution to the winds and slipped out into the garden with at least one of the male guests.

By the time she was able to retire to her room, her need was a terrible ache, which she begged Tessa to ease. The woman ignored the demand, admiring instead the brilliant sparkle of the diamond earrings.

'Oh take them,' snapped Jenny, 'but give me the ivory.'

'Not tonight, ma'am. I must return to my lover. His cock grows easily hard and he is impatient for my return.'

'You talk as if you are the only one who has ever had a good lover. Well, I have had many and I am determined that very soon I will take another. Then I won't need you. In fact I have a good mind to demand you give my earrings back to me.'

'I will give you back your diamonds – if that is what you want. Or, is this what you really want?'

The phallus was in her hand once more. This time she ran it down Jenny's abdomen to press the tip gently between her legs, knowing how the touch would arouse her petulant mistress. 'Do you want your earrings or the pleasure of the ivory.'

'Ooh, give it to me, Tessa.' Jenny's hands reached down in an attempt to take the shaft. Tessa was too quick. The phallus was rapidly placed out of sight as she walked out of the room. 'Tomorrow afternoon, ma'am. You must wait until then.'

So Jenny waited, her state of aroused anticipation rapidly giving way to angry frustration. It was gradually dawning on her just how strong was the hold her maid had over her; all because she was denied sex with a man. There must, Jenny decided miserably, be some way she could take a lover.

When the knock came on her door she hastily reached for her robe. It would not do for her mother-in-law to find her naked and masturbating on the bed. She called a hesitant, 'Come in,' bouncing to her feet in rage when Tessa entered the room.

'Where have you been,' she demanded. 'You gave your promise.'

'I am here, am I not?'

'You're late.' Jenny pouted.

'You must blame my lover, ma'am. His demands were great.'

'Oh, you and your lovers. I always had great lovers too.'

'Then tell me about them, ma'am, while I give you pleasure.'

Jenny did not progress very far with her tales. Naked on the bed she writhed and moaned, slave to the sexual enjoyment she could have only with this other woman. The black-haired, blackmailing maid used her fingers and tongue with devastating expertise, yet never asked Jenny to return the favour. Tessa preferred a man's touch on her sex parts and chose only those victims she could dominate.

On this afternoon she suckled Jenny's breasts, fingering deep into her moist slit and rubbing vigorously at her bud until she was almost ready to come. Deliberately and maliciously she teased and tantalised until the girl was writhing in the agony of denied release.

Tessa held up the ivory phallus. 'Do you want this now?'

'Oh please, please.' Jenny panted.

In a deliberately sadistic action Tessa thrust the ivory so deeply into Jenny's love hole that the girl's entire body arched with the shock. Tears sprang into her eyes and her cry was one of pain; wonderful, wonderful pain.

Tessa worked the shaft with a twisting, thrusting motion that carried Jenny to a long unknown height of sexual ecstasy.

'Have you ever known a man with a shaft so strong and hard?' asked Tessa as she increased the speed with which she manipulated the phallus.

Images of the night, and the man, undoubtedly responsible for her present situation, flitted through Jenny's mind. 'Once,' she gasped.

'Tell me about him.' coaxed Tessa.

'He – I – oh, Tessa, I'm coming, I'm coming! Oh, ooh, oooh! Don't stop Tessa, keep doing it. It feels so like a man, I want more.' Jenny was now jerking her own hips in her frenzy until she felt the second wave of orgasmic contraction. 'Yes!' she cried, 'Yes, yes, yees!'

Tessa withdrew the shaft, the ivory glistening with Jenny's love juices. With a faintly contemptuous smile curling her mouth, she placed the shaft against Jenny's lips. 'It was good, wasn't it, ma'am. Taste how good.'

Jenny's eyes opened wide and she would have spoken a denial except the sticky ivory was pushed into her mouth. Unable to resist, totally in Tessa's power, she tasted the saltiness of her lust.

A few discreet enquiries informed Dan the house in Bayview Crescent belonged to a certain Timothy Wetherby. A few more ascertained that Tessa was not his wife. Not even a man with the most limited vision could describe that dark temptress as fair and petite. Neither was it a description which fitted Ginny. With Tessa,

203

however, lay his one hope of discovering just where that particular jezebel might be.

With that intention he stepped from the shadow of a tree to accost her, when she was far enough from the house not to be observed by any of its occupants. Not expecting her to recognise him he began with a polite, 'Excuse me, ma'am. I wonder if you could help me?'

Tessa, always ready for any opportunity which might lead to interesting sex, gazed provocatively up at him only for her eyes to widen in surprise. 'You!' she declared.

'Do you know me?' Dan queried with understandable caution.

'But of course. Though I imagine you may now be using a different name?'

'Joe Gordon, at your service, Miss Tessa.'

A smile quirked Tessa's mouth. 'And how did you choose that particular name?'

Dan grinned in response, for some reason feeling rather more light-hearted than he had for many a month. 'My father was Joseph and my mother's maiden name was Gordon.'

'I see. It suits you well enough, especially with that beard.'

A rueful smile twisted Dan's lips as his hand fondled the profuse growth of whiskers. 'I thought this disguise enough. How was it that you knew me?'

'Would you expect me to forget a man with such a magnificent tool of pleasure?' she asked with a smile of unmistakable meaning.

Dan's own smile deepened and he, also for the first time in months, found himself anticipating the fun of some romping good sex. 'I have not forgotten your abilities either, Tessa. Is there some place we can go?'

'Of course there is.' She resumed her passage down the street and Dan fell into step beside her.

'Why were you looking for me?' she asked. 'And don't

tell me it was solely for sex, for I do not believe that was even in your mind when you stopped me.'

'You are quite right. I have been looking for Ginny. You remember her?'

Tessa glanced up at him from flashing eyes. 'As if I would forget the bitch.'

The vehemence of the statement took Dan by surprise. 'Do I take it you do not like her?'

'I detest her. She took Logan away from me.'

'Ah! So she is with him still.'

'Unless he has discarded her, then I suppose she is.'

'Do you know where they are?'

'No, I do not.' They had reached the small hotel where Dan first saw her. There she paused to question him. 'Why are you looking for her?'

The bitter expression in Dan's eyes and the harsh, 'Let's just say I've got a score to settle,' satisfied Tessa completely.

A middle-aged, bleary-eyed man at the reception desk glanced casually at them as they passed through the lobby then resumed reading his paper. It became apparent to Dan that the rooms in this hotel were let for one purpose only and that Tessa was a permanent lessee.

The room, too, was furnished for the one purpose with a large bed, wash-stand and mirror the only furnishings. Waiting only long enough to drop her bag on the floor, Tessa reached for the fastening of Dan's trousers. 'I must see whether my memory deceives me or not.'

Dan's trousers were pulled to his knees, his only half-awakened tool hanging forward.

'Ah, yes,' breathed Tessa. 'It is just as big as I remember, though as I recall it was far more eager for action.'

'It'll get there,' promised Dan. 'Especially if you suck it as expertly as I remember.'

Tessa went to work, it needing only the touch of her mouth encompassing his shaft for it to swell to its maximum size. For a while he allowed her to pleasure him with the special delight a man feels only with his tool in a woman's mouth. When her actions became more determined he pulled away. He did not want to come in her mouth yet; not until they were both naked and had satisfied each other in many ways.

Dan had forgotten just how thickly the dark hairs grew on her mound and he parted then impatiently to seek her sex folds with his tongue. But he had not forgotten how she liked a finger worked in the tight hole of her rear passage.

Her lusty cry of approval excited him even more. He twisted his body around, into a position which enabled her to suck him while he frigged her with a finger in each opening. In a sexual frenzy Tessa jerked her body against his fingers. Dan, in turn, worked his own rod in her mouth and, the moment he felt the tightening preceding his release, sucked hard on her love lips so that they both came at once.

'Christ, Tessa – ' he gasped, when they relaxed, head to heel, away from each other. 'You certainly know what it's all about.'

Tessa reached a hand to idly finger his balls. 'Do you want more?' she asked.

An involuntary chuckle escaped Dan's lips and he propped himself on an elbow to look at her. 'Insatiable slut. You'd wear a man out if he let you.'

Tessa smiled back at him. 'I'm not so sure. I rather think that great rod of yours could wear me out. I want it again, but this time I want it inside me.'

Under the expert touch of her hand, Dan's rod was rising to strength again. With a soft, triumphant laugh Tessa moved on top of him, easing her sheath over the hardened muscle. Giving loud animalistic grunts she ground herself down and around so that the head was pressing against her womb and the crisp hairs at the base chafed the soft folds of her sex lips.

Growling his approval Dan permitted the action for a while then rapidly rolled them over, still joined, to pump into her with increasing force as she demanded more and more.

'Will we meet again?' she asked, while they were dressing.

'Why not,' agreed Dan with a grin, 'we satisfy each other well enough.' Very well, as far as Dan was concerned. Neither was seeking any lasting or emotional involvement. Sex, and sex alone, was what drew them to each other.

Tessa reached her arms around his neck to press a lush kiss on his lips. 'I have enjoyed this afternoon so much that I will tell you something which might interest you.'

Dan was immediately alert. 'You know where Ginny is?'

'No, not that one. But my mistress is a certain spoiled young madam who once cried rape when things did not go her way.'

'Good grief! Jenny Townsend?'

'She is Mrs Timothy Wetherby now.'

A soft, and decidedly unpleasant, chuckle left Dan's lips. 'So,' he mused aloud, 'I have at least caught up with that little bitch.'

Chapter Thirteen

*T*essa became a willing conspirator in planning Jenny's downfall. Her own blackmailing activities rendered it unwise for her to remain in any household for too long. Some of her victims rebelled after only a short time. Others, like Jenny, she controlled as easily as if they were puppets whose strings she pulled. However she was becoming tired of that petulant, demanding beauty who, even after parting with so much money and jewellery, had no idea how deeply she was in Tessa's power. The time had come, Tessa decided, to move on to another household and another frustrated, unsuspecting wife.

Many and varied were the ideas they explored then discarded, none appealing to Dan as being just retribution. During one of their discussions, punctuated as usual with various acts of sex, Dan related the means of his escape from the Wattle Creek gaol.

Tessa, who would never fall into such a trap herself no matter how much she wanted a man, was highly amused. Only when she laughingly suggested he should do the same to Jenny were the seeds of their vengeful plan sown. A short time later, Dan – alias Joe Gordon – obtained a position as gardener on the Wetherby estate.

Dan held no fear of being recognised. Only Tessa and Jenny knew him from the past and the latter would be given no opportunity to discover his true identity until he was ready. On the night he took his revenge.

He had not been on the estate more than a week when he realised Jenny was watching him from her bedroom window. Giving no indication he was aware of her he straightened from the garden, flexed his shoulders, rubbed his balls to bring her attention to that part of his anatomy, then resumed weeding.

Jenny did not miss a single action. Though her mouth went dry, her love lips tingled with the wetness of arousal. She was more excited than she had been since the early days of her marriage; before she discovered how determined her husband was that she should have no affairs.

When Jenny first realised she was to be given no opportunity of arranging any secret rendezvous with any of the males of their social acquaintance, she turned her attention to the servants. To her immense chagrin, she discovered there was not a man among them worthy of pursuing. They were either old, simple or totally uncouth. Starved for sex she might be, but there was a certain point at which she drew the line. That being so she could hardly believe her eyes when she looked out of her window and saw the undoubtedly handsome and very, very masculine, new gardener.

At the sound of her door being opened, Jenny turned to call impatiently to her maid. 'Come here, Tessa. Look out there. Who is that man?'

'Why, that is the new gardener, Ma'am.'

'I realise that.' snapped Jenny. 'What is his name.'

'Joe Gordon, Ma'am.'

'Tell me about him, Tessa. What is he like?'

'He is a very good lover.'

'You would know that, of course. Do you ever think of anything but sex?'

'Do you, ma'am?'

'Oh, you are too impertinent. I don't know why I put up with you.'

'That is easily solved. I was intending to give notice anyway.'

Jenny's imperious attitude immediately changed. 'You can't leave me. What would I do without your piece of ivory?'

'Perhaps you should find a lover, ma'am.'

'I wish I could.' Jenny's gaze strayed back to the garden. 'I wonder if it would be possible for him to become my lover.'

'He is only a servant.'

'He is at least a man, and what else am I supposed to do? You will not give me the ivory.'

'It is too precious to part with. Its stimulation, as you know, is unique. Here, ma'am, I am feeling in a generous mood. I will let you pleasure yourself with it today. I wish to spend the afternoon with a lover.'

Jenny clutched at the ivory phallus with a covetous expression in her eyes. Tessa held back, a mocking smile curling her lips. 'You really do need a man. I had a mistress once with a similar problem to yours. She became very clever at showing her guests the library after dinner.'

'Oh,' said Jenny, her mind at once attempting to visualise such activities. 'But that would not be any fun. It would have to be all rushed, without taking any clothes off.'

'I am certain it would be better than nothing,' assured Tessa, relinquishing the phallus. 'Why don't you try it this evening? In the meantime, enjoy the ivory while you can.'

Jenny enjoyed it very much. It was good when Tessa used it on her, when she lay on the bed and imagined it was a man's hard shaft thrusting into her love canal. Now, when she had it to herself, she discovered there were many other ways it could be used. She wanted to watch the gardener while she worked it in her moist passage. She would pretend that it was his shaft which gave her pleasure.

For a while she stood where she could see him, though out of sight of anyone who should chance to look up. With one foot on a chair to open herself out, she rubbed the head of the phallus against her slit until she was almost ready to come. She then straddled the chair, and with one hand holding the ivory shaft upright on the seat, she rode frantically up and down on it to give herself an orgasm so strong the copious flow of juices stained the pale blue velvet of the chair.

So stimulating was the effect that she was still highly aroused when she went down to dinner that night. Her vulva pulsed so strongly with sexual awakening she found it extremely difficult to act the part of dutiful wife and charming hostess she was expected to play. A couple of times she did wriggle on her chair, pressing her thighs together to give herself some relief.

Jenny ate little of the meal. Her hunger was for sex with a man. As the majority of the male guests were either accompanied by their wives or particular friends of her husband, Jenny chose, as the experiment of Tessa's suggestion, a shy young man who always gazed upon her beauty with puppy-like adoration.

Everything went so well that by the time they were walking down the hall to the library, she was almost beside herself with excitement. Once they were alone in that room her plan began to go awry. Jenny, eager though she was for sex, was tempted to play yet again the sweet young thing who was being seduced. That act had the unfortunate effect of reaffirming her companion's belief she was a creature of such feminine perfection he was honoured merely to have the opportunity to be able to put his admiration into words.

This he did at such poetic length Jenny became both impatient and fearful of discovery. 'Perhaps you would like to kiss me,' she suggested, moving closer to him on the couch.

211

'Oh, Mrs Wetherby, I am too lowly a creature to taste the nectar of your lips. Your sweet mouth is as delicate as a newly opened rose bud. I could not soil such beauty with my touch,'

'Rot,' snapped Jenny, deciding he was the most tiresome young man. 'I see I must kiss you.'

Her kiss pressed him back against the couch, the sensual movement of her lips on his mouth and the pressure of her breasts against his chest, turning his pale complexion into a bright red.

The sudden opening of the door created further embarrassment. Like a battleship in black silk, Jenny's mother-in-law sailed into the room with a loud demand to know what was going on. The young couple sprang guiltily apart, the young man stammering a hasty apology before darting from the room like a scared rabbit. Mrs Wetherby senior turned the full force of her indignant wrath on the helpless Jenny.

Her castigation of the girl for such wanton behaviour was more than Jenny could bear. 'What do you expect,' she cried in self-defence, 'when your son is not a normal man.'

'My son was good enough to give you his name and provide you with a grand home and social standing.' Mrs Wetherby senior paused to look scornfully down her aristocratic nose at the girl. 'From what I heard of your past, you should consider yourself fortunate enough to have that. I have no doubt there would have been many willing to take you as a mistress, though not as a soiled wife.'

'Oooh!' Jenny stamped her foot in rage. 'I would far rather be someone's mistress than wife of a – a – '

'That is quite enough,' commanded the older woman. 'You will go to your room immediately.'

Uttering another futile exclamation of rage, Jenny fled, tears of frustration and anger on her cheeks.

Her frustration would have been even greater if she

had known what was going on in the servants quarters at that time.

Dan and Tessa were enjoying an evening of mutually pleasing sex. They paid no heed to the fact that the sounds of their activities could be heard through the wall by the occupant of the adjoining room. Lying awake in her bed and listening, the maid called Bess was becoming both highly aroused and envious. She had no doubt who was in Tessa's room and she lusted after the gardener herself. Very quietly she let herself into the passage and tiptoed up to the door of Tessa's room. The maids' rooms could not be locked and Bess silently opened the door.

Neither man nor woman heard her. The gardener lay on his back with his hands pillowing his head while Tessa knelt by the bed, sucking on his shaft. Bess was not about to let such an opportunity go by. Dropping her nightdress on the floor she hurried across to the bed and, with a minimum of words, straddled Dan's face.

Feeling a trifle bemused, and he had to admit highly aroused, Dan tongued the maid's slit with a thoroughness which brought forth cries of approval. Then the women changed places, and the moment Bess saw the full size of his shaft she was demanding to have it inside her.

Tessa made no objection when Bess slid her sheath over Dan's great rod. She moved to the chair and sat with her legs hooked over the arms so that her sex lips were stretched wide with all their creases and folds visible to the other two. In her hand she held the ivory phallus. The sight of her banging herself with that inanimate object stretched Dan's rod even further. He grasped Bess's hips, working her against his vigorous upwards thrusts. While Tessa brought herself to a climax he pumped hard into Bess until all three were gasping with the heightened thrill of their satisfaction.

* * *

The next day Jenny regaled her maid with her tale of woe. 'It will be even worse than before,' she sighed miserably. 'My door is to be locked each night to make sure I behave.'

'I am sorry, ma'am. It appears you must reconcile yourself to your fate. Unless, of course, you decided to leave your husband.'

'There are times, Tessa, when I am tempted to do just that. But if I did, what would become of me? It is true that he has given me social standing and he has threatened if I ever do anything to create a scandal he will turn me out on the streets.'

'I truly feel sorry for you, ma'am, especially as I will be leaving you next week.'

'I wish you would stay,' Jenny pouted. 'What if I had your wages increased?'

'It would make no difference. Perhaps, though, I might be able to help you before I leave.'

'In what way do you mean?'

'You lust for a man, any man. Look out the window, ma'am. How would you like a night of sex with such a man.'

Jenny looked out of the window and could see Dan working in the garden. 'Oh, Tessa, I dream about what it would be like with him. Is he really a good lover?'

'A very good lover. His shaft is so big and untiring I am worn out long before he is.'

Jenny gave a deep sigh. 'I become all wet and tingly just thinking about him. I want more than anything to have my love place filled with that magnificent shaft you describe.'

'He has noticed you, ma'am, and told me he has an equal desire to fill you with his shaft.'

'Really?' squeaked Jenny, almost beside herself with excitement. Was it really possible she might at last have a lover?

'Yes. However, he knows his place as a servant and would not presume to approach you.'

'Then I must approach him. Oh, Tessa, I am so excited. How can it be arranged.'

'I will think of something, but you must be patient.'

Patience was not Jenny's strong point, especially as Tessa refused to give her any assistance in obtaining sexual gratification. By the end of another week she was in a frenzy of anticipation. Then came the day she awaited.

'It is arranged,' said Tessa. 'He will be waiting for you in the summerhouse tonight.'

Disappointment quelled Jenny's excitement. 'I cannot get out. My door is always locked.'

'I can unlock it, ma'am. Your husband will be busy with his friends for they have, as you know, planned a hunt for tomorrow. I will see to it that you are able both to leave the house and to return unobserved.'

Barely able to control her excitement Jenny pleaded a headache and retired immediately after dinner. Clad only in a robe, her vulva swollen and throbbing with sexual anticipation, she paced nervously around her room, pausing every now and then to peer over the moonlit garden towards the barely visible summerhouse.

It was well after midnight before Tessa came. They crept stealthily down the darkened stairs and through the drawing room to the long window which Tessa silently unlocked. 'Quick now,' she said, giving Jenny a gentle push, 'he has waited impatiently for you to come.'

Jenny ran across the lawn hardly able to believe she was to know again the pleasure of being with a man. It had been so long. She was trembling with nervousness when she reached the summerhouse and saw him there in the shadows.

'I thought you had changed your mind,' he said. 'Come here and let me look at you.'

Jenny quickly undid her robe, allowing it to fall in a pool of silk at her feet. Posed alluringly in the moonlight she could not know the cold rage which surged through Dan as he recalled the last time he had seen her like that.

'Do you think I am beautiful,' she asked.

'Very beautiful.'

'Touch me,' she coaxed. 'Feel how wet and eager I am for love.' She guided Dan's hand between her thighs, exhaling with satisfaction when his finger slipped into her dripping hole. 'Oh, yes. I like that.'

'I like it too,' agreed Dan, lifting her off her feet to lay her on the rug spread in readiness on the floor.

He wasted no time in unnecessary preliminaries. Opening her legs wide, he pushed his rod gently against her slit then eased it part way into her canal. In an action that was almost teasing he pulled part way out and slid it slowly back in again.

'Oooh, yes,' sighed Jenny. 'That feels so good. Is it good for you too?'

Dan laughed then; an ugly mocking laugh. 'It is very good. I have waited a long time for this particular pleasure, Jenny Townsend.'

He thrust savagely into her and if his words had momentarily puzzled her she knew in that action who he was. It was too late. She was held captive by her lust and the weight of Dan's body as he used her far more ruthlessly than before.

'You claimed I raped you,' he panted. 'Well let's make that the truth.'

The sexual gratification Jenny had begun to feel was over-ridden by her fear. Begging forgiveness she cried that she was sorry. Dan neither took notice nor showed pity. Aroused by his anger and the vengeful bitterness he had carried for so long, he used her again and again. One time he withdrew and knelt over her, spraying his semen on her body, anointing her thoroughly with the smell of sex. Sobbing and enraged, climaxes giving her no pleasure, Jenny cursed her own foolishness and gullibility.

When at last Dan's anger was spent, he dragged

himself off her and refastened his trousers. 'You won't cry rape again, little bitch. You'll be too busy explaining to your husband.'

Sniffling back tears of self-pity, Jenny gazed up at him. 'W-what do you m-mean?'

Dan was rolling up her robe. 'You'll soon find out,' he declared. Then he was gone, striding across the lawn with her robe tucked under his arm.

Jenny dragged herself unsteadily to her feet. Shivering slightly from the chill in the air, she wrapped her arms around her naked body. With a shock of pure terror she realised it was almost daylight. Somehow she must get back into the house before anyone was up and about. Halfway across the lawn, she was struck to a standstill at the sight of Dan and Tessa leaving the grounds together. She knew, then, how cleverly she had been tricked.

It was too late. Her husband and his friends were spilling out of the house, ready for their hunt.

Chapter Fourteen

*T*here was not another house in Mackay to compare with the splendour of the one belonging to the Widow Leighton. It was built on a rise overlooking the town with a long gravel drive sweeping up a curve of manicured lawns.

Urns of brilliant flowers flanked the short flight of stone steps which led to the wide verandah. Adorned with white-painted iron-lace railings and trims, the verandah was the most striking feature of that tropical mansion. From the top of the stairs it curved around the pentagonal drawing room, swept both right and left along the front of the building and around the sides to the rear.

From one rear corner another, longer, flight of steps led down into the lush tropical garden which clothed the steeper incline at the back of the house. From there, one could look across many miles of virgin land to the western horizon, where the high peaks of the distant mountains loomed misty, dark and mysterious.

Everything about the house and its setting bespoke wealth; from the well-kept grounds, the grand exterior, the tasteful furnishings to the elegant gown of the woman who sat at a large oak desk putting her signature to a deed of purchase.

Satisfied, she carefully placed the pen back in its stand and looked up at the two gentlemen seated opposite. One reached across for the paper to add his own signature, then he returned the document to her with a nod of approval.

'Congratulations, Mrs Leighton, Plankton is now entirely yours. But tell me. Just what are you intending to do with a cane farm?'

'Make money, of course,' came the cool reply, 'exactly as I have done with all my other properties.'

'Of course,' agreed the solicitor, feeling a trifle foolish at having asked such an unnecessary question. This woman could be said to possess the touch of Midas, so rapidly did her wealth multiply. He was intrigued by her; attracted to her; wished to know her better.

She rose from behind the desk, indicating the meeting was at an end. Both men rose immediately, to take their reluctant leave. They had rather hoped they might be offered refreshments so they would be able to admire for a little longer the graceful perfection of her figure and the unmarred beauty of her face.

'If there is any other way in which I can be of service,' the solicitor offered, leaving the question hanging hopefully in the air. He might just as well have saved his breath. The cool expression in the brown eyes which turned in his direction made him feel that his unspoken suggestion had been a downright impertinence.

'Damned waste,' he commented to his companion when they were in their carriage and on their way back to their respective places of business. 'There is not a man in this town who does not want to take her to bed. If ever a woman was made to please a man, she was, but the merest suggestion one might like to know her better is quashed with that icy disdain.'

'I know what you mean,' sighed the bank manager. He was several years older than the solicitor and married to boot, with a wife and six offspring, yet their existence did not prevent him from indulging in erotic daydreams.

'It is not that she appears to take offence, rather that she views any such suggestion as being presumptuous. I have heard it remarked it is as though she considers there is not a man alive capable of pleasing her.'

The other was in wholehearted agreement. 'I wonder what she would be like to bed.' He spoke both wistfully and wishfully. 'If a man was given the chance to break through that reserve I do not think she would be cool and distant for too long. A woman who looks as she does must know what sexual passion is all about.'

'Perhaps she cared too much for her late husband to want another to take his place.'

Thus went the strain of their conversation, neither aware of just how close they were to the truth.

After they had driven away, Ginny left her study and walked around the verandah. She descended the stairs and followed a path which wound through a lush and colourful tropical shrubbery. Some distance from the house the path ended in a tiny clearing where a rustic wooden seat was conveniently situated beside a small, fern-fringed pool.

Of all the places in the garden where one could sit, this was Ginny's favourite. Here, with the tranquillity of water at her feet, the tuneful songs of the colourful birds which inhabited her garden to bring music to her ears, and the vista of distant mountains to soothe her eyes, she could feel at peace. This was where she always came to ease troubling thoughts, such as the ones which disturbed her now.

Exactly two years and three months had passed since she left Cumberland Downs. From that day on Ginny Leigh ceased to exist. In her place walked Mrs Virginia Leighton, wealthy widow, shrewd businesswoman; beautiful, clever and lonely.

On the morrow she would be 26 years old and the rest of her life stretched like a long and empty tunnel in front of her. True, she was wealthy, far wealthier than she had ever dreamed, but wealth alone could not warm a woman at night nor comfort her in her old age.

In the years since Logan died no man had shared her bed. Logan possessed her as totally in death as he had in life. Even now there were times when she missed him with a pain that was purely physical. Her body might appear outwardly unchanged, yet it was but the shell of the sensual, sexy woman men looked upon with desire. Inside there was no feeling.

Once, about a year after Logan's death, she took a man to her bed hoping to regain the part of herself she had lost. It was the only time; the experiment a terrible fiasco. Certainly it was not the fault of her would-be lover, who was a strong, handsome man well practised in the art of pleasing a woman. Ginny had tried to respond. It was no use. Even the touch of his hands caused her flesh to cringe, and before they were half naked she had sent him away. No man had touched her since.

All her thoughts and energy she put into increasing her wealth. As she suspected so long ago when she sought to buy a staging inn, she possessed a natural talent for business. It was that shrewd acumen which led her north to the tropics. Mackay, surrounded by sugar cane plantations and outlying cattle stations, was a growing town where she bought and sold property with outstanding pecuniary success.

Plankton, her new acquisition, was one of the most prosperous cane farms in the area. High though the price had been, she could well afford it for her two hotels and her block of shops were all providing good returns.

For some reason, on this particular afternoon, Ginny was unable to achieve her customary feeling of peace. The pool was as tranquil as ever, the mountains as misty, the birds both colourful and tuneful. In spite of all, she was unable to banish the restless, disjointed images of her past that were too vivid in her mind. Suddenly, she knew what she would do. She hurried back to the house to call her housekeeper and order her carriage for the morning. Tomorrow was her birthday and she would give herself a treat by visiting her cane farm.

Jack Williams was manager at Plankton; had been for many years. The original owner, preferring the social life of Sydney, had rarely visited the property and left all details of the running in Williams's, capable hands. He had been none too pleased when he heard a woman was thinking of buying the place. There was, therefore, an understandable wariness in the manner in which he welcomed the new owner. On seeing the carriage pull to a halt, he went forward rather reluctantly to greet this woman whom he imagined would be an old dowager. He was even less pleased to discover the Widow Leighton was both young and beautiful. Won't know a damned thing, he thought, and will want to change everything.

Her immediate assurance she wanted both Williams and his wife to remain on the property and continue their lives in the same manner as before made him feel a mite happier. The subsequent flow of pertinent and intelligent questions set him further at ease. In response to her request, he professed himself more than willing to spend what remained of the afternoon with her, riding around some of the fields.

Ginny found it all incredibly fascinating. There were fields that were lying fallow, others where the new cane grew at varying heights and the ones where the mature stalks were over twelve feet high. She listened intently to Williams's explanations of how the cane was planted and the yield each subsequent planting could be expected to give. In the fields of mature cane, harvesting had already begun and they sat upon their horses to watch.

The workers were all dark-skinned men of the South Pacific. The cutting of the cane was hard physical work, exacerbated by the searing heat of the tropical sun. No white man would tolerate working in such conditions

222

but the islanders both could and did. Willingly and unwillingly, they came on three year contracts, leaving their wives and families behind. They worked for a wage so insignificant it made little difference to the cane farmers' profits, yet it enabled them to return to their islands as men of relative wealth.

They worked clad only in loin cloths, the sweat glistening on their dark brown, muscular bodies. There was not a man among them who did not possess a splendid physique. Thick of thigh and strong of arm they worked with a smooth economy of movement that was a delight to watch. There was once a time when the sight of such near-naked manliness would have stirred Ginny's sexual appreciation. All she appreciated now was the deftness and speed with which they worked.

A few of the men glanced up with quick smiles before bending again to the rhythmic movements of their work. Most took little notice of the manager and the unknown woman who rode slowly back and forth along the line. Only when they rode on to another field did one pause in his work to stare hard at the departing woman.

Ginny dined with the Williamses that evening. The rooms of their house still held the heat of the day and, after their meal was complete, they adjourned to the verandah to enjoy the pleasant night air. The beat of drums and then of primitive music throbbed into the stillness of the night.

'What is that?' asked Ginny.

'The Kanakas,' replied Jack Williams, referring to the islanders by the commonly used name. 'They do this from time to time; apparently have a bit of a party. The noise could go on for several hours. It is frequently after midnight before they give it away. Beats me how they find the energy to get up early in the morning and do another hard day's work.' He looked directly at Ginny and there was genuine concern in his voice. 'I hope they do not disturb you, Mrs Leighton. They get a bit drunk and riotous at times. You can stay here with us if you are afraid.'

'Thank you, but I am not afraid,' Ginny assured him. 'I will sleep in my own house.'

'Then I will walk you across when you are ready.'

Less than 50 yards separated the two houses, both of which were moderately large with all rooms opening onto the wide verandahs intrinsic to tropical houses.

Lying in her net-draped bed, Ginny was unable to sleep, though the heat was not completely to blame. The french doors were wide open to admit fresh air. Drifting in with the air came the primitive, throbbing beat of the drums.

It seemed to reverberate against her flesh, finding an answering rhythm in the manner in which the blood pulsed through her veins. There came with it an awareness of the feminine shape of her body and a yearning for the sexual re-awakening of her womanhood. Ginny hooked back the net and slipped off the bed. Out on the verandah, she stood for a time gazing into the night and allowing the sensual message of the music to reach out to her.

A faint orange glow, the light from many fires, lit the sky above the Kanaka village. Built in the style of their island homes, it was less than half a mile away. Curiosity, and something else, propelled Ginny down the stairs and across the fields until she reached the belt of trees surrounding the village. Hidden in the shadows, she gazed in amazement at the scene before her eyes.

She was looking at a clearing in the centre of the group of huts. From the cooking pots near the fires and the utensils lying around, it was apparent there had been a grand feast. It was equally obvious a great deal of alcoholic liquid had been consumed during and after the feast.

Until this moment Ginny had not known there were any women in the village. It was impossible, watching them dance, to tell if they belonged to any man in particular, or were present for the pleasure of all. Both men and women danced to the music of the drums, their bodily movements uninhibited and sexually explicit. The erotism of their dancing sent the blood pulsing faster through Ginny's body as she felt the pull of their earthy message.

The islanders were also becoming highly aroused. One couple rushed from the group and in the shadow of the trees, barely out of sight of the others, they flung themselves to the ground to engage in a frenzied copulation.

Ginny's mouth went dry. She returned her gaze to the dancers in time to see the tallest and most magnificent of all discard his loin cloth to expose his rigid manhood. He appeared so god-like, Ginny sucked in her breath, only to exhale it with a gasp when he seized his partner by the waist and lifted her high to slide her over his shaft. Ginny experienced a quickening deep inside; knew herself highly stimulated as he continued his dance movements with the woman joined to him in that manner.

The night was apparently reaching its climax. In twos and threes, for there were far more men than women, the dancers left the clearing to satisfy their sex lust in whatever manner they would. Unseen by any, Ginny watched it all.

Suddenly, the young giant lifted his partner from his shaft and dragged her into the bushes; straight towards where Ginny stood. Fearful of being discovered, Ginny shrank back against the trunk of the tree, hoping she was concealed by its shadow.

The couple halted only feet away. The man pushed the woman down onto the ground and wasted no time in lowering his body over hers, and driving his great manhood between her open thighs. He did so with such force an involuntary gasp left Ginny's lips.

The man looked up – directly into her eyes. He made no sound, his dark gaze holding her wide-eyed one as he pumped his hard organ into the woman on the ground. Weak-kneed, unable to turn away, Ginny clung to the tree. Her body reacted as though she was the one who was coupled with him, who felt his powerful thrusts.

Deep within her woman's place, her nerve ends tingled with burning awareness. Her breathing became ragged, the pinpricks of flame igniting into a raging inferno, which seared her body in a hot flow. With a shock of disbelief, Ginny realised she was having an orgasm.

A faint smile seemed to curve the man's lips. Only then did he return his attention to his partner, increasing the speed of his thrusts to reach his own climax. Ginny fled.

There was a stitch in her side by the time she reached her house and she doubled up on the step taking several deep breaths to steady herself. The beat of the drums had ceased and there were only the normal night sounds to be heard.

Ginny stood up and slowly went into her room and to bed. Sleep was a long time coming. That night, she knew, marked a momentous change in her life. She felt vibrantly alive, aware once again of her body as an instrument for giving and receiving pleasure. The need to do both began to obsess her. Almost until the hour of dawn she tossed and turned on her bed, for it seemed the drums still beat with the pulse of desire.

The next day Ginny rode alone through the fields. There was no indication of the night's excesses in the energetic manner in which the Kanakas worked. She had not taken much notice of individual workers the previous day, assuming, because they were of a different race, that they would all look the same. Today she realised this was not so.

Without making her inspection too obvious, she studied them carefully, noting how individual their features

226

were. All were powerfully built and good looking. Some could be considered quite handsome.

Very slowly she walked her horse along the line of men. She looked only for one and wondered if she would recognise him. If her heart beat faster than normal, she told herself she only sought to prove the incredible orgasm she experienced was due solely to the earthy beat of the drums and not the strong sexuality of the man.

Some of the workers glanced up at her, others did not. It was very much a repeat of how it had been the previous afternoon when she was escorted by Williams. She was almost at the end of the line when one of the men straightened to look her directly in the eye.

With a lurch of her heart, Ginny brought her horse to a halt. The eye contact lasted only a few moments, yet was sufficient to tell Ginny he was the man she sought. There, in the bright sun of day, with no drums to beat their erotic message, she was forced to acknowledge his compelling sexuality.

Her blood pounded in her veins and it was as though she was naked before his eyes with every secret of her body visible to his dusky gaze. The unspoken message was clear between them. He wanted her and Ginny wanted him; could almost feel his shaft stroking to the depths of her canal. Then he bent again to the cane and the spell was broken.

That evening Ginny again dined with her manager and his wife. On this night the only sounds to be heard were the call of a night bird and the loud chirping of the cicadas. As before, Williams escorted Ginny to her house and bade her goodnight at the door. Instead of going inside, Ginny wandered slowly around the verandah to stare in the direction of the Kanaka village. There, in the dark, she deliberately recalled the events of the previous night and her incredible orgasm.

On an impulse she turned into her room and hastily

227

shed all her clothes. Her hair she loosened to fall in a heavy swathe around her shoulders. The light from the lamp was sufficient to enable her to see her reflection in the mirror. In a purely sensuous action Ginny ran her hands down her body, pleased at its perfection. Her breasts were firm and thrusting, her stomach smooth, her hips gently curved and her legs long and shapely, the small thatch of light-coloured hairs sheilding the delight to be found between them. How many times had she been told it was a body designed to drive men wild with desire? Tonight it was Ginny who was wild with desire for a man – one particular man.

A slight sound brought her spinning around. He stood framed in the doorway; tall, muscular, his thighs almost as thick as Ginny's waist. The brief loin cloth he wore was stretched forward by the rigid muscle of his manhood. With a single deft movement he discarded that garment as he stepped into the room and waited.

Without a word Ginny walked slowly up to him and halted in front of him. She looked into his eyes and he into hers. Large, strong hands gripped her waist and lifted her high to slide her eager, moist sheath over his rampant shaft.

Ginny exhaled her breath in a sigh of pure ecstasy. Never, it seemed, had anything felt so good. She clung with her hands to his shoulders; her legs hooked around his waist. For a time they remained thus, joined together in motionless pleasure. Then his hands slid under her buttocks to lift her again.

Eyes closed, head back, Ginny gave herself up to the fabulous sensations aroused by having her sheath worked up and down over his shaft. She came quickly, crying out with the burning intensity of her climax. It flooded from between her thighs to wet them both. His fingers pressed into her flesh as he held her down hard over his rod, forcing it into the very depths of her contracting womanhood.

Holding her thus, he sank to his knees, proving the

strength and incredible control of his muscles. They were still joined, with her legs hooked around his waist, when he lowered her onto her back on the floor. His thrusts were deep and powerful, awakening from their sleep every one of Ginny's erogenous nerve ends. She slid her own hands beneath her buttocks to lift herself against him and meet him thrust for thrust.

Much later, sated and content, Ginny lay alone in her bed reliving the delights of those hours of wonderful sex. At last it appeared as though Logan's spell had been broken. She would never forget the power of what had been between them, but she could again enjoy sex for no other reason than purely carnal pleasure. As her lids drooped heavily over her eyes and she began to drift off to sleep, Ginny vowed to make up for the lost years; the years when she could bear the touch of no man's hand.

Her Kanaka lover was more than willing to oblige. They never spoke for Ginny knew nothing of his language and he knew little of hers. Words, however, were unnecessary, for they instinctively understood each other's sexual desires. Night after night Badu came to her and their initial couplings were of an almost animalistic urgency.

Only after that frenzied, blood drumming need was satisfied, did they prolong the game of gratification. They thrilled each others bodies in every way imaginable. Badu's tool was a powerful one indeed and his superb control of that magnificent instrument of pleasure almost beyond belief. He could hold an erection for so long that Ginny invariably came two or three times before he allowed himself the satisfaction of his own orgasm.

One night Ginny lay on her back on the floor – they never used the bed – with her knees crooked and her sex place opened wide. Badu knelt between her legs. Twice already she had reached a climax and she caressed her own breasts as Badu stroked a finger along her opening. So unexpected that it was a shock, she felt the hard muscle of his manhood slapped against her vulva. A wildly erotic response flicked through her body. Ginny moaned and closed her eyes, giving herself up to the fabulous sensations that action aroused.

Harder and harder he slapped his rod against her. Little shocks fired into Ginny's love hole with each blow, her panting breaths responding to each slap. When he rubbed the head of his shaft unexpectedly down her slit she cried out loud, wanting it all. He was not, however, ready to give it to her, slapping and teasing her over and over until she felt she must almost go mad from the nigh unbearable state of her arousal and her need for coition. When eventually his rod slid deep between her throbbing sex lips she bucked against him in an almost demented frenzy.

Badu thrilled and stimulated her in the same manner at least once every night. Ginny knew only pleasure. She did not realise Badu performed the act of slapping her sex lips with his manhood as an assertion of his dominance. He was a proud man; a prince among his people. At such times he was the master and Ginny his slave in sex.

How long she would have remained at Plankton if the message had not come from her solicitor she did not know. But the message had come, and after three weeks of sex filled nights Ginny was compelled to return to Mackay. She did not tell Badu of her imminent departure. It did not occur to her that there was any need for him to know.

In the morning she took leave of the Williamses and set out for the town. Her driver did not go past the fields where the men were working and Ginny did not know that Badu watched the carriage depart with an angry glint in his eyes.

Back in Mackay, with her business affairs quickly put to rights, Ginny thought to pursue her renewed joy in sex. That was not to be. She had been, for so long, the cold unapproachable widow that it seemed she could not change. Or perhaps it was that the men who professed to desire her preferred to dream of her as the unattainable perfection rather than risk the disillusionment which sometimes went with possession.

Although she had not intended to do so, Ginny decided to return to Plankton.

For no reason other than what had been before, Ginny expected Badu would come to her on the first night. When he did not her disappointment was edged with anger. He was well aware that she had returned; she had made certain of that.

By morning Ginny's frustration had developed into a haughty determination. She had returned to Plankton solely for the pleasure of sex with Badu and that pleasure she intended to have. As the owner of Plankton, she was mistress of all who worked there. Badu might not be a slave, but the position of all the islanders was so close to slavery as made no difference. Ginny would command Badu to come to her that night. He could not refuse.

It was with that intention she rode out into the fields during the day. Most of the men now greeted her with friendly smiles whenever she rode in the fields to watch them work. Their flashing white grins showed their pleasure at seeing her again. Only one ignored her presence.

Ginny drew her horse to a halt and called him by name. He came slowly erect to glance up at her with insulting indifference before resuming his work on the cane. Any words Ginny might have spoken dried in her mouth. This was not a man to be commanded by a woman. The unspoken message was loud and clear. His pride had been insulted by the manner of her departure. He would not be coming to her house again.

High spots of angry colour were in her cheeks when she wheeled her horse away. Her anger was directed both at Badu for the manner in which he slighted her and at herself for the degree of her need. Sex was what she craved and Badu was only one of the many men who worked on Plankton.

In addition to Williams – who was out of the question – and the Kanaka labourers, there were about a dozen men employed in the crushing mill. It was now in full production with the syrupy smell sickly sweet in the air.

Wrinkling her nose in distaste Ginny wondered how anyone ever became accustomed to that smell for it was almost overpowering inside the mill. This season's sugar yield was high and it pleased Ginny to learn her investment was already returning a good profit. After an hour she left the mill totally satisfied with all she had seen – except the men. Not one had stirred within her even the tiniest flicker of sexual interest. If she wanted sex it appeared she must somehow make her peace with Badu.

When the drums beat their rhythm into the night they again found a response in the way the blood throbbed through Ginny's veins. For a time she sat on her verandah listening – feeling. Every part of her body was aware of the pulse of desire. The deepest place of her womanhood felt vibrant, alive; awakened to a need which must be fulfilled. And fulfilment lay in the beat of the drums. They called her to come to the village. This time she would not hide in the shadows; all would know she was there.

A wild, uncaring wantoness held her in its grip. Ginny left her hair loose and dressed only in a skirt and blouse with not a stitch of clothing underneath. The blouse she left with several buttons undone to reveal the shadow between her breasts. Through the thin material her hard peaked nipples were clearly visible. Ginny was ripe and ready for sex.

The scene at the village was the same as before with the islanders dancing in the flickering light of the fires. There were, Ginny knew, far more men than women in the village and it was with a nervous dryness in her throat she stepped out from the cover of the trees.

At first it appeared that no one had noticed her. There

232

was no pause in the erotic dancing; no faltering in the passionate beat of the drums. She did not know she had been seen until one man appeared suddenly at her side. In his hands was a wooden cup which he offered to her with an encouraging smile.

Ginny smiled in response and accepted the cup. The beverage was faintly bitter and undoubtedly highly alcoholic. When faint memories of another time she had drunk such a brew surfaced she pushed them firmly aside.

A sensual warmth flowed through her veins and she began to sway in time with the music. The tempo of the drums appeared to have increased. Men and women danced with movements of avid sexual suggestion, couples leaving the dancers to complete the act wherever they would.

Dark hands were laid on Ginny's arms, drawing her forward into the firelight, enticing her to dance. Something deep and primitive stirred within her and she began to mimic the movements of the women. Other hands reached to her clothes and soon she was naked. Totally uninhibited she swung her hips to the beat of the drum, her pelvic movements as suggestive as those of the men who surrounded her.

There were no other women still dancing; all were claimed for the night. Ginny knew she could have any one of the men, including Badu, who danced around her. The trouble was Ginny wanted them all.

Badu had scorned her so she would not look at him. All of the men had fully erect manhoods which they jerked towards her in carnal invitation. Ginny reached out to touch the shaft of one who was not much more than a lad.

The response was dramatic. The youth pulled her towards him to slide his shaft between her thighs. He did not seek entry but slid it up and down along her slit to arouse her even more. As though it was some pre-planned ritual, he broke the contact and passed her along to the next man for the act to be repeated. Around the circle she went, being touched and stroked externally by every man until at last she stood in front of Badu.

The drum beats suddenly ceased; the silence more dramatic by contrast.

Breathless, uncertain, Ginny gazed up in to Badu's eyes. There was an arrogance in their expression she had never seen before and she realised then he was a chieftain to his people. No other man would have her unless he turned her aside.

Eternity seemed to pass as they stared at each other. Then Badu lifted her as he had done the first night to fit her on his shaft. This time other hands supported her body and held her legs wide. Badu's arms were raised high in the air as if in a gesture of triumph.

The drums recommenced their beat with a slow, rhythmic thud – thud. In time with each beat, Badu drove into her with his shaft. For Ginny it was the most erotic sex she had ever experienced, supported in the air by men's hands while another thrust his powerful organ into her in a rhythm governed by the beat of the drums; a rhythmic movement which increased in tempo as the drumbeats rose to a crescendo.

It was as unbelievable as a dream; the thudding drumbeats; the hard strength of Badu's organ driving into her; the searing, indescribable ecstasy of her orgasm. Wave after never-ending wave, it flowed through her body, heightened by the frenetic increase in tempo of both the drums and Badu's thrusts. Faster and faster they went until Badu reached his climax.

That, however, was not the finish for the night. When Ginny awoke the next morning she thought she must have been dreaming. The ache in her head and the puffy soreness of her vulva told her otherwise. The night before had given her the most wonderful sexual fantasy she could have hoped to enjoy. Caution told her it would be unwise to seek a repeat.

Chapter Fifteen

*D*an Berrigan lounged on a bench on the shaded verandah of the Royal Hotel. The day was excessively hot, the steaminess so great that his shirt clung damply to his back. He had not been in Mackay for much longer than 36 hours and was not yet accustomed to the enervating humidity of the tropical summer heat. Another man, one of the locals, lounged beside him and from time to time they exchanged some desultory remark.

Dan settled himself more comfortably with his long legs stretched out in front of him and his hat tipped forward to shade his eyes from the glare. He had actually shut his eyes with the intention of catching forty winks when his ears picked up the sounds made by an approaching carriage.

On opening his eyes to see just what type of vehicle was passing down the street he pursed his lips in a long, low whistle of appreciation. The carriage itself was immaculate with shiny black paintwork decorated with gold scrolling but the pair of matched bays which drew it were magnificent beyond compare.

'Ve-ery nice,' he said.

'Sure is,' agreed his companion. 'It belongs to the Widow Leighton.'

'Yeah? I've heard of her; heard she's worth a quid or two.'

'Richest woman in the district. Owns this hotel in fact, plus quite a lot of other property.'

While they spoke the carriage drew abreast of them and passed by. Blinds drawn against the heat and glare hid the occupant from view. Dan stared after the carriage wishing he had been able to see inside.

'What is this Widow Leighton like? Old as the hills I suppose.'

'Crikey no. Reckon she'd be a mite younger than you.'

'Tell me about her. What does she look like?'

The man turned his head to give him a puzzled look. 'Why are you so interested?'

'I just am.' Dan's tone was carefully non-committal. 'What do you know about her?'

For a while the local continued to puzzle over the reasons for the stranger's questions before giving a metaphorical shrug of his shoulders. It was none of his business anyway. 'Like I said,' he continued, 'she's young and she's also beautiful.'

'What colour is her hair?'

'Sort of golden brown, I reckon. I've never been real close to her so I can't describe her better than that. But she sure is one good looking woman.'

'Where did she come from?'

'No one seems to know where she came from or even how she got to be so rich. Some reckon she must have been married to some rich old codger who conveniently died and left her the lot. It is well known she already had a stack of money before she arrived here a couple of years ago.'

Dan made no reply as he watched the carriage disappear from sight at the far end of the street. Neither was there any need to ask other questions. The man had confirmed that the widow was young and beautiful and if the source of her wealth was a mystery to the town's residents it was no mystery to Dan. If asked, he could have told them exactly from where it had come.

With an abruptness of movement which took his companion by surprise, Dan heaved himself to his feet and strode off down the street. He needed to think and wanted no interruptions. There was certain to be some place cooler down by the river where he could be alone.

Now that he had confirmation his journey north to Mackay had not been another wild goose chase, he was uncertain what action to take next. The trail which had led him to Ginny had been long and difficult. At times it had been one of terrible misery and great personal deprivation.

He had left Sydney immediately upon taking his revenge on Jenny Townsend, deeming the move to be prudent. Tessa had told him all she knew of her brother's plans and tracing Logan and Ginny to Cumberland Downs had been relatively easy. From there the trail became extremely difficult to follow. No one knew where Ginny had gone when she left.

Eventually, after hundreds of miles of travel and following numerous false leads, he came to Queensland. It was at a hotel in the capital that he first heard mention of the Widow Leighton. The man who spoke was a pastoralist from Mackay on a visit to Brisbane. Dan took little notice of what was being said until he heard the woman's full name.

'Virginia Leighton?' he had repeated. 'Spelt L-A-Y-T-O-N, I presume?'

'No, I believe it is L-E-I-G-H-T-O-N.'

Even then Dan had not allowed himself to become too excited or been overly optimistic. The similarity of names might just be a coincidence, the possibility it was, not sufficient to induce him to book his passage on the next boat going north.

So here he was in Mackay, caught up with Ginny after all this time. Now he must figure out the most devastating manner in which to take his revenge. And revenged he was determined to be. Ginny had betrayed him to the police, stolen his gold and lived in luxury while he battled his way around the country with little more than the shirt on his back and frequently no food in his stomach. There had been times when he was so destitute and wretched that the conviction he would one day find her was all that kept him going.

Ginny had wronged him in so many ways he nurtured an almost manic intent to hurt her as deeply as possible. Dan wanted to see her crushed; to take all her wealth away. The malevolence he felt towards Ginny was a hundred times greater than the rancour he harboured against Jenny Townsend.

A grim recollection of that act of vengeance impinged on his thoughts and he wondered if the conniving little bitch had managed to explain her way out of that predicament.

There was no way Dan could know just how dramatic the results of his night's work had been.

Timothy Wetherby, his pale effeminate face turned bright scarlet with embarrassment and fury, sought no explanation. He hastily wrapped his coat around his naked wife and hustled her indoors out of sight of his companions, every one of whom was agog with lewd curiosity. Wrinkling his nose in distaste at the strong sex odour given off by her soiled body, he called loudly for his mother.

Truly terrified, Jenny fully expected either to be beaten or thrown into the streets – perhaps both. The Wetherbys did neither. Nor did they ask the quivering, tearful girl for any explanations; their horrified imaginations provided ones vivid enough.

From that day on Jenny became a prisoner in her room, kept secluded from contact with others. Timothy Wetherby's friends and acquaintances offered him their deepest sympathy, commiserating with him because his beautiful wife had been discovered to be mentally unstable.

Indeed there were many times in the long year that followed when Jenny believed she really would become insane. Iron rods barred her window and a heavy lock secured her door. The middle-aged, taciturn servant who replaced Tessa possessed all the unpleasant attributes of a gaoler. Although Jenny did not know it, the woman had, in fact, been employed because of her experience in dealing with the mentally disturbed. Nothing even faintly resembling a smile ever touched the woman's harsh features and in her dour presence the poor girl became completely intimidated.

The few times when Jenny was permitted to leave her room to go downstairs or to take a walk in the garden the woman was close to her side. Not that Jenny was capable of taking advantage of her brief freedom to run away. On each occasion she was suitably sedated before she was allowed from her room.

This was the punitive wretchedness of Jenny's existence until the day Timothy Wetherby was thrown from his horse and broke his neck. His body was carried home and when it had been laid out, his coffin was placed in the parlour. Jenny, brought from her room to view his lifeless body, felt no emotion at all. While his mother grieved loudly and the servants filed past to pay their respects, Jenny walked sedately from the parlour, out of the front door, and fled.

Jenny was mingling with the crowds in the busiest part of the town before she began to worry about just where she was going to go. Her initial euphoria over the ease with which she had made her escape rapidly faded to an apprehensive state of mind. For the rest of the day she might be able to wander through the streets without arousing comment. But what would happen to her with the coming of the night?

For some time she roamed aimlessly up and down and in and out of different shops. Her anxiety increased so greatly with every minute which ticked by that, when she saw her former maid coming along the street, she hurried eagerly towards her. So pleased was she to see someone she knew, Jenny gave no thought to the part the woman had played in causing her misery. Neither did she pause to wonder at the dramatic change of the maid's appearance.

Tessa no longer wore the plain garb of a servant. Her mauve silk gown was of the latest fashion; her dark hair dressed in a stylish mode and topped by a ridiculous and patently expensive concoction of purple net and blue feathers which passed for a hat. Everything about her manner of dress gave the impression of a woman well able to afford the very best.

Recognising Jenny as she hurried towards her, Tessa was the one who received the greater surprise. Naturally she had learnt of the aftermath of that night. Although she had always held the spoilt little beauty in contempt and laughed with Dan over the success of their devious plan, she knew the punishment had been excessively harsh. In her own way she felt a little sorry for the girl who, after all, had been caught by her craving for sex. Even if that was something of which Tessa had taken advantage, it was also something which she understood.

'I am so relieved to see you,' Jenny cried now. 'Oh, Tessa, I need your help. I have nowhere to go and I am becoming afraid.'

The wan-faced girl did indeed appear to be on the verge of a nervous collapse. Tessa was surprised to discover in herself feelings of compassion. 'Are you alone?' she asked.

'Yes. I have run away and I do not have any money or even any clothes.'

'What of your husband?'

'He is dead.' Jenny's voice was shrill. Tears flowed into her eyes and she began to laugh in hiccuping giggles. 'He is dead – dead.'

Recognising the signs of approaching hysteria, Tessa

placed a comforting arm around the younger girl's shoulders. 'It is all right,' she soothed. 'You must come home with me. I have a spare room where you can stay.'

Jenny was far too relieved to wonder at Tessa's apparent change of circumstance. A cab was hailed to carry them to an elegant, narrow-fronted, three-storied town house where they were admitted by a liveried servant.

'Do you like it?' asked Tessa leading the way into a tastefully furnished parlour.

'It is very lovely,' Jenny agreed. 'But how can this be your house? I do not understand.'

'Don't you?' smiled Tessa. 'It was for this that I was saving. My house is the most exclusive establishment of its kind in Sydney. I have two girls from high class backgrounds who live here and work for me but there is place for another.'

Jenny's eyes were like blue saucers in the pale oval of her face. 'Do you mean this house is a brothel?'

Tessa's lips quirked in disapproval. 'I do not like to hear that word used. It suggests something low class and sleazy, which my establishment very definitely is not. Only the most refined of gentlemen gain entry here; ones who are willing to pay handsomely for a pleasant evening dining with, and being entertained by, beautiful, intelligent women who understand the varied pleasures of sex.'

She paused for a while to allow that information to be absorbed before she continued. 'What do you think, Jenny? You have always enjoyed sex and you possess the delicate type of beauty which appeals to many men.'

'I do not know.' Jenny was hesitant. Everything was too new and too strange. She had not yet accustomed herself to the fact she was free.

'Think about it,' suggested Tessa. 'There is no hurry, you may stay here as long as you like. In the meantime we will order you some new clothes and see the roses put back in your cheeks.'

'Oh, Tessa, you are being so kind.'

'Perhaps I am only being fair. I did, after all, take many of your jewels with me when I left.'

Jenny entertained her first client just three nights later. Over dinner and wine she played to perfection her role of a demure young virgin who was reluctantly allowing herself to be seduced. The act, which titillated and increased her gentleman's libido to a marvellous degree, continued in the bedroom right up until she was fully undressed and his hands were caressing her intimate places. Only then did she give rein to her sexual appetites with a wantoness which thrilled them both. And at some stage during that evening of unparalleled carnal pleasure, it dawned on Jenny that she had found her niche in life.

As was her custom in the mornings Ginny was seated at her desk going through her accounts. A little over a week had passed since her return from Plankton; a week during which her fantasy night of sex assumed an even greater aura of unreality. Dream-like though her recollection might be, she knew those things had indeed happened – and must never happen again. From now on Plankton would be left entirely in Williams's capable hands. Ginny would not be visiting there any more. At least not before Badu and his men returned to their islands.

She had paused in her work to consider again her need to find a lover among her own kind when her housekeeper knocked on the door and entered the room in a visible state of agitation.

'Whatever is the matter, Mrs Brown?' Ginny asked in concern, for the woman was a treasure of unflappable efficiency.

'There is a man outside, ma'am. Very insistent on seeing you he is, but I don't like the look of him.'

'Did he say why he wanted to see me or give you his name?'

242

'No, ma'am. He – ' Her words broke off as the door was pushed open behind her.

'I am quite certain, Mrs Brown, there is absolutely no need to give your mistress my name.'

Ginny felt the colour drain from her face and if she had not been already seated, she believed she would have fallen down. Her hands gripped the edge of the desk so hard her knuckles showed white beneath the skin. The housekeeper was flustering with indignation at the rudeness of the man's behaviour.

'It is all right, Mrs Brown,' Ginny spoke quietly 'you may go.'

Ginny took no notice of her housekeeper's puzzled departure for her eyes saw only the man. He had changed, and the change was not due solely to the beard he wore. There was a leanness to his body, an unforgiving hardness about his stance. The laughing light which once lit his eyes had been replaced with a bitter cynicism. Gone was the carefree boyishness she had loved.

Very slowly, her hands still on the desk to steady her, Ginny rose to her feet. 'Hello, Dan,' she said.

A dark brow arched upwards and his lips twisted in derision.

'Hello, Dan?' he mimicked. 'Is that all you can say?'

'I am surprised to see you.'

'I bet you are.' He came fully into the room and stood gazing around. The bitter twist to his lips became more pronounced. Very slowly he walked around the room, picking up objects to examine them, assessing with increasing bitterness the value of everything. Ginny watched him in trembling silence.

Returning a Dresden figurine to its place on a small table, he turned to look at her. 'You have done well for yourself, haven't you?'

Ginny flinched at the mocking acrimony in his voice. 'It was my gold too, Dan. After all, I was the one who found it.'

'True,' he acceded. 'I would not have minded if you

243

had taken only your share, but you took the lot; money, jewels, every damned thing.'

'What else did you expect me to do,' Ginny flared in self defence, 'after the way Charlie and Josh treated me?'

Dan's brows rose in contemptuous disbelief. 'From what I heard you were more than willing to have sex with both of them.'

The emphasis he placed on his words brought an uncomfortable flush to Ginny's face. 'That was later, after they had made me drink that brew. But Charlie tried to rape me first.'

For a long moment Dan stared hard at her, at the tautness of her expression, experiencing emotions that were both unexpected and unwelcome, 'Yes,' he agreed at last. 'I rather thought he had.'

He said nothing else for so long that the silence between them stretched Ginny's nerves. 'Dan, I – ' she began.

'Yes?' encouraged Dan when she faltered. 'I am waiting for your explanation.'

'Explanation of what? I told you why I took the gold.'

'You have not yet told me why you betrayed me to the police.'

'I never did!' cried Ginny in distressed denial.

'No? For Christ sake don't lie to me!' In an explosion of temper Dan slammed his fist so hard on the little table at his side that the figurine toppled to the floor and shattered. Neither of them took any notice.

Dan strode across the room until he was opposite her. With his hands on the desk he leant menacingly across to bring his face close. 'Don't lie to me, Ginny,' he repeated. 'You not only helped Ferguson set his trap you could hardly wait until I was in gaol to get your clothes off and start humping with him. Isn't that so, you damned conniving bitch?'

Ginny sat down abruptly. There was a terrible pain somewhere deep inside, a pain that wrenched her stomach and placed a constricting band around her heart. Uttering a tiny sob she buried her face in her hands, unable to bear what she saw in Dan's eyes.

Dan walked around the desk to pull her to her feet and drag her hands from her face. 'Tears will do you no good, Ginny.'

He was so close to her that their bodies were almost touching, his hands warm upon hers. Ginny gazed up at him; saw the expression in his eyes begin to change. The small space between them became charged with the emotiveness of remembrance. It was as though they kissed without their lips touching.

Dan was the one to break away and move to put distance between them. Ginny made no attempt to follow, sensing his regret of that intensely intimate moment.

'I did not betray you Dan,' she said quietly. 'Ferguson used me – completely. He promised to set you free, then would not. I went back to the hut with the intention of fetching Charlie and Josh to help.'

'They also thought you had betrayed me.'

'I know.'

Silence once more stretched between them. This time it held a different air. Dan spoke softly, his words edged with recrimination.

'I thought there was something special between us, Ginny.'

Ginny's reply was equally soft. 'It was you who sent me away.'

'After you had made your choice. Logan came and you went to him. Remember?' The bitterness returned to his expression. 'Maybe you did not betray me to the police, but you left me in gaol to go away with Logan. Did he mean so very much more to you?'

He saw the shadows of grief and pain in her eyes and felt an unwelcome stab of jealousy.

'Logan is dead,' she said.

'I know,' Dan replied quietly. 'I have no right to

question your feelings but I would like to know why he was the one.'

Ginny sighed deeply, setting aside her own pain. 'I cannot explain Logan to you, Dan. Please don't ask me to try. I, too, believed there was something special between you and I, but what bound me to Logan was too strong to deny.'

There was nothing in Dan's expression to tell her how deeply he was affected by her words. His steady regard held no hint of his inner turmoil; of the rush of jealousy which brought with it an unwelcome acknowledgement of how much he still cared.

'Why did you come here, Dan?' she asked.

'I came to find you, to take back what you owe me.'

'How much do you want?'

Dan's laugh was one of derision. 'Do you think you might write me a cheque so that I will go away and leave you to share this luxury with whatever lovers you have now. How many lovers do you have, Ginny?' he asked with an abrupt change of tone.

'None,' replied Ginny, though her teeth bit at her lip. What would Dan think of her if he knew with exactly how many dark-skinned lovers she had taken her pleasure the other night.

'Liar,' he stated, though he did not press the point. 'No, Ginny, I intend to share in all your good fortune. Your house will also be mine.'

'Do you mean you intend to live here?'

'That is precisely what I mean.'

Ginny's heart beat a little faster. 'What about your things?'

'All my worldly possessions are in a small bag which I left on your doorstep.'

If the rancour of his tone made Ginny inwardly flinch she gave no outward sign. Dan had come back into her life and she had no intention of allowing him to go out of it again. Dan might want retribution; Ginny simply wanted him.

'Very well. I will inform Mrs Brown. Perhaps you would like to see the rest of the house and the garden before lunch.'

Ginny took him on a guided tour and as he walked through the elegant rooms of that beautiful house his anger and bitterness increased tenfold. To think she had enjoyed all this while he had dodged the law, living at times a life little better than an animal. When he looked at the luxury of her bedroom he recalled the many times when wet or cold and sometimes both, he had slept under a bush or in a deserted hut. Following Ginny down the flight of stairs into the tropical garden, Dan again vowed to turn the tables and take everything for his own.

They reached Ginny's favourite place near the tranquil pool and she smiled up at him. 'What do you think of this? I like to sit here and look out at the mountains and listen to the birds. It is lovely, isn't it?'

'Very,' agreed Dan, barely able to force the word past the constriction of emotion in his throat. How could she stand there looking so proud, so serene and, confound her traitorous heart, so utterly desirable.

'Come,' she said. 'There is another place I want to show you.'

Ginny led the way back a short distance to turn into another more natural path which led deep into the virgin bush. After some distance it began to follow a tiny, gurgling stream and she halted when they reached a place where the clear water tumbled over some rocks in a series of small rapids before spreading into a deeper pool.

'Does this remind you of anything?' she asked.

Dan stared at the pool forcibly reminded, as she had intended he should be, of the first time they met. There was a sickened feeling in his gut. Why should he be remembering how wonderful it was between them when he had spent the past few years nurturing his hatred.

When he turned his gaze to her he saw she was

regarding him with desire in her eyes. Well she could desire as much as she liked. She had turned from him and now he would enjoy spurning her. This would just be the beginning of his revenge. When Ginny stepped towards him he grabbed her wrists to hold her off.

He knew instantly it had been a mistake to touch her, to allow her to come near enough for her special aura of sexuality to tease his senses. Against his will his arms closed around her and his mouth sought her lips. They kissed with the hunger of long-parted lovers, igniting a wild passion of mutual desire.

It was as though they had never been apart, their bodies succumbing to the urgent joy of their coupling. When Dan lay heavily upon her with his breath coming in ragged gasps Ginny held him in a close embrace enjoying the feel of his quiescent shaft within her love canal.

'Do you remember', she whispered in his ear, 'how we washed each other in the pool? Shall we do that again?'

Dan propped himself on his hands to look down at her, moving his shaft in a manner which made her wriggle in delight beneath him. 'You are a seductive witch, Ginny, do you know that. I never intended this to happen.'

'Liar,' she laughed softly, mocking his earlier statement. 'Why else did you want to stay?' She gave another little laugh of triumph. 'I can feel you growing hard again already.'

Indeed his manhood was rapidly regaining full rigidity and the nerves of her womanhood pulsed in response.

'Oh Dan, Dan,' she cried, lifting her knees high to open herself wide and gripping his buttocks to pull him deeper within. His lips sought hers, crushing them in a passionate kiss as their bodies thrust wildly against each other to carry them to another peak of mutual sexual pleasure.

* * *

Rumours very quickly began to circulate around the town about the strange man who was living at the home of, and no doubt with, the beautiful Widow Leighton. There was a great degree of lewdly envious speculation among the male populace which suggested the stranger might be screwing his way to her fortune. Ginny's solicitor, who had his own interests to protect as well as those of his client, sought to investigate.

This he did with a bluntness of manner which aroused her indignation and brought forth her haughtiest and most dismissive demeanour.

'My personal affairs, Mr Webb, are no concern of yours. My *business* affairs are. I trust there is no reason for me to find your management of those unsatisfactory.'

Although she had put the presumptuous solicitor firmly in his place, it bothered Ginny to know people were talking about them. Her concern was neither for herself nor her reputation; it was entirely for Dan. Ginny knew Dan had escaped from gaol, though not the full details of how. At first she demanded to be told but now she no longer asked. There were certain events of their years apart which she realised he would never disclose. It was sufficient to have him sharing her home, even if he could not openly share her life. The reasons why he could not worried her, and she spoke of her fear that evening.

Dan lay on his back on the bed with his hands pillowing his head watching Ginny undress. He enjoyed seeing each garment come off to reveal more and more of her delightful body. Sometimes, knowing how greatly the sight of her undressing aroused him, she would tease him with a seductive act. This night her mind was apparently too preoccupied for her actions were mechanical.

'People are talking about you, Dan. I do not think there is a person in town who does not know you are here.'

'Are you bothered by what people think.'

'I am quite certain gossip has correctly assigned you the role of my lover, and that does not worry me in the least. But people are wondering who you really are.'

'There is no way anyone can find out. Is there?' he questioned, regarding her intently.

'I would not betray you, Dan. I never betrayed you before. I thought you believed me.'

'Perhaps I do,' he said, unwilling to admit to either of them how much his thoughts and feelings had changed. 'Why are you so concerned by a bit of gossip?'

'The police must have heard the gossip and I am terrified they will discover the truth. I could not bear it if you were arrested and taken away.'

'Are you trying to tell me that you really care?'

'Care? Oh, Dan, I love you. Haven't you realised that?'

Dan gave no indication of the triumphant satisfaction he received on hearing her utter those words. His lips curved into an easy smile. 'If I am to believe you love me, then you had better come to bed and prove it.'

Ginny removed the last of her garments and walked across to the bed. Dan's manhood already jutted stiffly from his prone body. A teasing smile touched her lips as she regarded its magnificence. With a knee resting on the edge of the bed Ginny leant forward to flick her tongue over the tip of her lover's shaft before encompassing it with her lips.

A shock of surprised delight coursed through Dan's body.

Ginny had never willingly performed such an act with him before. She sucked him with an expertise which aroused a flare of bitter jealousy. Just where had she learnt to pleasure a man so well?

Finding that speculation far too disturbing he pulled her away and turned her on the bed so that his own tongue could seek the sweetness of her slit. He used it to arouse her as intensely as she aroused him with her little moans of delight and in the manner in which she cried his name. Desire far stronger than any he had ever felt before surged through his body. Desire and something else to which he refused to give a name.

When he felt her approaching her climax he heaved his body over hers and thrust deeply into her, mindless of anything but the need for possession. He pushed his shaft so completely into her womanhood that her fingers dug into his back and she cried aloud with the excess of passion. His lips captured hers in a brief, hard kiss.

Over and over Dan thrust into her, revelling in the warm, silky feel of her sheath which fitted so perfectly around his shaft. He wanted her with a desperation of intensity he had never experienced before, pumping into her as if he could never have enough, as if he must savour to the full what he intended to turn aside.

Later, when Ginny lay asleep in his arms, Dan stared into the darkness, dragging up memories of the past to steel himself for what he had long ago vowed to do. In the morning he asked her to marry him.

The expression of absolute joy on Ginny's face and the manner in which she flew into his arms almost unnerved him. She kissed him in delight before the shine dimmed in her eyes.

'How can we marry, when you are on the run from the law?'

'Money is a powerful silencer, even for a man of the cloth. I want you for my own; my wife, not my mistress. We will be properly married in a church, Ginny, using our real names. Though none but the priest and witnesses will know.'

A week later Ginny became Dan's wife. When the gold band slid on to her finger happiness surged through her and she smiled at her new husband with all her love in her eyes.

'Happy?' Dan asked when they were returning home.

'I am the happiest woman alive.' She gave a little laugh and snuggled up to him to emphasise the declaration.

Dan turned away from the joyous expression on her

face and his own inner discomfort. He should be totally satisfied. The deeper her love the more devastating would be his revenge.

That night in bed he turned his back on her and Ginny endured the bewildering frustration of having her sexual advances spurned. The next night was the same and through sleepless hours of darkness, Ginny began to realise something was wrong. When she would have demanded an explanation by light of day it was to discover he had risen before her and again gone into town.

Dan did not return until late in the afternoon when he found her arranging a bowl of flowers in the drawing room. He ignored her tight-lipped query as to where he had been.

'You love this house, don't you, Ginny.'

'Of course I do.'

'Then I suggest you enjoy living in it while you still can.' Ginny looked fully at him; at the hard, tense set of his features. Perplexity creased her brow. 'I do not understand.'

'You would if you thought about it. It is very simple, really. From the day you betrayed me I was determined to have my revenge. You fell so easily into my plan.'

'Exactly what was that plan?' Ginny spoke with a quiet preciseness necessary to keep her voice steady. 'Have the past two nights been part of it?'

'They have. You betrayed me, spurned me and stole my gold. I hated you, Ginny, and every night I spent cold and hungry I hated you a little more. I wanted you to suffer the way I suffered, to experience the pain and despair. I did not know how I was going to do that until I saw you again. You gave me the answer yourself when you revealed how much you wanted me.'

'Didn't you want me?'

Dan ignored the truth behind her query. 'I wanted you to fall in love with me, to agree to marry me. You see, my dear, now that I am your husband all your possessions are legally mine. There is, as you are aware, a price on my head and I have no desire to go back to gaol. On my instructions every one of your properties has been put up for sale.'

All colour had drained from Ginny's face while he spoke but she would not give him the satisfaction of seeing her pain. 'Why is it necessary for everything to be sold. I willingly share it all with you.'

'But I have no intention of sharing it with you. The bank has already given me an advance against the proceeds of sale. Tomorrow I leave for Brisbane and from there will take passage to New Zealand. In that country, where no one has heard of Dan Berrigan, I will be able to start my life anew.'

'I see.' The words were spoken so softly he barely heard them. Ginny turned away from him to stare out of the window. Dan watched her, suddenly uncertain of himself. He had spent the day working himself into a cold rage to gain the courage to confront her and she had not reacted as he expected. He had thought she would become angry and protest, to cry and to beg. He especially wanted to hear her beg. Her silence perplexed him and he wished he could know what thoughts were going through her head.

He would have been surprised if he could have seen the expression on her face, for it held more cunning than pain. Of the many thoughts which tumbled chaotically through her mind two were uppermost; the knowledge a new life grew within her womb and a determination her child would know its father's love.

'You don't say anything,' Dan prompted.

Ginny turned slowly around to face him with a faint provocative smile tilting her lips. Her fingers were already unfastening the buttons of her gown.

'What is there to say?' she asked as her bodice parted to reveal the swell of her breasts. 'I think, dear husband, that living in New Zealand will be very nice.'

BLACK
lace

NO LADY – Saskia Hope
ISBN 0 352 32857 6

WEB OF DESIRE – Sophie Danson
ISBN 0 352 32856 8

BLUE HOTEL – Cherri Pickford
ISBN 0 352 32858 4

CASSANDRA'S CONFLICT – Fredrica Alleyn
ISBN 0 352 32859 2

THE CAPTIVE FLESH – Cleo Cordell
ISBN 0 352 32872 X

PLEASURE HUNT – Sophie Danson
ISBN 0 352 32880 0

OUTLANDIA – Georgia Angelis
ISBN 0 352 32883 5

BLACK ORCHID – Roxanne Carr
ISBN 0 352 32888 6

ODALISQUE – Fleur Reynolds
ISBN 0 352 32887 8

OUTLAW LOVER – Saskia Hope
ISBN 0 352 32909 2

THE SENSES BEJEWELLED – Cleo Cordell
ISBN 0 352 32904 1

GEMINI HEAT – Portia Da Costa
ISBN 0 352 32912 2

THE HOUSE IN NEW ORLEANS – Fleur Reynolds
ISBN 0 352 32951 3

ELENA'S CONQUEST – Lisette Allen
ISBN 0 352 32950 5

CASSANDRA'S CHATEAU – Fredrica Alleyn
ISBN 0 352 32955 6

WICKED WORK – Pamela Kyle
ISBN 0 352 32958 0

DREAM LOVER – Katrina Vincenzi
ISBN 0 352 32956 4

PATH OF THE TIGER – Cleo Cordell
ISBN 0 352 32959 9

BELLA'S BLADE – Georgia Angelis
ISBN 0 352 32965 3

THE DEVIL AND THE DEEP BLUE SEA – Cheryl
Mildenhall
ISBN 0 352 32966 1

WESTERN STAR – Roxanne Carr
ISBN 0 352 32969 6

A PRIVATE COLLECTION – Sarah Fisher
ISBN 0 352 32970 X

NICOLE'S REVENGE – Lisette Allen
ISBN 0 352 32984 X

UNFINISHED BUSINESS – Sarah Hope-Walker
ISBN 0 352 32983 1

CRIMSON BUCCANEER – Cleo Cordell
ISBN 0 352 32987 4

Published in November

JEWEL OF XANADU
Roxanne Carr

In the land of the Tartar warriors lies the pleasure palace of the Kublai Khan. But Cirina has grown up knowing only the harsh life of the caravanserai. When she is captured and taken to the palace, she meets Venetian artist Antonio Balleri, who is making his way across the Gobi desert to reclaim a priceless Byzantine jewel. Together, they embark on an erotically-charged mission to recover the jewel together.

ISBN 0 352 33037 6

RUDE AWAKENING
Pamela Kyle

Alison is a control freak. She loves giving orders to her wealthy, masochistic husband and spending her time shopping and relaxing. But when she and her friend Belinda are kidnapped and held to ransom in less than salubrious surroundings, they have to come to terms with their most secret selves and draw on reserves of inner strength and cunning.

ISBN 0 352 33036 8

Published in December

GOLD FEVER
Louisa Francis

The Australian outback is a harsh place by anyone's judgement. But in the 1860s, things were especially tough for women. The feisty Ginny Leigh is caught in a stifling marriage and yearns for fun and adventure. Dan Berrigan is on the run, accused of a crime he didn't commit. When they meet up in Wattle Creek, their lust for each other is immediate. There's gold in the hills and their happiness seems certain. But can Ginny outwit those determined to ruin her with scandal?

ISBN 0 352 33043 0

EYE OF THE STORM
Georgina Brown

Antonia thought she was in a long-term relationship with a globe-trotting bachelor. She was not. His wife told her so. Seething with anger, Toni decides to run away to sea. She gets a job on a yacht but her new employers turn out to be far from normal. The owner of the craft is in a constant state of bitter rivalry with his half-brother and the arrival of their outrageous mother throws everyone into a spin. But the one thing they all have in common is a love of bizarre sex.

ISBN 0 352 330044 9

To be published in January

WHITE ROSE ENSNARED
Juliet Hastings

When the elderly Lionel, Lord de Verney, is killed in battle, his beautiful widow Rosamund finds herself at the mercy of Sir Ralph Aycliffe, a dark knight, who will stop at nothing to humiliate her and seize her property. Set against the Wars of the Roses, only the young squire Geoffrey Lymington will risk all he owns to save the woman he has loved for a single night. Who will prevail in the struggle for her body?

ISBN 0 352 33052 X

A SENSE OF ENTITLEMENT
Cheryl Mildenhall

When 24-year-old Angelique is summoned to the reading of her late father's will, there are a few surprises in store for her. Not only was her late father not her real father, but he's left her a large sum of money and a half share in a Buckinghamshire hotel. The trouble is, Angelique is going to have to learn to share the running of this particularly strange hotel with the enigmatic Jordan; a man who knew her as a child and now wants to know her as a woman.

ISBN 0 352 33053 8

If you would like a complete list of plot summaries of Black Lace titles, please fill out the questionnaire overleaf or send a stamped addressed envelope to:-

Black Lace
332 Ladbroke Grove
London W10 5AH

BLACK
lace

WE NEED YOUR HELP ...
to plan the future of women's erotic fiction –

– and no stamp required!

Yours are the only opinions that matter.

Black Lace is the first series of books devoted to erotic fiction by women for women.

We intend to keep providing the best-written, sexiest books you can buy. And we'd appreciate your help and valued opinion of the books so far. Tell us what you want to read.

THE BLACK LACE QUESTIONNAIRE

SECTION ONE: ABOUT YOU

1.1 Sex (*we presume you are female, but so as not to discriminate*)
     Are you?
     Male ☐
     Female ☐

1.2 Age
     under 21 ☐   21–30 ☐
     31–40 ☐   41–50 ☐
     51–60 ☐   over 60 ☐

1.3 At what age did you leave full-time education?
     still in education ☐   16 or younger ☐
     17–19 ☐   20 or older ☐

1.4 Occupation _____

1.5 Annual household income

       under £10,000 ☐   £10–£20,000 ☐

       £20–£30,000 ☐   £30–£40,000 ☐

       over £40,000 ☐

1.6 We are perfectly happy for you to remain anonymous; but if you would like to receive information on other publications available, please insert your name and address

_____

_____

_____

_____

SECTION TWO: ABOUT BUYING BLACK LACE BOOKS

2.1 How did you acquire this copy of *Gold Fever*?

    I bought it myself ☐   My partner bought it ☐

    I borrowed/found it ☐

2.2 How did you find out about Black Lace books?

    I saw them in a shop ☐

    I saw them advertised in a magazine ☐

    I saw the London Underground posters ☐

    I read about them in _____

    Other _____

2.3 Please tick the following statements you agree with:

    I would be less embarrassed about buying Black Lace books if the cover pictures were less explicit ☐

    I think that in general the pictures on Black Lace books are about right ☐

    I think Black Lace cover pictures should be as explicit as possible ☐

2.4 Would you read a Black Lace book in a public place – on a train for instance?

    Yes ☐   No ☐

SECTION THREE: ABOUT THIS BLACK LACE BOOK

3.1 Do you think the sex content in this book is:
  Too much ☐   About right ☐
  Not enough ☐

3.2 Do you think the writing style in this book is:
  Too unreal/escapist ☐   About right ☐
  Too down to earth ☐

3.3 Do you think the story in this book is:
  Too complicated ☐   About right ☐
  Too boring/simple ☐

3.4 Do you think the cover of this book is:
  Too explicit ☐   About right ☐
  Not explicit enough ☐

Here's a space for any other comments:

SECTION FOUR: ABOUT OTHER BLACK LACE BOOKS

4.1 How many Black Lace books have you read? ☐

4.2 If more than one, which one did you prefer?

4.3 Why?

SECTION FIVE: ABOUT YOUR IDEAL EROTIC NOVEL

We want to publish the books you want to read – so this is your chance to tell us exactly what your ideal erotic novel would be like.

5.1   Using a scale of 1 to 5 (1 = no interest at all, 5 = your ideal), please rate the following possible settings for an erotic novel:

Medieval/barbarian/sword 'n' sorcery ☐
Renaissance/Elizabethan/Restoration ☐
Victorian/Edwardian ☐
1920s & 1930s – the Jazz Age ☐
Present day ☐
Future/Science Fiction ☐

5.2   Using the same scale of 1 to 5, please rate the following themes you may find in an erotic novel:

Submissive male/dominant female ☐
Submissive female/dominant male ☐
Lesbianism ☐
Bondage/fetishism ☐
Romantic love ☐
Experimental sex e.g. anal/watersports/sex toys ☐
Gay male sex ☐
Group sex ☐

Using the same scale of 1 to 5, please rate the following styles in which an erotic novel could be written:

Realistic, down to earth, set in real life ☐
Escapist fantasy, but just about believable ☐
Completely unreal, impressionistic, dreamlike ☐

5.3   Would you prefer your ideal erotic novel to be written from the viewpoint of the main male characters or the main female characters?

Male ☐   Female ☐
Both ☐

5.4 What would your ideal Black Lace heroine be like? Tick as many as you like:

Dominant	☐	Glamorous	☐
Extroverted	☐	Contemporary	☐
Independent	☐	Bisexual	☐
Adventurous	☐	Naive	☐
Intellectual	☐	Introverted	☐
Professional	☐	Kinky	☐
Submissive	☐	Anything else?	☐
Ordinary	☐		

5.5 What would your ideal male lead character be like? Again, tick as many as you like:

Rugged	☐		
Athletic	☐	Caring	☐
Sophisticated	☐	Cruel	☐
Retiring	☐	Debonair	☐
Outdoor-type	☐	Naive	☐
Executive-type	☐	Intellectual	☐
Ordinary	☐	Professional	☐
Kinky	☐	Romantic	☐
Hunky	☐		
Sexually dominant	☐	Anything else?	☐
Sexually submissive	☐		

5.6 Is there one particular setting or subject matter that your ideal erotic novel would contain?

_____

SECTION SIX: LAST WORDS

6.1 What do you like best about Black Lace books?

_____

6.2 What do you most dislike about Black Lace books?

_____

6.3 In what way, if any, would you like to change Black Lace covers?

_____

6.4 Here's a space for any other comments:

_____

_____

_____

_____

Thank you for completing this questionnaire. Now tear it out of the book – carefully! – put it in an envelope and send it to:

Black Lace
FREEPOST
London
W10 5BR

No stamp is required if you are resident in the U.K.